LV

AUGUST 28, 2014

LUKE JEN...
BOUNTY HUNTER
BLOODY SUNDAY

LUKE JENSEN, BOUNTY HUNTER
BLOODY SUNDAY

WILLIAM W. JOHNSTONE
WITH J. A. JOHNSTONE

PINNACLE BOOKS
Kensington Publishing Corp.
www.kensingtonbooks.com

PINNACLE BOOKS are published by

Kensington Publishing Corp.
119 West 40th Street
New York, NY 10018

Copyright © 2014 J. A. Johnstone

PUBLISHER'S NOTE
Following the death of William W. Johnstone, the Johnstone family is
working with a carefully selected writer to organize and complete Mr.
Johnstone's outlines and many unfinished manuscripts to create addi-
tional novels in all of his series like The Last Gunfighter, Mountain
Man, and Eagles, among others. This novel was inspired by Mr. Johnstone's superb storytelling.

All Kensington titles, imprints, and distributed lines are available at
special quantity discounts for bulk purchases for sales promotions, pre-
miums, fund-raising, educational, or institutional use. Special book ex-
cerpts or customized printings can also be created to fit specific needs.
For details, write or phone the office of the Kensington special sales
manager: Kensington Publishing Corp., 119 West 40th Street, New
York, NY 10018, attn: Special Sales Department; phone 1-800-221-2647.

PINNACLE BOOKS and the Pinnacle logo are Reg. U.S. Pat. & TM Off.
The WWJ steer head logo is a trademark of Kensington Publishing
Corp.

ISBN-13: 978-0-7860-3352-2
ISBN-10: 0-7860-3352-5

First printing: July 2014

10   9   8   7   6   5   4   3   2   1

Printed in the United States of America

First electronic edition: July 2014

ISBN-13: 978-0-7860-3353-9
ISBN-10: 0-7860-3353-3

CHAPTER 1

Some people said that a bullet going close past a man's ear sounded like a hornet, but Luke Jensen knew better than that because he had heard plenty of them.

What it sounded like was a bullet coming too blasted close to blowing his brains out.

He kicked his feet free of the stirrups and left the saddle in a dive that landed him on the hard ground with a jolt he felt all through his body. He was getting too old for this, he thought as he rolled behind a rock barely big enough to give him any cover. Another slug ricocheted off the rock with a wicked whine.

Luke hadn't been expecting trouble, so he hadn't been riding with his Winchester across his saddle's pommel as he did when he knew hell might start to pop. Nor had he had time to drag it from its sheath as he was diving off the dun's back.

That meant his only weapons were the twin Remington revolvers he carried in cross-draw holsters and a sheathed knife on his left hip, just behind the gun on that side. None of them were any good for distance work.

He thought back a few seconds to the moment when he had spotted a glint of reflected sunlight on top of a sandstone bluff in front of him. That warning had barely had time to register before the bullet buzzed past his ear.

The bluff was at least a hundred yards away. The Remingtons wouldn't carry that far, not with any degree of accuracy, anyway.

Luke looked to his left. The dun had bolted off in that direction, spooked not so much by the gunfire as by Luke's reaction to it. The horse, like Luke, was accustomed to violence. In one sense, they were partners in the bounty hunting business.

Another shot rang out in the hot, still air. It hit just in front of the rock and threw up a shower of dirt and grit that spilled over into Luke's face. He lowered his head and muttered a curse as he blinked.

He had no idea who was trying to kill him or how he was going to get out of this.

A frown creased his forehead as a quick spattering of gunshots followed the latest crack of the rifle. Somebody else was horning in on this fight, which was fine with him. He could use the distraction.

He surged to his feet and ran toward the dun. No more slugs ripped the air around him. He grabbed the horn, went into the saddle in a hurry, and leaned forward over the horse's neck to make himself a smaller target as he kicked it into a gallop.

A cloud of dust boiled into the air near the bluff ahead of him. It headed to his right, telling him that a group of men on horseback were fleeing in that direction. He hauled the dun's head around and rode hard to intercept them.

The bluff hemmed them in. Luke caught sight of four or five men as their mounts raced through the chaparral along its base. More men rode along the top of the bluff and fired down at the fleeing riders.

The fugitives tried to veer away from the rise, but Luke had the angle on them from that direction. He had the dun's reins in his left hand. He used his right to draw one of the Remingtons and thumbed off a pair of shots.

He didn't hope to hit anything but rather to herd the riders back toward the bluff. So he was surprised when one of the men threw his arms in the air and pitched from the saddle in an obvious death sprawl.

Luke didn't like killing a stranger when he didn't even know the reason for it, but one of this bunch had been the rifleman who nearly put a bullet through his head, so he wasn't going to lose a lot of sleep over it. He fired again.

Without any warning, the four men who still fled abruptly disappeared. Luke didn't have any idea where they had gone until he drew closer and saw a dry wash twisting away across the West Texas landscape.

The wash gave them the cover they needed to get away from the men on top of the bluff. Those men reined in and continued firing rifles and handguns toward the arroyo, but they were shooting blind. The bluff was too steep here for them to get their horses down.

Luke thought about pursuing the men into the wash, but he decided there were too many places where they could stop and ambush him.

Instead, he turned his horse and rode toward the man he had shot, who still lay motionless on the ground where he had landed next to a scrubby mesquite bush.

As he brought the dun to a halt not far from the dead man, somebody hailed him from the top of the bluff.

"Stay right there, mister!" the man called, then disappeared as he turned his horse away from the rimrock.

Luke didn't like being told what to do, but he was curious about what had happened here and waiting for the others to join him seemed like the quickest, easiest way to find out.

As long as they didn't start taking potshots at him, too.

He swung down from the saddle and left the dun's reins hanging. The man he had shot lay on his side in a pool of blood that the thirsty ground would soon soak up. Luke could see part of the hombre's face as he approached. He slipped one of the Remingtons from its holster just in case, even though he was convinced the man wasn't playing possum.

As a bounty hunter, Luke had seen more outlaws than he liked to think about. This man fit the type. He wore rough range clothes and had a beard-stubbled face that bore marks of dissolution. As far as Luke could remember, he had never seen the man before, either in person or as a likeness on a wanted poster.

The men in the second bunch must have found a way down off the bluff. Luke heard hoofbeats and looked up to see them riding toward him. He kept the Remington in his hand but let it hang beside his leg as they approached.

This group consisted of eight men. They reined in when they were about twenty feet away and watched Luke warily. One man walked his horse forward to close the gap between them. His hand rested on the butt of the gun holstered on his right hip.

Luke understood why they were being cautious. He was a stranger to them, and a heavily armed one, at that. Dressed in black from head to foot, his hat, clothes, and boots were covered with a layer of gray trail dust that showed he'd been traveling for quite a ways. His craggy face and dark, narrow mustache gave him a somewhat sinister air. He looked like a bad man to have for an enemy.

That much was true about him, anyway.

What didn't show was the real nature of the man. Luke Jensen was a bounty hunter, a ruthless man-hunter, and a dangerous foe, no doubt about that. He was also a very well-read man who knew the classics, who enjoyed a fine cigar and a snifter of cognac, who was just as much at home in an opera house as he was in a trail town saloon. He carried the scars of a violent life on his body and the scars of a tragic past on his soul, although he wasn't the sort to brood about either.

But none of the cowboys confronting him now with their guns ready for trouble knew about any of that, so he just gave their apparent leader a noncommittal nod and said, "Howdy."

"You're on MacCrae range, mister," the man said. "Mind telling me who you are?"

"I assume you have a right to ask that question?"

The man grunted and said, "Damned right I do. I ramrod the crew. Name's Gabe Pendleton. Now, I've told you who I am, so I'd appreciate it if you'd return the favor."

Pendleton was a stocky man with a thatch of straw-like hair under his battered brown hat. His eyes were a washed-out blue, Luke noted, and at the moment were narrow with suspicion.

"I'm Luke Jensen," Luke introduced himself. He was used to people asking him if he was related to Smoke Jensen, the famous gunfighter. As a matter of fact, he and Smoke were brothers, although Luke didn't go out of his way to publicize that relationship.

He had made plenty of enemies of his own without having everybody with a grudge against his brother gunning for him, too.

"What are you doing here?"

"I was riding along minding my own business when somebody on top of that bluff started shooting at me. Whoever it was had me pinned down. Then you and your friends came along and rousted him out, and he and his friends lit a shuck. I owe you some thanks for that, by the way." Luke shrugged. "Now you know as much about this dustup as I do. More, I would guess."

Pendleton nodded toward the dead man and asked, "You know who that is?"

"I never saw him before," Luke said.

"We don't mean you any harm. How about pouching that iron?"

"I'd be glad to . . . as soon as you and these other men take your hands off your guns."

Pendleton jerked his head in a command, and the other men relaxed and lifted hands from gun butts. Luke slid the Remington he held back into its holster.

Pendleton motioned to his men and said, "Take a look at that hombre and see if any of you know him."

He dismounted, and the others followed suit and gathered around the corpse while Luke and Pendleton moved to one side. One of the cowboys said, "I think I've seen him before, Gabe, maybe in one of the saloons at Painted Post, but I don't know his name."

"His name don't matter," another man said. "All that counts is that he works for Harry Elston."

Pendleton said, "We don't know that for a fact."

That brought a snort of disbelief from the man who had just spoken.

"Who else would be out here usin' a runnin' iron on our critters?" the man wanted to know.

Pendleton just grunted and didn't have any other answer for the question.

A swift, sudden rataplan of hoofbeats would have kept him from replying, anyway. The sound made all the men look around, including Luke. He saw a single rider coming toward them on a big white horse.

"That looks like the boss," one of the men said.

"Yeah," Pendleton agreed. A nervous expression appeared on his face. The owner of this ranch must have been a real fire-breather to have that effect on the tough foreman, Luke thought. From everything he had heard about Sam MacCrae, that was the case.

But the newcomer wasn't the old Scotsman, Luke realized a moment later. The rider's faded blue shirt hugged curves that were undeniably female. Luke spotted long, black hair that was pulled back and tied in a ponytail that hung down the woman's back. She wore a flat-crowned black hat with its neck strap tight under her chin.

When she reined her mount to a halt and swung down from the saddle, Luke saw that she wore a divided canvas riding skirt as well, which explained how she was able to ride astride the way she did. She led the horse toward them. She didn't walk like a man, but there was nothing mincing or affected about her stride, either.

"I saw the branding fire, Gabe," she said.

Pendleton nodded and said, "Yes, ma'am." Luke noticed that the foreman had moved so that he stood between the woman and the man on the ground.

It didn't do any good, because she asked, "Is that a dead man behind you?"

"Yes, ma'am, but you don't want to be looking at him."

"Is he one of our men, or one of the rustlers?"

"He's not one of us," Pendleton said.

"Let me have a look."

Pendleton hesitated. Clearly, he didn't want to expose her to the sight of a grisly corpse. Luke's bullet had ripped through the man's torso from side to side, and there was a lot of blood on the ground around him.

The woman wore a determined expression, though, so after a few seconds Pendleton gave a tiny shrug and stepped aside. The woman came forward a few steps to peer down at the dead man.

Her face went pale for a second under its healthy tan, but her expression remained steady and composed. She shook her head and said, "I don't know him."

"None of us do," Pendleton told her, "although Chuck said he might've seen the man in one of the saloons in Painted Post."

"That doesn't mean anything. It's the closest place for Harry Elston's men to drink."

"Yeah, that's true."

The woman turned her head to look at Luke. She said bluntly, "I don't think I know you."

"This fella is the one who downed that rustler," Pendleton explained. "The way I figure it, a couple of them were working the branding fire while two more drove our steers up. They put one man up on top of the bluff to keep a lookout and make sure they weren't disturbed. When Jensen here came along, the sentry got spooked and started shooting. The boys and I heard the shots and got here as quick as we could."

"Mr. Jensen, is it?" the woman said to Luke.

"That's right," he said. "Luke Jensen."

She wore riding gloves, but she used her left hand

to pull the glove off her right and then stuck it out like a man.

"I'm Glory MacCrae," she introduced herself.

Luke shook hands with her, and as he did he thought that she had just confirmed what he already suspected. She was the woman he had come here to find.

The woman who had a price on her head for murder.

CHAPTER 2

It had started a few weeks earlier in San Antonio, where Luke had brought the body of an outlaw named Joe Jack Talcott. Luke had caught up to Talcott at a road ranch between Schulenberg and San Antonio and gotten the drop on him—or so he'd thought—while the outlaw was in bed with a soiled dove named Juanita.

What Luke didn't find out until later was that Juanita's brother, who was something of a desperado himself, had been gunned down by a bounty hunter a couple of years earlier, so when Talcott, with his hands up and his long underwear down, had paused in his cussing long enough to call Luke a no-good bounty hunter, Juanita had gone loco.

Practically spitting fire, she had rolled out of the sheets with a flash of sleek, golden-brown skin and grabbed a bottle of tequila from the little table beside the bed. She flung it at Luke's head, and her aim was good. He had to throw his left arm up to block the bottle.

The next instant, Talcott crashed into him, desperation prompting the outlaw to try a diving tackle despite the fact that Luke's gun was still pointed in his general direction.

The Remington had gone off as the collision drove Luke backwards off his feet, but the bullet missed Talcott and tore through the oilcloth shade over the room's single window instead. Outside, it creased the rump of one of the horses tied at a hitch rack and set off an explosion of bucking and squealing that spooked the other mounts and made them jerk their reins loose and stampede away.

While that was going on, Luke was locked in a deadly struggle with Joe Jack Talcott. The outlaw got a hand on the barrel of Luke's gun and tried to twist the weapon around so that it pointed at its owner. Luke resisted that effort. Juanita came up and tried to kick him in the head with a bare foot. Actually, she was bare all over, which was very evident from Luke's vantage point on the floor, although he was in no position, physical or otherwise, to appreciate the view.

After jerking his head out of the way of Juanita's foot a couple of times, he grabbed her ankle with his free hand and heaved. She went over backwards and landed hard enough on her rump to knock the breath out of her and take her out of the fight for the moment. Luke balled that hand into a fist and slammed it a couple of times into the side of Talcott's head. The outlaw's eyes glazed over. He lost his grip on Luke's gun and Luke shoved him away.

Unfortunately, Talcott rolled within reach of his Colt, which rested in a holster attached to a shell belt hung over one of the posts at the foot of the bed. He regained his wits enough to make a grab for the gun, even though Luke yelled for him not to do it. The Colt slid out of leather and Talcott started to swing it up.

Luke shot him in the chest.

The Remington boomed three times and made Juanita scream and clap her hands over her ears. The first shot probably killed Talcott instantly, but Luke knew there was nothing worse than thinking some varmint was dead and then finding out that he wasn't, so he put two more slugs into the outlaw, each within a few inches of the blood-pouring hole where the first bullet had struck him. With the Colt still in his hand, Talcott sagged sideways on the floor.

Luke pushed himself onto one knee, then onto his feet and took a step back so he could cover Talcott and Juanita at the same time. Neither appeared to be a threat anymore. Talcott was dead and Juanita was curled up in a ball, sobbing in fear.

The fella who ran the place came in the door with a shotgun. He was a fat, bald-headed gent named Edwards with a long gray beard that hung down over his chest. Luke was ready to shoot him, too, if need be, but Edwards quickly pointed the shotgun at the floor and backed off.

"Take it easy, mister," he said in an urgent voice. "Just take it easy."

After that it was just a matter of explaining everything and showing Edwards the wanted poster with Joe

Jack Talcott's picture on it. The proprietor insisted that he hadn't known the man who had taken Juanita into one of the rooms was really a wanted killer. Luke didn't know whether or not Edwards was telling the truth and didn't really care one way or the other.

The only ones who were really upset were the men whose horses had run off, and after taking a look at Luke they appeared to decide it wasn't worth raising a ruckus over.

All that was left was getting some clothes on Talcott's corpse, throwing it over the saddle on his horse, lashing the dead outlaw in place, and taking him to San Antonio. The State of Texas had placed the bounty on Talcott's head, so Luke figured the easiest way to collect would be to turn the body over to the Rangers.

That was how he came to find himself in the office of Major John B. Jones, the head of the Frontier Battalion.

The major didn't seem to be overly fond of bounty hunters, but what Luke did for a living wasn't illegal and there was a reward for Talcott, dead or alive, so Luke had $800 coming to him.

"Next time you should just take the body to the nearest undertaker and get a local lawman or other official to vouch for the fact that you brought him in," Jones said. "You didn't have to haul Talcott all the way here to San Antonio."

"The place where I caught up with him was halfway between here and Schuelenberg," Luke explained. "I thought I'd probably get my money faster if I brought him to you."

Jones grunted and said, "The money's all that matters to you, isn't it?"

"Talcott's killed three men in the commission of his crimes, that we know of," Luke pointed out. "There's a good chance he's also the one who burned down that store in Hallettsville after it was robbed, and the bodies of two more men were found in the ashes. I'd say it's a pretty good thing Talcott won't be around to keep on robbing and killing, because I don't think he planned on stopping anytime soon."

The bearded ranger inclined his head in acknowledgment of Luke's argument.

"I'll have the voucher for your reward drawn up right away," he said. "You can come back by the office and pick it up later this afternoon. Take it to any bank in San Antonio and they'll honor it."

"I'm obliged to you." Luke nodded toward a stack of papers on Jones's desk. "That looks like a bunch of new wanted posters."

"Already thinking about where your next payoff is coming from, eh?" Jones shoved the reward dodgers toward Luke. "You can take a look at them, but don't carry any of them off with you. My men haven't even seen them yet."

"Obliged again," Luke said as he picked up the stack.

The first dozen posters he flipped through were the usual motley assortment of bank, train, and stagecoach robbers, rustlers, horse thieves, backshooters, and rapists.

Many of them were illustrated with crude drawings of the wanted men, and a few didn't have pictures at all.

But then Luke came to one that made him pause as his eyebrows rose in surprise. He said, "What do we have here?"

"What?" Major Jones asked distractedly without looking up from the paperwork he had already gone back to.

Luke turned the reward dodger around and held it out so that Jones could see the picture on it. This was a photograph, not a drawing, and the portrait was of an undeniably beautiful young woman with dark hair.

Jones grunted as he leaned forward to take a look at the wanted poster. He started rummaging through some of the papers on his desk as he said, "I think I've got a notice about her somewhere here. Yeah, there it is."

He handed a couple of pages to Luke. One was a letter from the chief of police in Baltimore, Maryland, asking the Rangers to be on the lookout for a fugitive, and the other was a report from a Pinkerton Detective Agency operative.

"Gloria Jennings," Luke mused as he studied the documents. "Wanted for murder. That's a little unusual, isn't it?"

"You've never hunted down a female killer before?"

"Actually I have, several times, in fact. But it's still not all that common. I see here that she murdered her husband."

"Alfred Jennings," Major Jones said. "A rich man,

considerably older than Mrs. Jennings, who was his, ah, second wife."

"Funny how often it happens that way," Luke said. "This says that Jennings had interests in banks, warehouses, even a shipping line. He must've had a lot of money."

"Less when his wife got through with him. In addition to the murder, there's a hundred thousand dollars missing."

Luke let out a low whistle.

"I suppose that's why the family can afford to post a five thousand dollar reward."

The amount of the bounty was the second thing Luke had noticed, the first being the fact that Mrs. Gloria Jennings was an exceptionally good-looking woman. Most of the time he brought in outlaws who were worth less than a thousand dollars, like Joe Jack Talcott. He made a decent living doing that, but most likely he would never get rich at it.

He tapped the detective's report and said, "It says here the Pinks tracked her to Fort Worth."

"That's right, and while she was there she boarded a train bound for San Antonio."

"Do you know if she ever got here?"

"I have no idea," Major Jones said. "I'm not a Pinkerton detective or a bounty hunter. I've got a big stretch of country between here and the border to ride herd on. I can't go out looking for one fugitive who hasn't committed any crimes in Texas that I know of, and my men can't, either. I'll make sure they know about

Mrs. Jennings, in case they happen to run across her, but capturing her isn't going to be a priority."

"How long ago was this?" Luke asked.

"The dates are on the paperwork."

Luke looked at the documents again, then said, "She killed her husband and vanished from Baltimore almost a year ago. This report saying she was in Fort Worth is almost eight months old. You're just getting a wanted poster on her now?"

"I don't have any control over when those things are sent out," Jones said testily. "Paperwork takes a long time."

"Why were these documents still on your desk?"

"They weren't. I had a vague memory of the case, so I had my clerk go through the files and pull them out after I saw the lady's picture on the poster. I wanted to refresh my memory on the details."

Luke grinned and said, "You wanted to know more about the pretty lady."

"If we're done here, Jensen . . ."

Luke tossed the documents back onto the desk and stood up. He would have liked to take them with him, along with the reward poster, but he had a good memory for facts.

And for faces as well, when they were as attractive as the one belonging to Gloria Jennings.

"Since this particular fugitive isn't a high priority of yours, I don't suppose you'd mind if I took a shot at tracking her down, would you, major?"

"Help yourself," Jones said. "As long as you don't break the law or interfere with me or my men, I don't care what you do. The trail's bound to be pretty cold by now, though."

"I've picked up colder ones," Luke said.

As it turned out, it took him a week of asking questions at hotels, boardinghouses, and the railroad station before he found someone who remembered seeing Gloria Jennings. That led him to a porter who recalled helping her with her bags as she boarded a westbound train. More searching and asking questions turned up the conductor on that run, who told Luke, "The lady didn't go all the way to El Paso, I remember that for sure. It's not every day you come across a woman who's so easy on the eyes."

"Where did she get off?" Luke asked.

The conductor, a pudgy, mostly bald gent with a high-pitched voice, took off his cap and scratched his bare scalp.

"I don't rightly recall," he said.

Luke reached for his pocket.

"No, no, I'm not hinting for a bribe, mister," the conductor said quickly. "I honestly don't remember. I'm pretty sure it was somewhere pretty far west, but not all the way to El Paso. There are several little towns in that ranching country out there north of the Big Bend. That's where it was she got off the train, in one of those settlements."

Well, that narrowed it down some, anyway, Luke thought. He thanked the conductor, put together a load of supplies, picked up his horse from the livery stable, and headed west.

He could have taken the train and retraced Gloria's

route that way, but he preferred to ride. As cold as the trail already was, a little more time wouldn't make any difference. Besides, if she was trying to elude pursuit she might have doubled back, and this would give him a chance to stop and ask questions in every little town he came to.

He was in a wide place in the road called Bracken's Crossing when the man who ran the general store listened to his description of Gloria Jennings and then said, "That sounds a lot like the gal who married old Sam MacCrae a while back. She's from back East somewhere, I hear tell. Young and a real looker, too. That ol' dog Sam."

"Who's MacCrae?" Luke asked. "Where does he live?"

"He owns a ranch over on the other side of Painted Post, about fifty miles from here."

Luke's interest picked up at that news. He said, "A good-sized spread, is it? Or just a little greasy sack outfit?"

The storekeeper snorted.

"Greasy sack, my hind foot. The MacCrae spread is the biggest outfit in that part of Texas. Takes up the whole of Sabado Valley and more besides."

"So MacCrae's a rich man," Luke said. "You called him old Sam. How old?"

"Shoot, I don't know for sure. He's in his fifties, I'd say."

So far, everything Luke was hearing meshed perfectly with what he knew about Gloria Jennings. She had married a rich, older man back in Baltimore. There was no reason to think she wouldn't marry another one here in Texas if she got the chance.

Of course, she had already stolen a hundred thousand dollars from Alfred Jennings when she killed him, so she probably didn't need money, but for some people, plenty was never enough. No matter how much they had, they always wanted more, especially when it came to money and power.

"Do you recall the name of MacCrae's new wife?" Luke asked the storekeeper.

"Don't know that I ever heard it," the man replied. "All I know is some of my customers gossiped about ol' Sam getting himself a young, pretty wife. That's all I can tell you, mister."

"There's one more thing you can tell me," Luke said. "How to get to Painted Post."

The storekeeper was glad to supply him with directions, especially after Luke bought some supplies. A couple of days' ride brought him to Painted Post, a sleepy cow town not much different from a hundred others Luke had seen. While he was there, he picked up some more gossip about Sam MacCrae and the rancher's new wife.

MacCrae had been a widower for quite a few years, and evidently he had fallen hard for the young woman who had gotten off the train and settled in at the hotel. A whirlwind courtship later, the couple had gotten married in the Painted Post Baptist Church, and the woman—her name was Glory, Luke was told—had gone off to live on the ranch with her new husband.

All that information combined to convince Luke that

he was on the right trail. Glory MacCrae had to be the fugitive murderer Gloria Jennings.

All he needed to do was get a look at her to be absolutely certain of her identity. Even though it had been a while, in his mind's eye he could still see the portrait of the woman he had seen on that wanted poster in Major Jones's office.

Now, as he stood there with Glory MacCrae's warm hand gripped in his, he was dead solid sure.

CHAPTER 3

"Welcome to the MC Ranch, Mr. Jensen," Glory said. "I don't know what brings you here, but you've done us a favor." She nodded toward the dead man. "This is one less gunnie to do Harry Elston's bidding."

She gave his hand a final squeeze and let go of it. Luke was a little sorry not to be holding her hand anymore. She was the sort of woman whose beauty possessed a raw, primitive power over men, and Luke wasn't immune to it . . . although he would never let it make his decisions for him, either.

"I don't know anything about this fella Elston," he said. "All I know is that somebody in that bunch tried to kill me, and I don't take kindly to that. Could've even been this hombre. If it wasn't . . ." A cold smile curved Luke's mouth under the mustache. "Then I reckon he was guilty by association."

"Elston's men are all guilty of one thing: associating with a skunk." Glory turned to Pendleton and went on: "Put him on a horse and take him back to headquarters,

Gabe. From there one of the men can take the body to Painted Post in a wagon and leave it at the undertaker's."

"You aim to pay for planting him, Miz MacCrae?" the foreman asked.

"Not if there's enough of Harry Elston's dirty money in his pockets to pay for a pine box, I don't," Glory answered without hesitation. Then she shrugged and added, "But whoever takes the body to town can tell the undertaker that I'll cover the difference, if there is any."

Pendleton's voice hardened as he said, "I'll make sure you get an honest accounting, ma'am."

"Thank you, Gabe." Glory turned back to Luke. "If you're not in a hurry, Mr. Jensen, I hope you'll come on to the ranch house with us and have supper. You're welcome to spend the night in the bunkhouse, as well."

"That's kind of you," Luke said with a nod. "I accept."

"Not at all. Like I said, you did us a favor . . . and I like to repay any favors that I owe."

She was a plainspoken, straightforward woman, Luke thought as they mounted up. He liked that about her, over and above her good looks.

It was a shame he was going to have to take her in and turn her over to the law. It would be even more of a shame when they put a hang rope around that pretty neck of hers and stretched it for murdering her husband.

Her *other* husband, Luke corrected himself as he moved the dun alongside her horse and they began to ride along the base of the bluff. Behind them, a couple of the hands rounded up the dead man's horse so they could throw the corpse over the saddle.

"Are you from somewhere around these parts,

Mr. Jensen?" Glory MacCrae asked. "I don't think I've heard your name before."

"No, ma'am. Originally I'm from Missouri, but I've moved around a lot in recent years. I consider myself a citizen of the world."

"I like that," she said with a smile.

"Where are you from?" he asked. "You don't really sound like a Texan."

She laughed and said, "Those can be fighting words around here. Although a lot of people in Texas these days weren't born here."

Luke knew that was true. After the end of the war, there had been nothing left in the conquered Southern states for many of the returning Confederate soldiers. The brutal, vindictive Yankee reconstructionists and carpetbaggers had seen to that.

So most of those men had headed west, looking for new lives on the frontier. Luke's experience had been different in some details, although there were certain similarities. He didn't consider himself an unreconstructed rebel, though. The war was too far in the past for that.

He noticed that Glory had dodged his question about where she was from, but he didn't press her on the issue. Anyway, he already knew the answer. Her voice had a slight trace of a Southern accent, another indication that she was from Baltimore, which straddled the cultural line dividing north from south.

To pass the time, Luke said, "Tell me about this hombre Elston. Why would he want his men to rustle some of your stock?"

"Why will a rattlesnake sink its fangs in anything that moves?" Glory asked in return. "It's filled with venom, and that venom has to come out somewhere." As they passed the embers of a fire that had burned down to almost nothing, she pointed at them and went on: "They were using that as a branding fire, venting the MC brand into a Lazy EO with a running iron. We've caught them doing it before."

Luke frowned and said, "I don't see how they thought they could get away with that. It would be easy enough to spot an altered brand if you killed the cow and peeled the hide off. Don't you have a cattleman's association to send in some brand inspectors and put a stop to it?"

"The brand inspectors have been in, and they've warned Elston," Glory said. "He claimed his men were doing it without his knowledge. He fired some of them, ran them off." She laughed, but there was no humor in the sound. "Paid them off, is more like it. He put on a show of being angry about it, but he really gave the men money to go somewhere else and find another job. I'm convinced of that."

They left the branding fire behind. Luke said, "It doesn't seem like you could steal enough cattle that way to make it worthwhile unless you had a little outfit and were just barely hanging on."

"Well, it's not like Harry Elston is trying to stock his ranch. He has his own herds. What he really wants is my range and my water. Sabado Creek runs through the valley and is the best source of water around here.

Elston just wants to make enough of a nuisance of himself that I'll give up and sell out to him."

Starting out, Luke hadn't been sure why he was questioning Glory MacCrae about what was going on around here. He didn't care about the ranch's troubles. He was just here to make sure she was the fugitive he was after and then figure out a way to get her behind bars.

She had said some things that intrigued him, though, and his interest grew even stronger when he recalled how one of the ranch hands had referred to her as "the boss" when he spotted Glory approaching.

"Mrs. MacCrae," he said, "how does your husband feel about all this?"

Glory's horse broke stride a little, and Luke knew his question had caused her to jerk the reins. She looked over at him and said, "My husband is dead, Mr. Jensen. The MC Ranch is mine now."

Well, thought Luke, given this woman's history, that wasn't really much of a surprise.

"I'm sorry," he said. "I didn't know."

She shrugged and said, "Since you're a stranger in these parts, there's no reason you should have."

That storekeeper back in Bracken's Crossing could have told him, he thought. Of course, it was possible the man hadn't known about Sam MacCrae's death, especially if it had occurred recently.

"You have my condolences," Luke said. "If you don't mind my asking, how long ago . . . ?"

"Three months." Glory glanced down at the riding clothes she wore and went on: "I know, these aren't exactly widow's weeds, are they? But I don't have time to sit around in a dark room with a veil over my face, weeping and wailing. There's a ranch that has to be run. The last thing in the world Sam would have wanted was for me to let things go to hell around here."

She was good, Luke thought. Every word out of her mouth sounded genuine and sincere, but he knew she was lying through her teeth. The most likely explanation was that she had killed Sam MacCrae, gotten away with it somehow without being suspected, and now intended to strip her late husband's ranch of every penny she could before she disappeared again.

"I did my mourning for a few days," Glory was saying as those thoughts ran through Luke's brain. "Gabe and the other men kept things going. But then it was time to move forward again instead of looking back. I had my time with Sam. It was too short, but other than that it . . . it was everything a woman could ask for."

That little catch in her voice was perfect. Anybody else hearing it would believe that deep down she was still devastated by the loss of her husband.

"How long were you married?" Luke asked.

"Three months. Like I said, not nearly long enough."

But long enough for Sam MacCrae to have changed his will, Luke was willing to bet. Wasn't anybody around here suspicious of this woman? Had she managed to fool them all just because she was beautiful?

They came to a place where the bluff had caved in, a long time in the past. An easy trail led to the top. As they rode up it, Luke glanced back and saw Pendleton and the other MC hands strung out behind them. One of the cowboys was leading a horse with the dead man draped over the saddle.

"How far is it to your headquarters?"

"About five miles," Glory said. "It's over there at the edge of those foothills to the west."

A couple of ranges of small mountains, not much more than hills themselves, bordered the valley on the northeast and southwest. The settlement of Painted Post was ten or twelve miles back to the southeast. This whole area between the mountain ranges was known as Sabado Valley—Sabbath Valley, in English—and it all belonged to Glory MacCrae now. Some of the landscape Luke could see was brown and arid, but a large swath of the valley was verdant with grass and brush. Luke wasn't a cattleman, but he had been around enough ranches to know good grazing land when he saw it.

Maybe Glory wasn't planning on running out after all. Maybe she was sincere about keeping the ranch going. It was possible she had lucked into something by marrying Sam MacCrae, something that would allow her to settle down.

Of course, she still had a murder charge hanging over her head, and unless Luke missed his guess, that wasn't the only murder she had committed. He had to pretend to be taken in by the web of lies she was spinning, but he couldn't let himself actually be convinced she was telling the truth.

She was worth five thousand dollars, after all!

They passed more cattle as they rode, good-looking animals, Luke thought, although he wasn't really a judge of such things. After a few minutes, Glory said, "You never did tell me what you're doing on this range, Mr. Jensen."

"I'm headed for El Paso," Luke said, "but I'm taking my time getting there and seeing some of the country while I'm at it."

"What's in El Paso? Family? Friends?"

For a long time after the war, Luke hadn't had either of those things in his life. He hadn't even known at first that the famous gunman Smoke Jensen was really his little brother Kirby.

Since then he had met not only Smoke, but also their adopted brother, Matt, along with the old mountain man known as Preacher who had been Smoke's mentor for many years. So, yeah, he had family now, and friends, and they were the same.

But in answer to Glory's question he said, "No, none of that. But I'm told there's always a big poker game going on in the bar of the Camino Real Hotel."

Glory laughed and said, "So you're a gambler?"

"When you get up in the morning, you're betting that you'll make it through the day, aren't you? And when you lay your head down at night, you've made a wager that you'll wake up again."

"That's a rather . . . fatalistic way of looking at things, isn't it?"

"I suppose you're right," Luke said with a chuckle of his own. "Let's just say I enjoy a good game of cards."

"Fine. That means it won't be keeping you from anything important if you have dinner with me tonight and stay a day or two."

It didn't escape Luke's notice that she had gone from asking him to spend the night at the ranch to saying that he could stay a day or two. He didn't comment on it, though.

They came within sight of the ranch headquarters. It was a fine-looking place. The house was whitewashed adobe with a tile roof and several cottonwood trees around it. A long, low adobe bunkhouse sat to one side. There were a couple of barns built of rough-planed lumber with a network of corrals between and around them. Other outbuildings were scattered here and there. Luke could tell the ranch was successful.

A couple of big, shaggy dogs, one yellow, and one gray and brown, ran out to greet them with full-throated barks. A woman with gray hair braided and wrapped around her head came out of the main house, and a couple of young punchers emerged from one of the barns. One of the youngsters hurried up and took hold of the headstall on Glory's horse as she reined to a halt.

"I'll put him up for you, ma'am," the boy said. He was a stocky, redheaded youngster with a scattering of freckles across his face.

"Thank you, Ernie," Glory told him, and as she expressed her gratitude a smile as bright as the sun broke out on the boy's face. He looked like he'd just been given the world's best present on Christmas morning.

Glory swung down from the saddle, and so did Luke. Glory said to the other young man, "Vince, take care of Mr. Jensen's horse, will you?"

"Sure," Vince said. He was taller, leaner, and darker than Ernie, and he looked like it would take a lot more than a fleeting smile from Glory MacCrae to make him beam like the sun.

The other hands who had been with Gabe Pendleton during the fight with the rustlers were headed for the barn, except for Pendleton and the cowboy leading the dead man's horse. Pendleton hipped around slightly in his saddle, peered to the north, and said, "Company coming, Miz MacCrae."

"Can you tell who it is?" Glory asked.

Pendleton's voice hardened as he said, "Looks like a buggy with three or four riders trailing it. Coming from that direction, you know what that means."

"Yes," Glory said. Her voice had gone flinty, too. "Harry Elston is coming to pay us a visit."

CHAPTER 4

The gray-haired woman came closer. She said to Glory, "You should go inside, señora. Let Gabe deal with Señor Elston."

Her lined face was nut brown, her eyes dark and piercing. Luke couldn't tell for sure how old she was. She could have been anywhere from fifty to eighty.

"I'm not going to let Harry Elston make me hide in the house, Teresa," Glory said. "Whatever he wants, he can deal with me."

"Señor MacCrae would not want you doing this, señora."

"I think I'm a better judge of what Sam would want," Glory snapped. "After all, I was his wife."

Luke saw the older woman's already grim mouth draw down into an even thinner line, but Teresa didn't say anything else. Luke had a hunch that she had been Sam MacCrae's cook, housekeeper, something like that, quite possibly for many years, ever since MacCrae's first wife passed away.

It wouldn't surprise him if Teresa had been in love with MacCrae, too, although as a servant she'd probably kept that emotion to herself. She was bound to resent Glory for coming in and first marrying MacCrae, then taking over the ranch after his death.

Glory turned away dismissively from the older woman and strode across the ranch yard toward the approaching buggy with its trailing riders. The buggy was close enough now for Luke to see that a thickset man in a gray tweed suit and narrow-brimmed dark brown hat was handling the reins. That would be Harry Elston, he thought, owner of the Lazy EO.

The men on horseback behind the buggy rode with easy, arrogant slouches. They wore range clothes, but they were all armed with holstered handguns, which meant they weren't regular cowboys. A man who worked with cows all day from horseback generally didn't pack an iron, just a rifle for shooting snakes or coyotes.

Luke glanced over at Gabe Pendleton, who looked pretty tense.

"Is this fixing to be trouble?" Luke asked quietly.

"Don't know." Pendleton bit out the words with his jaw clenched. "See that lean fella with the sandy hair?"

Luke knew Pendleton was referring to one of the riders following Elston's buggy. He said, "I see him."

"That's Verne Finn. You know the name?"

"Vaguely," Luke said. "He's a gunman, isn't he?"

"Hired killer," Pendleton said. "He's a backshooter and a bushwhacker, but the law's never been able to prove it. All of his face-to-face killings have come in fair fights. He's fast enough to have lived this long."

Actually, Verne Finn was a rather mild-looking hombre, Luke thought. But that didn't mean anything. Some of the most dangerous men he'd come across in his career as a bounty hunter hadn't looked all that threatening.

"If you want to," Pendleton went on, "drift on into the barn. You'll be safe enough there if any trouble starts."

"I never said I was worried about it," Luke drawled. "Just curious, that's all. Reckon I'm fine where I am."

Pendleton grunted, and when he glanced over at Luke there was a little more respect in his eyes.

"All right," he said. "But don't say I didn't warn you."

Elston brought the buggy to a halt. Glory was about fifteen feet away and slightly to one side. She said, "What are you doing here, Mr. Elston?"

"That's not a very friendly greeting, Mrs. MacCrae," Elston said. He was in his forties, with a beefy face and short, grizzled hair under his hat.

"It wasn't intended to be," Glory said. "Actually, though, I'm glad you're here."

Elston looked a little surprised by that comment. He said, "Oh? Why is that?"

Glory pointed to the corpse still draped over the saddle a few yards away.

"You can take the body of one of your rustlers to the undertaker and save my men the trouble of having to do it."

Luke had seen the glances the horsemen had thrown toward the corpse and taken note of the way some of them stiffened in their saddles. That told him they recognized the horse or the dead man or both. That was all the proof he needed that the rustlers had been working for Elston, although it was hardly the sort of evidence that would stand up in a court of law.

Elston's already florid face flushed an even deeper shade of red as he scowled angrily. He said, "I don't know what you're talking about. I came over to pay a friendly visit, not to be accused of something."

"Since when are we friends?" Glory demanded.

Elston fiddled with the reins and said, "We're neighbors—"

"That doesn't make us friends."

"Blast it, woman, you've got me all wrong!" Elston burst out. "You act like I'm trying to cause trouble for you, when all I wanted to do was make sure you're all right over here. It hasn't been that long since you lost poor Sam—"

"I'll thank you not to mention my husband," Glory said coldly.

Elston tried to defend himself by saying, "Sam and I were friends—"

Glory interrupted him again.

"That's funny. There you go again with that friend business. I never heard my husband refer to you as anything except a no-good range hog."

One of the men with Elston—but not Verne Finn, Luke noted, Finn stayed calm and apparently emotionless—prodded his horse forward and said hotly, "That's just about damned well enough from a—"

Gabe Pendleton took a step and said, "You'd better

think long and hard about what you're gonna say next, Carter."

The gunman sneered at him.

"If I didn't know better, I'd say you're actin' like you're fast on the draw, cow nurse. If you think you can beat me, you're welcome to try your luck."

"I don't have to outdraw you," Pendleton said. "There are a dozen rifles trained on the whole sorry lot of you right now."

Luke had spotted four or five rifle barrels poking from the barn and the bunkhouse. Maybe Pendleton was bluffing about there being a dozen, or maybe Luke just couldn't see them from where he was. Either way, the tension in the air ratcheted up a few notches. Luke could almost smell the blood that was about to be spilled.

"Carter, stop it!" Elston's voice held a note of desperation as it lashed out. If bullets started to fly, he'd be right in the middle of them. "Back off, you hear me? Now!"

Clearly, Carter didn't appreciate being ordered around like that, nor did he like the idea of backing off from the confrontation with Pendleton. But he rode for the Lazy EO brand, and Harry Elston was the boss.

"Another day," he growled at Pendleton.

"You call it," the MC foreman said.

Carter backed his horse until he was behind the buggy again. Then Glory said, "If you don't have any real business here, Mr. Elston, I'll bid you good day."

"Hold on a minute," Elston said. He was going to try to save a little face by refusing to be dismissed that easily, Luke thought. The rancher went on: "What did you mean by accusing me of rustling that way? And who's that dead man?"

"Gabe," Glory said as she inclined her head toward the corpse.

Pendleton stepped over to the mount, took hold of its reins, and turned it so the dead man's head was toward the visitors. Grasping the corpse's hair, Pendleton lifted the head so the face was visible.

"That's Dave Randall," Elston said. "I fired him last week. So whatever mischief he was up to today, you can hardly blame me for it."

"I suppose the rest of your men will vouch for the fact that you fired Randall?" Glory asked.

"I don't see why not. That's the way it happened."

Glory's contemptuous snort made it clear she didn't believe a word Elston was saying. The man's face flushed again, but he kept a visibly tight rein on his temper.

"You can take the body to Painted Post anyway," Glory said. "Since he *used* to work for you."

Curtly, Elston jerked his head toward the body. One of his men rode forward and took the reins from Pendleton, then led the horse as he went back to join the others.

"I'm sorry for the hard feelings between us, Mrs. MacCrae," Elston said. "It doesn't have to be this way, you know."

"Yes," Glory said, "I'm afraid it does."

Elston lifted the buggy horse's reins. He clucked to the animal and turned it, then slapped the reins against its rump and drove out of the yard. The man who had taken charge of Randall's horse rode southeast, toward

Painted Post. The other gunmen followed Elston as he headed back northwest, presumably toward his ranch.

Verne Finn was a little slower about turning his horse than the others were. As he lingered slightly, his hooded gaze studied Luke, seeming to appraise him. Obviously, Finn was curious about this newcomer to the MacCrae ranch.

Luke returned the gunman's regard with a cool, level look of his own. After a moment, the corners of Finn's mouth quirked in an almost invisible smile. He lifted his left hand, touched a finger to the brim of his hat in a mocking salute, then wheeled his horse and rode after the others.

"What was that about?" Pendleton asked.

"Just taking stock," Luke said.

"You sure you and Finn aren't acquainted?"

"I never laid eyes on the man until today."

Pendleton still looked a little doubtful, but he didn't press the issue. Instead, he turned to Glory and said, "I can ride to Painted Post and tell the deputy sheriff who's usually around there about the brand-blotting."

"What good would it do?" Glory asked, and for the first time in the admittedly short period Luke had known her, he thought she sounded tired. She went on: "Be careful for the next few days. This is the first time we've killed one of them. They may strike back at us."

"We didn't actually kill that fella," Pendleton pointed out as he looked at Luke.

"It happened on our range, and Mr. Jensen is our guest. I don't think that'll make any difference to Elston's bunch of hired killers."

"Probably not," Pendleton admitted.

Glory summoned up a smile for Luke and invited, "Come on in the house."

She led him through an arched gateway and a little garden to the big wooden door. The old woman, Teresa, had already vanished back into the house. Luke and Glory stepped into the shady interior where the air held a welcome hint of coolness behind thick adobe walls.

"Would you like a drink?" Glory asked as she loosened her hat's chin strap and took it off. She placed the hat on a heavy table that gleamed with polish.

"That sounds good."

"Being a proper Scotsman, my late husband had an ample supply of fine Scotch."

Luke smiled and said, "Even better."

He looked around the room while Glory went to a massive sideboard to pour the drinks. The furnishings appeared comfortable without being ostentatious. Heavy, overstuffed chairs, big tables, woven rugs on the floor, a fireplace that dominated one side of the room. A long-barreled flintlock rifle and a saber hung on pegs over the fireplace, flanked by a pair of flintlock pistols.

Glory came back with squat, thick glasses, each with a finger of amber liquid in it. When she saw Luke looking at the weapons hanging on the wall, she said, "My husband's father fought with Sam Houston during the revolution against Mexico. He was an officer and carried those during the battle of San Jacinto."

"For somebody who's not from Texas, you seem to know something about the place's history," Luke said.

"Sam wasn't your typical closemouthed, tightfisted

Scotsman," she said with a smile. "He liked to talk, and he was generous to a fault. That's how he inspired such loyalty among his friends and the men who worked for him. We spent many hours with him telling me all about his family and how they came from Tennessee to Texas back in the days when it was still a Mexican colony. I thought all the history was fascinating."

"I would have expected most women to find it boring."

"I'm not like most women." She lifted her glass. "To absent friends."

Luke clinked his glass against hers and nodded. When he sipped the whiskey, he found that it was as good as she had said it would be.

He told her as much, and she said, "You have an appreciation for fine liquor beyond the sort of rotgut flavored with gunpowder and rattlesnake heads you usually find around here?"

"I'd like to think I have an appreciation for all sorts of fine things in life."

She gave him an appraising look, too, but it was different from the one Verne Finn had directed at him. Then she said, "You're not the saddle tramp you appear to be, Mr. Jensen."

"There's a lot of that going around," Luke said. Glory cocked her head to the side quizzically, but he didn't elaborate. Instead, he said, "I hope you don't think I'm trying to stir up unpleasant emotions, but if you'll forgive my curiosity . . . how did your husband die?"

Her fingers tightened slightly on the glass. She had already taken a couple of sips of the liquor, but now she threw back the rest of the whiskey. As she lowered the glass, she said, "You really must be just passing through, as you said. If you'd been around these parts for very long, you would have heard the rumors."

"Rumors?" Luke repeated.

"About my husband's death. And I can tell you, Mr. Jensen, they're more than just rumors. They're true." She paused. "Sam MacCrae was murdered."

CHAPTER 5

Luke had plenty of practice at concealing his emotions. With nothing showing on his face except mild surprise, he said, "I'm sorry to hear that. It must've been pretty hard on you."

"Losing Sam would have been hard no matter how it happened. To have him stolen away like that . . ." Her voice trailed off as she shook her head.

"What happened? That is, if you don't mind talking about it."

Luke was curious what her story was going to be. He was sure she wasn't going to come right out and admit that she had killed her husband, although he had little doubt that was what had happened. Such a crime fit her pattern, after all.

"Sam liked to ride out on the range early every morning," Glory said. "For years he was up well before the crack of dawn every day, and he put in just as many hours in the saddle as any of the men who worked for him. But he was getting on in age, you understand, and

I'd convinced him it would be all right for him to take it a little easier." She smiled. "I admit, I had a selfish motive. I wanted him to spend more time with me."

"Nothing wrong with that," Luke said.

"But I still couldn't break him of the habit of spending a couple of hours every morning checking on things around the ranch. He had to make sure everything was running smoothly, even though he had a perfectly good crew to take care of things."

"Something happened to him while he was out on one of those rides?" Luke guessed.

"He wasn't back by the time he normally came in," Glory said, "so I went out to look for him."

"By yourself?"

"I didn't really think anything had happened to him," she said with a slightly impatient shake of her head. "It was just hard to conceive of anything bad happening to Sam. He always seemed so big and . . . invulnerable."

"Nobody's invulnerable," Luke said quietly.

"I know, but some people seem like they are. You can almost believe it of them. Sam was like that. I just thought he'd gotten delayed somehow. Maybe his horse had thrown a shoe or come up lame. At the very worst I thought maybe a rattlesnake spooked the horse and Sam was thrown, so that he was having to walk back in. But I wasn't really that worried."

"You didn't take any of the hands with you when you went to look for him?"

"No, it didn't seem necessary. I'm an excellent rider, and I had my carbine if I ran into any wild animals. I headed up into the hills, because that was the way Sam had gone when he left that morning."

Luke didn't hear anything except sincerity in her words. But she'd had several months to practice the story, he reminded himself. She should have been good at telling it by now.

"I hadn't been searching for very long when I heard a shot," Glory went on. "As soon as I heard it, I knew somehow that something terrible had happened. I headed in the direction of the shot, and a few minutes later when I came over a rise, I saw Sam's horse down at the bottom of the slope. The horse moved aside, and I . . . I saw him lying there."

She was really good at those little hesitations, Luke thought. They made what she was saying sound even more believable. She had to be telling the truth, people would think, because look how emotional it made her.

"You heard just one shot?" he asked.

"Just one. But it was enough. Sam was dead when I reached him. He'd been shot in the back."

"I'm sorry," Luke said. "What did you do then?"

"I got my carbine and fired three shots in the air. I knew that would bring any of the hands who were close enough to hear them."

It was true that three shots, fired at regular, fairly close intervals, was a universal signal for trouble on the frontier. That was an understandable reaction for a woman who had just found her husband gunned down.

But it was also a good excuse for her to fire her carbine, so it would smell of burnt gunpowder. She could have thumbed an extra cartridge through the loading gate, too, so that only three rounds would be gone from the carbine's magazine in case anybody checked.

Luke suddenly seemed to hear Gabe Pendleton's words in his head again. Pendleton had said that Verne Finn was "a backshooter and a bushwhacker." If there was trouble between the two spreads, wasn't it possible that Finn or another of Harry Elston's hired guns had ambushed Sam MacCrae? Because of Glory's true background, he had jumped to the conclusion that she was responsible for her husband's death, but that didn't necessarily have to be the case, did it?

Those thoughts raced through Luke's head. He still leaned toward Glory MacCrae being the killer, but he asked, "How long has the trouble with Elston been going on?"

"Longer than I've been here. More than a year, according to the things Sam told me. But it's only really started to boil over since . . . since Sam's been gone. I'm sure that Elston thinks I'm just a defenseless, hysterical woman and he can bully me into doing whatever he wants." She turned to the sideboard, splashed more whiskey into her glass, and downed it. "He's going to find out just how wrong he is."

"You think one of Elston's men murdered your husband?"

"What other reasonable explanation is there?" Glory asked.

Luke could have answered that. He could have pointed out how convenient an excuse this range-war-in-the-making was for a woman who wanted to get rid of her wealthy husband and inherit everything he owned.

But for the time being, until he could figure out a way to get Glory off the ranch and into the nearest jail without having to fight his way through Gabe Pendleton and the rest of the crew in order to do it, he had to act like he believed her. He had to act like he sympathized with her.

It wasn't that much of a stretch. She was convincing, no doubt about that.

"Have you thought about hiring some gunmen of your own?" he asked.

"Gabe and his men are pretty tough."

"They might not be a match for Elston's gun-wolves."

"Are you applying for a job, Mr. Jensen?" Glory asked with a faint, sardonic smile.

"What makes you think I'm a hired gun?"

"You carry two Remingtons and a knife, and I saw a Winchester on your saddle. Your hands don't have the same sort of calluses they would if you worked with a rope all the time. You obviously know your way around firearms, or you wouldn't have been able to shoot that rustler out of his saddle."

"That doesn't mean my gun's for hire," he said. A harsh note crept into his voice, and he didn't try to stop it.

"I meant no offense," she said with a shake of her head. "It was rude of me to say such a thing to a guest. I hope you'll forgive me."

"There's nothing to forgive," Luke said. "I'm sorry if I seemed thin-skinned. Why don't we start again?"

She smiled.

"That sounds like a good idea to me. And we can start by putting some more whiskey in your glass."

"An excellent beginning," Luke said.

Glory told Teresa, who turned out to be both cook and housekeeper, that there would be a guest for dinner. Luke asked where he could wash up before the meal, and she directed him to the pump next to the bunkhouse. He thanked her and left the house.

He had a clean shirt in his saddlebags he wanted to put on, so he headed for the barn where he had seen the young man called Vince lead his horse earlier. He figured his gear was in there somewhere.

When he came into the barn, he saw the other young wrangler, the redhead Glory had addressed as Ernie. He was in one of the stalls using a currycomb on the big white horse Glory had been riding. Ernie appeared to be the only person in the barn.

He turned to look over his shoulder when he heard Luke come in and said, "Oh, hey, mister. Are you looking for your horse?"

"My saddlebags, actually, Ernie. My name is Luke, by the way."

"Yeah, I know. Mr. Pendleton told me." Ernie put the comb aside and came out of the stall with an eager expression on his freckled face. He held out his hand and introduced himself. "I'm Ernie Frazier."

"Pleased to meet you, Ernie," Luke said as he shook hands with the young man.

"Mr. Pendleton also said you're the one who shot that rustler."

"Only because someone in his bunch had been shooting at me."

"I'm not surprised. That crew of Elston's is no good."

"Have you been here on the MC for a while, Ernie?" Luke asked. A talkative youngster was often a good source of information.

"About a year and a half, sir."

"Then it was Mr. MacCrae who hired you."

"Actually, it was Mr. Pendleton who hired me on, but I reckon he cleared it with Mr. MacCrae."

"How do you feel about working for Mrs. MacCrae?"

Just the mention of Glory's name was enough to put that brilliant smile back on Ernie's face. He said, "Why, it's just fine. She's the boss now, Gabe—Mr. Pendleton—says, so we've got to do what she tells us same as if Mr. MacCrae was still alive. Of course, I'd do that anyway, no matter what Mr. Pendleton said."

"It's a shame about Mr. MacCrae being killed," Luke said.

That was enough to make the smile disappear from Ernie's face. He said, "You've heard about that?"

"Mrs. MacCrae told me."

"Yeah, it was awful." Ernie thumbed his hat back. "That was sure a sad day. When we had the buryin', I mean. You never saw anybody braver than Mrs. MacCrae.

I could tell she wanted to cry, but she never did. Not one tear."

That was a little surprising to Luke. He would figured that Glory could summon up at least one tear for the occasion, just to make it look good.

"Who do you think shot Mr. MacCrae?" Luke asked.

"My money's on that fella Verne Finn. He's a snake-blooded hombre if there ever was one. It gives me the fantods just lookin' at him. But if it wasn't Finn, it was one of Elston's other men. I'd stake my life on it."

Luke changed the subject by saying, "How did Mr. MacCrae come to marry a woman like Mrs. MacCrae? I understand that he was a widower for a long time."

"Yeah, that's the way I heard it, too." Ernie was so open and unsuspecting that the words came out of him without any hesitation at all. "They met in town a while back."

"In Painted Post, you mean."

"Yeah. Mrs. MacCrae—well, her name was Miss Jenkins then, I guess—she'd come out here to Texas from somewhere back East. For her health, you understand. Something about the climate bein' better here. You sure wouldn't think she'd ever been sick a day in her life to look at her, would you? She looks like the picture of health."

"She does," Luke agreed dryly. He was sure it wasn't any sort of medical condition that had prompted Gloria Jennings to get off the train in Painted Post and call herself Glory Jenkins. She had probably thought the little cow town looked like a good place to lie low for a while until any pursuit that was behind her cooled off.

Then she had stumbled upon another target for her wiles in Sam MacCrae and had been unable to withstand the temptation.

He wondered what her real name was. She might have had so many aliases that she would have a hard time herself remembering the name she'd been born with.

"Anyway, it didn't take any time at all for Mr. MacCrae to fall for her," Ernie continued. "Shoot, I can understand that. All you've got to do is look at her. It's not just that she's so pretty, though. She's kind, too, and sweet. And she'll talk to you straight out, no beatin' around the bush like some gals do. To tell you the truth, Mr. Jensen, I wasn't sure at first about a woman runnin' a ranch, but now there's no doubt in my mind that she can do it."

From the door of the barn, Gabe Pendleton said, "Well, I'm sure we're all glad to know you think Mrs. MacCrae's got a right to run her own ranch, Ernie." His voice was sharp enough to make the garrulous young wrangler jump a little.

"I, ah, didn't see you there, Mr. Pendleton," he said.

"I reckon you didn't, or you would have been tending to your chores instead of flapping your gums."

Luke said, "I'm afraid I'm the one who made Ernie here neglect his work. I was asking him some questions."

"Is that what you came in here for, Jensen? Seems to me you're a mite curious about the workings of this spread."

Luke saw the suspicion on Pendleton's face and

heard it in his voice. Keeping his own response casual, Luke said, "Not at all. Ernie and I just got to talking, that's all. I came in to get a clean shirt from my saddlebags before I wash up for dinner."

"That's right, you're having dinner in the big house." Pendleton hooked his thumbs in his gun belt. "But after dinner, you'll be coming back out to the bunkhouse to sleep."

"I never thought otherwise," Luke said.

Pendleton gave him a curt nod, then said to Ernie, "There are other horses that needed tending to, not just Mrs. MacCrae's saddle mount."

"Sure," Ernie said. "I'll get right to 'em."

"See that you do."

With that, Pendleton turned and walked away from the barn.

"He's a mite touchy, isn't he?" Luke said.

"I don't reckon I'd better talk anymore, Mr. Jensen. Like Gabe said, I've got work to do."

"Of course. Do you happen to know where my saddlebags are?"

Ernie pointed and said, "All your gear's in the tack room, right over there."

"Thanks."

Luke found his saddlebags and got out the clean shirt. He said so long to Ernie and walked out to find the pump Glory had told him about.

As he did so, he thought about Pendleton's reaction. The foreman didn't want Ernie running his mouth about Glory MacCrae. Maybe that was just a ramrod being normally protective of his employer, especially since that boss was a woman.

Luke couldn't help but wonder, though, if it was more than that. When Gabe Pendleton looked at Glory, did he see just his boss . . . or something else?

Like a beautiful woman he was a little bit in love with. Maybe more than a little bit.

CHAPTER 6

Luke beat as much of the dust from his hat and trousers as he could, then got a rag wet at the pump and used it to clean off his boots. He took off his shirt, stuck his head under the stream of water, and sluiced more dust from his hair and bare torso. It felt good to be at least a little bit clean again, he thought as he pulled on the fresh shirt. It stuck to his damp skin in places.

When he turned toward the house, he thought he saw one of the curtains move slightly as it fell back into place.

Had Glory been watching him wash up?

Luke didn't have any false modesty. He knew that many women found him attractive, despite the fact that he wasn't what anyone would call handsome. And he certainly enjoyed the company of women in return.

But even if Glory MacCrae was drawn to him, he wasn't going to try to take advantage of that to capture her and turn her in for the reward on her head. Such behavior just wouldn't be honorable as far as he was concerned. He might be just a no-account bounty hunter with more blood on his hands than he liked to think about, but he had his limits.

When he went back inside the house, Glory greeted him by saying, "Why don't you hang your gun belt there on that peg beside the door?" When Luke hesitated, she added, "Surely you don't intend to sit down to dinner armed to the teeth?"

"That would interfere with eating, now wouldn't it?" he said with a smile. He didn't like taking off his Remingtons, but he didn't want to make Glory suspicious, either. So he unbuckled his gun belt and hung it on the peg she had pointed out.

Anyway, he thought, he still had a pair of two-shot, .41 caliber derringers, one in each pocket, so it wasn't like he was defenseless.

Graciously, she showed him to a dining room with a long mahogany table in the center of it. The table was already set for dinner, and platters of food awaited them. Luke saw slabs of roast beef and mounds of potatoes and rolls, but in that mix of cultures common here in West Texas where the border wasn't all that far away, there were also beans and chilies and tortillas. Everything looked and smelled delicious.

Glasses of wine waited for them on the table as well, and the bottle sat to one side.

"I opened the best bottle I could find," Glory said. "I thought you would appreciate it, Mr. Jensen."

"I'm sure I will. And you can call me Luke, you know."

"Would that be proper, since we've only known each other a short time?"

"You're the mistress of this ranch," Luke said. "I figure you can make your own rules."

She smiled and said, "That's true. Let's have a seat."

She certainly looked like the mistress of all she surveyed, he thought. Instead of the utilitarian riding clothes she had worn earlier, she had changed into an ivory-colored dress that set off her tanned skin. The dress hugged her waist, left most of her arms bare, and swooped low enough at the neck to reveal the upper swells of her bosom. A simple but elegant necklace was her only piece of jewelry other than the wedding band she still wore. She had put her dark hair up on her head in an elaborate arrangement of raven curls.

She was lovely enough to take a man's breath away, no doubt about that.

They sat down across from each other with the seat at the head of the table—old Sam MacCrae's seat, Luke assumed—left vacant.

Glory took a sip of her wine and said, "I know, this isn't the proper mourning garb, either. Teresa doesn't approve of my choices. She'd have me wear black for a year, at the very least. But to be honest, Mr. Jensen— Luke—you're the first visitor to the ranch since Sam's death. The first welcome visitor, I should say, since I don't count Harry Elston and his gunmen. I just didn't feel like wallowing in my grief tonight."

Or maybe she didn't have any real grief to wallow in, Luke thought. He said, "You won't hear me complaining, Mrs. MacCrae. Or should I call you Glory?"

She smiled and said, "I think that would be very nice."

Luke picked up his wineglass and said, "To the future, then."

"To the future."

And to five thousand dollars, he thought.

Teresa emerged from somewhere else in the house and served them. She wore a dour expression, and Luke could imagine how she had looked at Glory when she had seen the younger woman's garb for the evening. She probably thought Glory was dishonoring Sam MacCrae's memory. She probably believed as well that Glory was going to go to bed with the visitor.

That wasn't going to happen, Luke told himself. Not when he knew what the future held for both of them if everything went according to his plan. But if the circumstances had been different . . .

He put that thought out of his head and concentrated on enjoying the meal, which was not difficult at all. The food tasted as good as he expected it to. Teresa might not have a sparkling personality, but she was a fine cook.

The evening passed without Luke really taking note of the time. That came from being in such pleasant company. Glory was witty, intelligent, well-read, familiar with many of the same books and plays and operas that Luke had enjoyed in the past. She could discuss Fielding and Defoe, Hawthorne, Whitman, and Longfellow, Verdi and Wagner, Shakespeare and Sophocles. She disagreed with some of Luke's opinions, but in such a charming way that the disagreements could never be called arguments.

In short, she was so blasted charming it was easy to forget that she was also a murderess and a fugitive from the law.

Luke had to force his mind back onto the real business at hand. As they lingered over snifters of brandy, he said, "Tell me, do you go out riding to oversee the ranch's operation the way your husband did?"

The light had dimmed in the room. A short time earlier, Teresa had lit the candles in a silver candelabra at the other end of the table, as well as in several oil lamps in brass wall sconces around the room. The soft glow of candle flame washed over Glory's face and struck highlights from her hair and made her even more beautiful, but it also revealed a slight tightening around her mouth as Luke asked that question.

"I do," she said. "And Gabe does everything short of telling me I'm a stubborn fool for doing it, too."

"He's just worried about you," Luke said. "After what happened to your husband, I don't think you can blame him. Elston might hesitate to have a woman killed . . . but he might not. Do you take any of the hands with you?"

"Sometimes," she replied with a shrug. "It depends on what needs to be done. Keeping the ranch going is the most important consideration."

"I'm sure Sam MacCrae would be proud of you for feeling that way."

"I hope so," she said, and once again there was the faintest of catches in her voice.

The wheels of Luke's brain turned rapidly. He had a good reason for asking Glory about her habits. If she rode out from the ranch headquarters on a regular basis, that might be his best chance to get his hands on her and take her somewhere she could be locked up. Painted Post was the closest town, but he didn't know how sturdy its jail was. Since it was on the railroad, chances were he could find a telegraph office there, too, and wire the Rangers that he had arrested the fugitive Gloria Jennings. He had to worry, though, about Gabe Pendleton and the rest of the MC crew coming to town to bust her out of jail as soon as they got wind of what had happened.

Would they do that once they found out the truth about her? Would they be willing to put themselves on the wrong side of the law for a woman who had murdered at least one husband and maybe two, including their former boss?

Luke didn't know the answers to those questions, and he probably wouldn't be able to find out and deal with them until the time came.

There was another potential problem to consider. What he had just said to Glory was true as far as it went. If Harry Elston really wanted to grab this ranch, he might decide it would be quicker and easier just to have Glory killed, especially if he had been responsible for Sam MacCrae's death instead of her. In that case, she really was risking her life by leaving the ranch and making herself an easier target for bushwhackers.

Luke thought he might have a glimmer of a way to address both issues, but he needed to give it some more thought first.

In the meantime, there was no reason for him not to

enjoy this evening. He said, "I didn't mean to veer off into unpleasant territory. Let's get back to books. What do you think of *The Adventures of Tom Sawyer*? I'm sure you've read it."

"Indeed I have. It was quite good . . . for a burlesque. But I think Mr. Mark Twain has even better, more serious work in him, and I'm eager to read whatever he publishes next."

Luke would have responded to that—he always enjoyed a vigorous discussion of literature—but at that moment several gunshots slammed through the night outside. The reports were muffled slightly by the thick adobe walls, but Luke heard them clearly enough to know what they were.

"Good Lord!" Glory exclaimed as she lifted her head. "Is that—"

"It is," Luke said. He had already started to his feet. "Stay here. I'll find out what's going on."

She stood up, too, and said, "I can handle a carbine. I'll get it."

"Well, then, stay inside, anyway," Luke told her. "If you have to shoot, do it from a window and keep your head down."

At first he had hoped the commotion was just some high-spirited cowboys letting off steam. The gunfire continued, though, the heavier boom of handguns mingling with the sharper cracks of rifle shots. He even heard the dull roar of a shotgun as he hurried through the front room and grabbed his gun belt from the peg beside the door.

He buckled on the Remingtons, but he didn't rush

out without knowing what was going on. Instead, he blew out the lamps burning in this room and went to one of the windows. As he peered through the glass he saw scattered muzzle flashes blooming like crimson flowers in the darkness. Night had settled down over the ranch, but it hadn't brought peace with it.

Some of the shots came from the bunkhouse, but plenty of others originated outside. The men firing them seemed to be moving around, and after a second Luke realized they were on horseback. The continuing gun-thunder drowned out most other sounds, but he thought he heard hoofbeats, too.

"Can you tell what's going on out there?" Glory asked from beside him.

At that moment one of the bullets flying around hit the window, shattering the glass. As sharp splinters flew through the air around them, Luke grabbed Glory and dragged her to the floor with him. He sprawled on top of her, shielding her with his body as more slugs whined through the broken window.

"Blast it, I told you to stay back!" he said. "They must've spotted us."

"Who . . . is it?" Glory gasped. Luke supposed she was a little breathless because he was lying on top of her and his weight kept her from getting as much air.

"I don't know. Night riders. Elston's men, if I had to guess, trying to settle the score for that dead rustler."

"The one . . . you killed."

"Well, it seemed like the thing to do at the time."

"It was. But now . . . you need to get off of me. I'll keep my head down."

Luke pushed himself up on hands and knees so she could breathe easier. He knelt beside her as she scooted over next to the wall and sat up with her back against it. In the light from the dining room, where the candles were still burning, he saw the Winchester carbine she held across her lap.

"We can't let them get away with this," she said.

"Your men are putting up a good fight. The raiders won't keep up the attack for long. They have to know how thick the walls of this house and the bunkhouse are. They're just trying to do a little damage. Then they'll pull out and head back where they came from. If they get in a lucky shot or two and kill some of your men, so much the better for them."

"Elston's declaring war on the MC," Glory said grimly.

Luke shook his head.

"I'd bet the fanciest hat in a San Francisco haberdashery that Elston is in Painted Post right now, in a saloon or a restaurant where dozens of people can see him. If the law ever asked him any questions about tonight, he'd claim that he didn't know anything about it. His men will be the same way. They'll all swear they were back at the Lazy EO together."

"Then what can I do?" Glory asked with a note of desperation in her voice. "I can't let Elston just attack me at will."

"He's hoping a few of these raids will convince you to sell out to him."

"Never!"

Bullets had stopped coming through the window, so

after telling Glory again to stay down, Luke risked another look.

Just as he raised his head over the sill, he saw what appeared to be a giant ball of fire coming straight at his face.

He got out of the way so fast he went over backwards. As he hit the floor, the blazing torch one of the night riders had just thrown flew through the window and landed on the rug behind him. The walls wouldn't burn, and torches flung onto the tile roof wouldn't have any effect, either, but if the raiders threw enough of those blazing brands through the bullet-shattered windows, they could catch the inside of the house on fire.

"There are more of them coming!" Glory cried. She had ignored Luke's warning and gotten up to look through the window.

Luke surged to his feet and started trying to stomp out the flames as they tried to spread. It was the rug that was burning, so he told Glory, "See if you can roll it up and smother the flames!"

While she did, he lunged to the window with a Remington in each hand. She'd been right: Two more riders carrying burning torches galloped toward the house. The raiders were bent low to present smaller targets, but Luke didn't aim at them as he opened fire. He shot at the torches instead, the Remingtons roaring and bucking against his palms.

One of the blazing brands suddenly pinwheeled through the night air, and he knew one of his bullets had struck it and ripped it out of the raider's hand. He hoped he had winged the man, too.

The other night rider threw his torch, but Luke's bullets whipping around his head made him hurry too much. The torch struck the wall next to the window and bounced off to land in the garden and lie guttering on the ground.

As if suddenly realizing their danger, the raiders tried to wheel their mounts and flee. Luke triggered two more shots and saw one of the men jerk in the saddle.

Beside Luke, Glory's carbine cracked as she crowded up to the window and joined in the fight. The stench of the scorched rug competed with the tang of gunsmoke, but when he glanced over his shoulder he saw that the fire was out.

"You're not in the habit of doing what people tell you to do, are you?" he said.

"Not so that you'd notice," she replied without looking at him as she worked the Winchester's lever and jacked another round into the chamber.

"I've got to go out there," he said. "There are too many windows. They could be trying to throw torches through some of them. I need to be able to see better . . . but I need you to stay in here, too."

He might still be able to collect the bounty if a stray slug cut her down, but he didn't want to run that risk.

"Be careful!" she told him, but he noticed that she didn't promise to do as he asked.

He paused long enough to reload both Remingtons. The revolvers, originally percussion weapons, had been converted for metallic cartridges by a top-notch gunsmith Luke knew, which certainly came in handy at moments like this when time was important.

With the cylinders of both guns full, Luke holstered the left-hand weapon and used that hand to open the door. He went through it in a low dive that landed him on the flagstone walk. He rolled over and came up on a knee as he drew the second gun again.

Some of the night riders were still concentrating their gunfire on the bunkhouse. The long, low structure had only small windows, and throwing torches through one of them would be almost impossible, especially with a gun-toting cowboy at each opening to discourage any of the raiders from getting too close.

No, the would-be arsonists were targeting the main house instead, and from the corner of his eye Luke saw flames again as two more torch-wielding riders raced toward the house. They were trying for windows at the end of the building this time.

Still on one knee, Luke twisted toward the raiders and triggered the Remingtons. One man dropped his torch, bent double, and grabbed at the saddlehorn to keep from toppling off his horse. The other raider kept coming, though, and drew back his torch to sling it.

The boom of a shotgun filled the night. The man went backwards, blown right out of the saddle by the load of buckshot that slammed into him. As far as Luke knew, the only other person in the house was Teresa. He wouldn't have thought the little gray-haired Mexican woman could handle a scattergun, but evidently he would have been wrong.

At that instant, hoofbeats pounded the ground close behind him. He looked over his shoulder and saw another of the night riders closing in on him. This man didn't have a torch, but he had a Colt in his hand and had already drawn a bead on Luke at almost point-blank range.

And in that shaved second of time, Luke knew that if he tried to turn and fire before the man's gun erupted in deadly flame, he would be too late.

CHAPTER 7

A rifle cracked suddenly, and the raider pitched sideways from his saddle before he could pull the trigger. Luke still had to dive out of the way to avoid being trampled by the charging horse. The slashing hooves barely missed him.

As he rolled over and came up on a knee, he saw Glory standing in the doorway with the carbine at her shoulder. She worked the lever and swung the barrel to the right, tracking another of the raiders. She fired again but evidently missed, because the man she was aiming at kept going without showing any signs of being hit.

It didn't matter, thought Luke. The shot just before that had been accurate.

And it had saved his life.

He came to his feet as the night riders began to break off their attack. They peeled away from the buildings and galloped into the darkness. Luke threw a couple of shots after them, as did Glory, but it would be pure luck if they hit any of the raiders and Luke knew it.

As she lowered her Winchester, Glory asked, "Are you all right, Luke?"

"Thanks to you I am," he said. "That was a nice shot."

"I had to hurry. I was afraid I was going to miss."

"You didn't." Luke holstered his left-hand gun and quickly reloaded the other Remington. Keeping the revolver leveled and ready, he cautiously approached the man Glory had shot out of the saddle.

The man had rolled over a couple of times when he landed and now lay sprawled on his back. He wasn't moving. Luke used a booted foot to prod his shoulder roughly enough to make the man's head loll back and forth. The limp motion convinced Luke the raider was dead.

The light wasn't good out here. He fished a lucifer from his pocket and snapped it to life with his thumbnail. By the little flame's glare, he saw that Glory's bullet had caught the man in the left side, bored all the way through his body, and come out on the right just above the ribs. It had gotten both lungs and possibly the heart.

Good shooting indeed, especially under pressure. She hadn't been lying when she said she knew how to handle a rifle.

Unfortunately, that was just one more indication that she could have bushwhacked her husband.

Luke held the match closer to the dead man's face and asked, "Do you know him?"

"No," Glory said.

"You haven't seen him before with Elston?"

"No. I'd tell you if I had."

Luke dropped the match in the dirt just before the flame reached his fingers. The dead man was a stranger to him, as well. He thought back to Elston's visit to the MacCrae ranch a few hours earlier and tried to remember the faces of the gunmen Elston had brought with him. Luke was pretty sure this man hadn't been one of them.

That was unfortunate. But maybe some of the other raiders had been left behind, and their corpses could serve as evidence against Elston.

"Mrs. MacCrae! Mrs. MacCrae!" Gabe Pendleton called as he ran toward them with a Colt in his hand. His boots were off, and he wore his trousers over a pair of long red underwear. "Are you all right?"

"I'm fine, Gabe," she told him. "Are any of the men hurt?"

"A couple of them," Pendleton said, "but they were just winged. They'll be all right."

"We'll take them to the doctor in Painted Post. Or you can send a rider to bring him back out here, if you think they're hurt too badly to travel."

The foreman shook his head and said, "I don't think that'll be necessary. Kaintuck ought to be able to patch them up. But if he says they need a real sawbones, we'll sure tend to it."

"All right," Glory said with a nod. "I'll leave that to your judgment."

Pendleton looked at Luke and said, "You appear to be all right, Jensen."

"A couple of close calls, but no damage done," Luke said.

Pendleton nodded toward the dead man lying almost at their feet.

"Brought one of the bas—I mean, varmints down, I see."

"Actually, Mrs. MacCrae deserves the credit for that," Luke said, smiling slightly. "She drilled him as neat as you please and saved my life."

Several other members of the crew had followed Pendleton over to the main house, including the two young wranglers Ernie and Vince. At Luke's words, Ernie let out an admiring whistle and said, "That's some shootin', ma'am!"

Pendleton turned to the men and said, "Spread out and make sure those skunks didn't do any more damage. Somebody needs to mount up and check on the herds and the men riding nighthawk, too. This raid could've been just a distraction to cover up some wide-looping on a larger scale."

That possibility had just occurred to Luke as well. Pendleton was already taking care of it, though, so he didn't have to make the suggestion himself.

"Bullets shattered some of the windows," Glory said. "They'll need to be boarded up until we can get them repaired."

Pendleton sighed and said, "Mr. MacCrae had those windows brought out here from San Antonio on the train and then we hauled 'em in the wagon to the ranch. He set great store by them."

"I know," Glory said quietly. "We'll put them back as

good as new. But right now I need to go make sure Teresa is all right."

Luke followed her into the house. They found the little Mexican woman sweeping up broken glass. She was unharmed but angry.

"The men should saddle and ride and unleash hell on Señor Elston," she proclaimed as she waved her broom in the air for emphasis.

"I'd agree," Glory said, "except that we have no proof."

"Proof!" Teresa snorted in disgust. "When you see a rattlesnake, you do not ask for proof that he is a venomous serpent. You just cut his head off!"

Nobody could argue much with that sentiment, Luke thought as he smiled to himself.

The violent raid brought the pleasant evening to an unexpected, unwanted end. Luke knew there was no point in trying to recapture what had been going on between him and Glory. It had been mostly a lie anyway, at least on his part, as he tried to figure out his next move.

He couldn't have said what she was feeling. He had a hunch Glory MacCrae was good at keeping her true thoughts and emotions to herself.

He pitched in to help board up the broken windows and then said good night. As they stood in front of the main house's doorway, Glory put a hand on his arm and said, "Thank you for everything you've done."

"You're the one who saved my life, remember?" Luke reminded her. "As far as I can tell, the only thing

I've accomplished is to make things worse between you and Harry Elston by killing that rustler."

"I promise you, this trouble was coming whether you were here or not, Luke. It's been inevitable since someone killed Sam and Elston decided he could force me out of Sabado Valley." Glory smiled sadly. "If you're as intelligent as you seem to be, you'll get on your horse in the morning and head for El Paso as fast as you can get there. Forget about everything that's going on here."

"I'm not sure I can do that," Luke said.

Glory's face grew solemn as she said, "I don't want to be responsible for anything happening to you."

"You won't be. I make my own decisions." He paused. "And right about now I'm not feeling any too kindly toward Mr. Harry Elston."

That was true, he reflected as he walked out to the bunkhouse. He didn't like range hogs who hired vicious killers. He didn't like men who tried to take advantage of women. And he sure as hell didn't like being shot at and nearly trampled. He might have come here on business, but now he had a personal score to settle, too.

It didn't look like Glory planned to go anywhere anytime soon. He didn't have to get in a hurry about taking her in. There was no reason he couldn't afford to hang around for a while and see what happened with this brewing range war.

With that decision made, he went into the bunkhouse, stretched out on an empty bunk that Ernie Frazier pointed out to him, and fell into his usual light but restful sleep.

* * *

As was always the case on a ranch, the men were awakened well before dawn the next morning. A tall, skinny old-timer with a black patch over his left eye stalked into the bunkhouse when the eastern sky was barely touched with gray and held a lantern high over his head in his right hand. In his left hand he carried a cowbell that he started clanging in a raucous racket.

"Get your butts outta them bunks 'fore I come around and kick 'em out!" the old man threatened in a leather-lunged bellow. "On your feet or I'll flang a hydrophobia skunk in here and let *him* roust you good-for-nothin' cow nurses!"

One of the men groaned and pulled his thin pillow over his head.

"Shut up that caterwaulin', you old pelican!" he yelled from under the pillow.

"Old pelican, is it!" The man with the eye patch strode over to the bunk where the complaining cowboy huddled and started lambasting him with the bell, which made its strident clamor even louder. "Get outta there, or I'll beat you within an inch o' your worthless life!"

Gabe Pendleton came out of the tiny private room that was his by right of being the foreman and said, "Take it easy, Kaintuck. If you kill him that's one less waddy I've got to do the work today."

Kaintuck snorted disgustedly, but he stopped whaling away at the cowboy. He said, "I'm sick and tired of these varmints carryin' on like it's early. Ain't I already been up for a couple o' hours boilin' coffee and cookin' bacon and biscuits?"

"If you can call that stuff coffee," came a voice from a corner of the bunkhouse. "It's thick as axle grease and tastes about as good."

Another man said, "If you been up cookin' that bacon for a couple hours, Kaintuck, shouldn't it be, you know, actually cooked and not half raw?"

"Not to mention those biscuits'd do for proppin' up a wagon, they're so danged hard!" somebody else jibed.

Kaintuck glared around and snapped, "Keep it up, you smart-mouthed golliwogs! See if you like your own cookin'! I quit!"

He stalked out of the bunkhouse, muttering curses as he disappeared into the predawn darkness.

Luke had watched the byplay with a smile on his face as he sat up in his bunk. The camaraderie among these men was obvious. He had seen the same thing with his brother Smoke's crew on the Sugarloaf Ranch in Colorado. Pearlie, Cal, and the rest of Smoke's men were cut from the same cloth as these Texas cowboys. They were, in a very real sense, family.

That was something Luke had missed out on for the most part. Looking back on his life, he could see that he had spent most of it in solitude, alone even when he was in a crowded saloon or café. Even most of his relations with women had been impersonal.

From time to time, he gave some thought to trying to change, but after all this time he wasn't sure he wanted to. He wasn't sure he even knew how.

Gabe Pendleton came over to his bunk. The foreman

was already fully dressed and looked like he was ready to begin the day's work.

"Well, now you've met our cook, Kaintuck," Pendleton said.

"We haven't been formally introduced," Luke said, "but I doubt if I'll forget him anytime soon. Of course, since he quit I don't suppose it really matters."

Pendleton chuckled and shook his head.

"Kaintuck quits three or four times a week. It doesn't mean anything. He's back in the cook shack right now, out back of the mess hall."

"You don't eat in the main house?"

"That's Mrs. MacCrae's house," Pendleton said, his voice hardening slightly. "She's got her place, and we've got ours. If you were going to be staying around here, Jensen, you'd need to understand that. But I guess since you're moving on, like you say, it doesn't matter."

Luke swung his legs off the bunk and stood up. He said, "I don't recall telling anybody that I was moving on."

"And I don't recall anybody inviting you to stay," Pendleton shot back. "If you're thinking about parlaying what happened yesterday into a riding job, you'd better think again. We're not hiring. Our crew's full up."

At one of the nearby bunks, Ernie Frazier pulled a shirt over his head and then said, "I figured we could always use another good hand around here, Mr. Pendleton. Anyway, you haven't replaced Jimmy Applewhite since he quit and went back down to South Texas. . . ."

The young wrangler's voice trailed off as Pendleton gave him a hard look.

"I handle the hiring and firing around here, Ernie," the foreman said. "You'd do well to remember that."

"Yes, sir," Ernie mumbled as he looked down at the plank floor.

Pendleton turned back to Luke and went on: "You're welcome to stay for breakfast, of course. If your horse needs to rest for a day or two, I reckon even that would be all right. But don't get the idea this is something that it's not, Jensen."

Pendleton had him pegged as just another drifting saddle tramp, one step below even a grub line rider. That was all right, Luke thought. The ramrod's opinion of him didn't really matter.

It was a lot more important what Glory MacCrae thought.

Luke didn't respond to Pendleton. After a moment, Pendleton turned and walked away, speaking quietly to several of the other men as he left the bunkhouse. Luke pulled on his boots and buckled his gun belt around his waist, then settled his hat on his head as he joined the others on their way to the mess hall.

True to Pendleton's prediction, Kaintuck was hustling around the room with its long table flanked by benches. The old cook filled coffee cups and set out platters of bacon—which as far as Luke could see was cooked just fine—biscuits, flapjacks, and fried eggs. There were bowls of gravy and molasses with spoons in them.

Luke sat down at one of the empty places and filled the tin plate in front of him. The food was simple but good. The coffee was better than good. Not as thick as axle grease, as the jocular cowboy had claimed, but plenty potent.

The crew ate without a lot of talking. Breakfast was serious business on a ranch, where hours of hard work awaited before the men would have a chance to eat again. Even then, their lunch was liable to be rather skimpy, maybe some jerky and a biscuit or two they would take with them from breakfast and stash in their saddlebags. So while they had the chance, they packed away the food to keep their strength up.

Luke didn't have that much work waiting for him today, as far as he knew, but he ate heartily anyway, because it was good and because there had been plenty of times in his life when he'd been hungry. Gut-wrenchingly, soul-crushingly hungry a few times. No one who had ever gone through that passed up the opportunity to enjoy some good food.

The eastern sky was starting to turn gold with the approach of the sun as the men left the mess hall and started drifting toward the barns and corrals to pick out their mounts for the day and get saddled up. The early morning air had a crisp, cool tang to it. Luke wondered if Glory was up yet.

He didn't have to wonder long. She came out of the house dressed in her riding clothes again and strode straight toward him. Getting right down to business as usual, she greeted him by saying, "Good morning, Luke. I'm on my way to Painted Post, and I'd like for you to come with me."

CHAPTER 8

Before Luke could respond, Gabe Pendleton said, "I can have one of the boys go into town with you, Mrs. MacCrae."

Glory shook her head.

"No, I don't want to take any of the men away from their work," she said. "Unless, of course, Mr. Jensen doesn't want to come with me."

"I'd be glad to accompany you, Mrs. MacCrae," Luke said. He and Glory had been using their first names with each other the night before, but since she had referred to him as "Mister" this morning he figured she wanted to maintain a certain level of formality in front of the crew. He didn't mind playing along with that.

Pendleton didn't look happy about the decision, but he didn't argue. Glory asked him, "Did you find out if anyone bothered the herds last night?"

"It was quiet out on the range," Pendleton reported. "No run-ins with rustlers."

"So the raid was just a blatant attack on us after all, not a distraction."

Pendleton shrugged and said, "That's the way it looks."

"Did you find the bodies of any other night riders?"

"No, ma'am. Either we didn't kill any more of them, or they took the rest of their dead with them."

Luke said, "Some of them were hit. I'm certain of that."

"Yeah, so am I," Pendleton said. "We didn't knock anybody out of the saddle, though, so I don't see what good it does us."

"You might keep your eyes and ears open in case there's any news of Elston's men suffering gunshot wounds."

Pendleton grunted.

"Elston's not gonna let word of that get out," he declared. "He'll make sure he's covered in the eyes of the law."

"We'll see about that," Glory said. "Where's the body of the man I killed?"

Pendleton jerked a thumb over his shoulder and said, "We put him in the barn. He's wrapped up in a horse blanket."

"Put him in the back of the wagon. I'm going to deliver him to Sheriff Whittaker's office myself."

"Are you sure that's a good idea, ma'am?" Pendleton asked with a frown.

"Mr. Jensen is going with me," Glory replied as she

nodded toward Luke. "I'm sure that between us we can handle any trouble we run into."

Again Pendleton looked like he wanted to argue but didn't. He just nodded and said, "I'll take care of it." He turned and started off toward the barn.

Luke told Glory, "I'll go get my horse saddled."

"You don't want to ride on the wagon with me?" she asked.

"If you can handle the team—and to be honest, you seem so capable I'll be surprised if you can't—I'd rather be mounted so I can move around better in case of trouble."

"So you can run out on me if any shooting starts?"

Luke felt a flash of anger. He said, "I won't dignify that with a response."

"I didn't think you would," she said. "But I wanted to be certain."

"I wouldn't run out on any woman who was in trouble."

And sure as hell not one who's worth five grand, he added silently to himself.

"If we're going to be spending the day together, let's not get off on the wrong foot," Glory said. "I see now I shouldn't have asked you that. I didn't mean anything by it, honestly. It's just that in my experience, men often promise one thing . . . and deliver another."

Luke didn't know what she meant by that, but he nodded and said, "It's all right. I'll be ready to go in a few minutes."

He had been pushing the dun fairly hard in recent

days, and he wanted to give the horse more time to rest if he could. When he went into the barn he found Vince there and said, "I'm riding into Painted Post with Mrs. MacCrae. I was wondering if I could use one of the ranch's saddle string and let my horse take it easy today."

"Sure," the solemn-faced youth said.

"Well . . . you know the horses a lot better than I do. Maybe you can recommend one."

Vince shrugged. He seemed to be a young man of few words. He and Luke went out to the corral and Vince pointed to one of the horses.

"Nobody's using that roan gelding today. Want me to put your saddle on him?"

The offer took Luke a little by surprise. He said, "That would be fine. Thanks, Vince."

The wrangler just shrugged again, wordlessly.

A few minutes later, he led the roan out of the barn and handed the reins to Luke, who had been watching a couple of the hands hitching up a team to the wagon. A grim, blanket-shrouded shape was already in the back of the vehicle. Rope had been tied around the corpse to hold the blanket in place.

Luke checked the cinches on the saddle before he mounted. He noticed Vince watching him and saw the frown creasing the young man's forehead.

"I always check my saddle when I don't do it myself," he explained. "It's just a matter of habit. Nothing against you, son."

Vince turned away without saying anything.

"Don't mind him," Ernie said quietly as he sidled up

next to Luke. "He's that way with everybody. His folks died when he was young, and he got shuffled around from relation to relation. That's a hard way to grow up."

"I suppose it is," Luke said. At least when he was a kid he'd had his ma and pa, as well as his younger brother and sister, so he had known what it was like to have a loving family before he went off to war and everything changed.

His parents were dead now, and Smoke had told him that their sister, Janey, had passed away several years earlier, too. Luke regretted never seeing her again after he enlisted. She had made some foolish decisions in her life and had come to a bad end, and he thought that if he'd been around he might have been able to help her avoid that fate.

She had left home before the war was even over, though, so logically he knew that wasn't the case. Nothing he could have done would have prevented Janey from following her own trail in life, no matter where it led.

When the wagon team was ready to go, Glory came over and climbed onto the high seat. Luke swung into the saddle, and they set out for Painted Post as the sun rose over the hills to the east, on the other side of Sabado Valley.

Luke didn't think Elston's men would try anything else so soon after the attack on the ranch, especially not anything as blatant as bushwhacking the MC's owner. But as he rode beside the wagon, his gaze remained in constant motion anyway, roaming over the rangeland around them in search of anything that might signal danger. Such caution was a requirement in his line of work. Without it he might not live long.

To make conversation, he said, "I was told that you came west for your health. If you don't mind my saying so, you appear to be a remarkably healthy individual."

"I don't mind," Glory answered, "but who told you that?"

"I heard it on the ranch," Luke said. "I don't recall exactly who mentioned it."

He didn't want to take a chance on getting young Ernie Frazier in trouble with the boss, even though Glory didn't seem bothered by the question.

"It doesn't matter," she said. "It's common knowledge. I had a problem with my breathing, but it got better almost immediately in the drier air out here."

She would have had trouble with her breathing if she'd stayed back in Baltimore, Luke thought. It was hard to breathe past a hang rope.

"That's just one reason I'm glad I came to Texas," Glory went on. "The other is that I met Sam, of course. The day we were married was the happiest day of my life."

"Is that so?"

She looked over at him and smiled.

"You sound skeptical. Don't you believe in marriage, Luke?"

"I believe it exists."

"But not in its benefits."

He shrugged and said, "I can't really testify one way

or the other. I've never indulged in the state of wedded bliss, myself."

"You've never been married?"

"Never even came close."

She flicked the reins and clucked to the horses, then said, "That's a shame. I'm sure you'd make some woman a fine husband."

That caused a genuine laugh to erupt from his lips. He shook his head and said, "Lady, you are about as far wrong on that score as you could be. I'd feel sorry for any woman who got herself saddled with the likes of me."

"Maybe you underestimate yourself."

"I don't think so," he said.

They rode on in silence for a few seconds. Then Glory said, "Well, I believe in marriage. I've been married twice, in fact."

He was a little surprised that she would admit that, but he kept his face and voice only casually curious as he said again, "Is that so?"

"Yes, I was married back East, before I came west. My husband . . . passed away."

"I'm sorry." He figured she might think it odd if he didn't comment on what she had just said, so he went on: "It sounds like you haven't had very good luck when it comes to husbands."

"On the contrary. I've had very good luck. Both of them were fine men. Wonderful men. They were the ones who were unlucky." A trace of bitterness tinged her voice as she added, "Unlucky enough to have married me."

"I don't see how you figure that."

"It's obvious, isn't it? I'm a jinx. At least my first marriage lasted for several years before something terrible happened. With Sam, it was only a matter of months."

Luke wondered just how much she would confess to, now that she had started talking. He said, "What happened to your first husband?"

Glory shook her head, though, and replied, "I'm sorry. I don't want to talk about it. It's still too painful."

"All right," Luke told her. "I didn't mean to open up old wounds."

"That's all right. I'm the one who brought it up. Perhaps we should talk about something more pleasant . . . like this blasted range war."

"You mentioned the sheriff in Painted Post. You reckon he'll step in and do anything about Elston?"

"I think it's highly doubtful. Jared Whittaker is a politician, first and foremost, and I think he's betting that in the long run Harry Elston will be more powerful and influential in the county than I will. I wouldn't go quite so far as to say that he's in Elston's pocket, but I don't think he'll go out of his way to help me, either."

"He's a lawman," Luke said. "It's his job to do what's right and legal."

Glory laughed and said, "You're not such a babe in the woods as to believe that, are you, Luke? Carrying a badge is like any other job. In the end you wind up working for whoever has the most money."

Luke thought that was a pretty cynical attitude, but in most cases she was probably right.

Not in all of them, though. There was such a thing as justice in this world, and in his occasional philosophical moments he liked to think that he served that end. Hunting down fugitives wasn't just a matter of collecting the bounties on their heads.

The road followed the hills, and as the ranges on both sides of the valley petered out, it continued southeast across semi-arid, chaparral-dotted flats that ran all the way down to the Rio Grande and the Mexican border. Luke had come through Painted Post the previous day, so he knew it lay only a few more miles ahead of them.

It wasn't long before he spotted the elevated water tank at the railroad station and a couple of church steeples. Those were the highest structures in town.

Painted Post owed most of its existence to the railroad and to the ranches in the hills to the north and west. It was also close enough to the border to serve as a supply point for the gold and silver mines in the mountains across the river in Mexico. So it was a dusty, sleepy little settlement most of the time, when the ranch crews or the miners weren't there on payday, spending their wages on a blowout of whiskey, women, and cards.

The town's main avenue was McDowell Street, which ran north from the railroad depot for several blocks. It was a wide, sun-blasted road crossed by several smaller streets lined with businesses for the first block before becoming residential neighborhoods where the town's inhabitants lived in a mixture of frame and adobe houses.

Most of the businesses on McDowell Street were frame as well, some with false fronts, but the bank was constructed of large blocks of sandstone, as was the county courthouse and jail. A few cottonwood and aspen and willow trees struggled to grow here and there. This region was more suited to cactus and bunch grass when it came to vegetation.

It was midday when Luke and Glory reached the settlement, so quite a few people were moving around. In another couple of hours, as the temperature began to heat up more, a lot of those folks would disappear until late afternoon when things began to cool off. Right now, though, wagons were parked in front of the stores, horses were tied at hitch racks, and people made their way along the boardwalks in front of some of the buildings. Many of them paused to turn and look as Glory drove by with Luke riding beside the wagon.

He was a stranger in town, having spent only a few minutes there the day before. Some of the citizens probably recognized Glory, and they would have looked at her anyway, especially the men.

Luke didn't get the feeling that Painted Post was overly friendly toward Glory MacCrae.

She kept her gaze directed straight ahead and her chin up. If the stares bothered her, she wasn't going to show it. Instead, she drove to the courthouse and pulled back on the reins to bring the two horses to a stop there.

Luke reined in as well and dismounted. As he looped the roan's reins around a hitch rail, he saw two men lounging in the open double doorway of the courthouse. One was a burly hombre whose hat looked a little too small for his block of a head. His face was sun-blistered, and the hair that poked out from under his hat was prematurely white.

His companion was smaller, but still broad-shouldered and well-built, with a black Stetson thumbed back on reddish-brown hair.

Luke turned to the wagon and said to Glory, "Let me give you a hand down."

For a second she looked like she was going to tell him she was perfectly capable of climbing down from the wagon by herself, but then she relented and let him assist her. With both hands on her waist, he set her on the ground and asked her in a half-whisper, "Who are the two gents in the door?"

"The big one is Whitey Singletary," Glory replied, equally quietly. "They're very original in their nicknames around here. He's the chief deputy. The other man is Jared Whittaker."

"The sheriff."

"That's right."

As the wagon had passed the people on the boardwalks, some of them had noticed the blanket-wrapped shape in back, and now they came along the street to find out what was going on. Anything out of the ordinary, anything that might break the monotony, was of extreme interest in a place like this.

Sheriff Whittaker straightened from his casual pose with one shoulder propped against the doorjamb and started toward the wagon. Deputy Singletary fell in behind him, hulking along like a bear. A polar bear, Luke thought, considering the white hair and pale skin.

"Mrs. MacCrae," Whittaker greeted Glory as she and Luke turned to meet the two lawman. He lifted a hand and carelessly touched a finger to his hat brim. "What in the world have you got there?"

Singletary leaned to the side to peer past them and said, "Looks like a body to me, Sheriff." The words seemed to have to strain to get past the muscles in his thick neck.

"It is a body," Glory said.

"One of your men?" Whittaker asked.

"No. One of the raiders who attacked my ranch last night and tried to burn down my house and kill me and my crew." Glory's voice was sharp, lashing the words. "In other words, one of your friend Harry Elston's men."

CHAPTER 9

Whittaker stiffened. He said, "That's a mighty serious accusation, Mrs. MacCrae. You know for a fact that this dead man worked for Mr. Elston?"

"Who else would send hired killers skulking through the night against me?" Glory demanded.

Whittaker cocked his head to the side and clucked his tongue.

"We're not that far from the border, you know. I try to keep an eye on things, but there's a lot of empty country out there. It would be easy enough for a bunch of bandidos to slip across the river, circle around the town, and raid some of the ranches around here."

"This man isn't a Mexican bandit," Glory said. "You can have a look for yourself."

"Oh, I intend to. Let's get that blanket off of him." Whittaker motioned toward the wagon. "Whitey."

Singletary stepped to the back of the wagon and pulled a folding knife from his pocket.

Before he could cut the ropes holding the blanket

around the corpse, though, Luke said, "There's no need for that. Just untie the knots, deputy. That's easy enough."

Singletary's moonlike face twisted in a sneer. He said, "Who're you to be givin' me orders, mister?"

"I'm a man who doesn't believe in cutting a perfectly good rope that can be untied."

Luke started to step past the deputy.

He didn't really care that much about the rope, but Singletary rubbed him the wrong way. The man's piggish eyes had a brutal cast to them. Luke had seen plenty of men like this before. Pin a badge to their sweat-stained shirts and they thought they had a right to lord it over other men. That made Luke want to get a rise out of him.

He did. Singletary grunted and swung a hamlike fist at Luke's head. It was the fist with the knife in it.

Luke jerked his head back. The blade flashed in front of his eyes, missing his face by bare inches. Singletary was off balance because of the miss, so Luke threw a looping, overhand left that smashed into the right side of the deputy's jaw and knocked him in the direction he was already going. Singletary stumbled and fell. He sprawled on his belly in the dust of the street.

Moving quickly, Luke brought his right foot down on Singletary's wrist, not hard enough to break any bones, but with sufficient force to keep that hand pinned to the ground. He reached down and plucked the knife from the deputy's fingers, then straightened and stepped back. He closed the knife and tossed it in the back of the wagon.

Sheriff Whittaker looked angry. He had his hand on the butt of his holstered Colt as he said, "You're under arrest, mister!"

"On what charges?" Glory demanded.

"Interfering with an officer of the law and assaulting him!"

"Deputy Singletary attacked Mr. Jensen with no provocation," Glory insisted. "Mr. Jensen was just defending himself. We all saw it."

Mutters of agreement came from some of the people in the crowd. Glory might not be a favorite of theirs, but evidently Singletary wasn't, either. That came as no surprise to Luke. He had been able to tell by looking at him that the deputy liked to run roughshod over people. Some of the citizens probably felt like they had been treated unfairly by him in the past.

"Now hold on there," Whittaker said. "I told Whitey to cut those ropes. Jensen had no right to stop him."

Luke said, "Actually, you didn't say that. You just told Deputy Singletary to get the blanket off the corpse. Cutting the rope was his idea. All I tried to do was untie it, and he nearly cut my throat."

From the ground, Whitey Singletary growled and said, "I'll do more than that, you son of a bitch. I'll bash your brains out!"

He surged up from the ground and charged at Luke like a maddened bull.

"Sheriff, stop this!" Glory cried.

Jared Whittaker just stood there, though, with an interested look on his face.

Singletary swung a wild punch that had the power of his burly body behind it. His fist moved slowly, however, and Luke had no trouble avoiding it.

But then he discovered that Singletary was smarter than he appeared to be, at least when it came to fighting. When he dodged to the side, Singletary's other hand was waiting. That was when Luke realized that the telegraphed punch had been a feint. Singletary grabbed the front of his shirt and swung him hard against the wagon's sideboards.

The impact jolted Luke and sent his hat flying into the street, but it didn't knock the breath out of him. Singletary let go of his shirt. Luke guessed the deputy's next move would be to throw those bearlike arms around him and try to crush his ribs. He couldn't let that happen, so he snapped a short but powerful punch to Singletary's nose, jabbing it with enough force to make Singletary jerk his head back and howl in pain.

Luke bored after him. His left pistoned back and forth a couple of times, landing with stinging splats on the deputy's nose. Luke felt hot blood gush over his knuckles. Singletary staggered back a step as he tried to get away from the persistent punishment. That gave Luke room to swing another right. It crashed into Singletary's slablike jaw.

That punch would have been enough to knock most men off their feet. It actually carried more strength than the blow that had landed the deputy in the street a few moments earlier.

But even though he was a little off-balance now, he

was able to catch himself and swing his right arm around in a scything backhand. Singletary might lumber when he was walking, but he moved fast in a fight. Luke couldn't avoid the sweeping blow. It caught him on the side of his head and knocked him spinning to the ground.

Vaguely, he heard shouts from the crowd as he rolled over. Glory yelled at Sheriff Whittaker to stop the fight, but the lawman ignored her. Mainly, though, what Luke heard was the blood roaring in his head.

Singletary was roaring, too, as he charged after Luke, evidently intent on kicking and stomping him to death. The deputy had lost his hat, and his thatch of white hair was in wild disarray.

Luke rolled desperately as Singletary launched a kick at him. Singletary's boot scraped Luke's shoulder hard enough to hurt, but without enough force to do any real damage. Luke twisted on the ground, grabbed Singletary's leg, and heaved. At the same time he scissored his legs around the deputy's other leg and swept it out from under Singletary. The white-haired man landed so hard it seemed like the whole world should have trembled under the impact.

Luke got a hand on the ground and levered himself up. A dive landed him on top of Singletary. He drove his knee into the man's stomach, then clubbed his hands together and sledged them down into Singletary's face. Singletary's nose was already broken, and the terrific blow just flattened it that much more. The bottom half of the deputy's pale face was smeared crimson with blood, and more splattered out across his pale skin.

That ended the fight. Singletary wasn't completely unconscious, but he lay there in a battered stupor, unable to move. Luke knelt on top of him, his chest heaving as he tried to catch his breath.

He heard the unmistakable metallic sound of a gun being cocked.

"That's it, mister," Sheriff Whittaker said as he leveled his Colt. "Make another move and I'll kill you. I said you're under arrest, and I meant it."

"But you were willing to stand by and let this thuggish bruiser of a deputy beat me to death if he could," Luke accused. After the exertion of the fight, it was a strain for him to keep his voice steady, but he managed.

"You were resisting arrest. That puts whatever happened on your head."

"Sheriff," Glory said, "you can't do this. Again, Mr. Jensen was only defending himself from your deputy's unlawful attack."

"Whitey's wearing a star," Whittaker said. "Whatever he does is legal."

"Is that what you really think, Sheriff?" Luke asked as he pushed himself to his feet. He looked around at the crowd. "Is that what the citizens of Painted Post believe? That just because these men carry badges, that puts them above the law?"

"You leave them out of it."

Whittaker darted a glance at the onlookers, though, Luke noted. While some of them were edging away nervously, obviously unwilling to go against the local star packers, others wore angry, defiant expressions. Like any politician, Whittaker clearly had his enemies.

"Mr. Jensen isn't going to jail," Glory said.

"He is if I say he is," Whittaker replied stubbornly.

"No, he's not. If you insist on arresting him, we'll all march down to Judge Marbright's office right now and the judge can assess a fine, which I'll pay. Mr. Jensen came to town with me today because I asked him to, and I'll be damned if I'm going to let him be locked up just because he stood up to your bullying hulk of a deputy!"

Glory stood there with her hands on her hips, looking beautiful as she berated the sheriff. Luke had to admit that she cut a mighty impressive figure.

Whittaker stood there with an angry frown on his face, but then he smiled abruptly and holstered his gun. He said, "I reckon this is all just a big misunderstanding. There's no need to involve the judge in it."

"I can see why you'd feel that way," Glory said. "The judge is an honest man."

Whittaker kept the insincere smile on his face, but his lips tightened. With a visible effort, he controlled his anger at Glory's gibe and went on: "We'll just drop it . . . this time." He turned his head to give Luke a cold stare. "But if you cause any more trouble in my town, mister, you'll regret it."

"I'm not here to cause trouble," Luke said. He bent and picked up his hat, then slapped it against his leg to get some of the dust off. After he settled the hat on his head, he turned to the wagon and reached into the back to untie the knot in the rope holding the blanket around the body of the dead night rider. He pulled the blankets back to reveal the man's face.

"Do you recognize him, Sheriff?" Glory asked.

Whittaker stepped closer to the wagon and rested his hands on the side as he looked at the corpse. After a long moment he shook his head.

"I don't think I've ever seen this man before," Whittaker said.

Luke addressed the crowd, asking, "What about the rest of you?"

Whittaker glared. He probably didn't like the way Luke had asked for help from the bystanders, many of whom crowded forward to take a better look at the dead man.

One man pointed at the corpse and said, "I think I've seen him around town before, but I ain't sure."

"Same here," another man chimed in. "I couldn't tell you his name, though, or even where I saw him. Probably in one of the saloons."

From the back of the crowd, somebody called, "If you saw him, Riley, it was bound to have been in a saloon!"

The man called Riley, who had the red-veined face of a heavy drinker, turned sharply and demanded, "Dadgummit, who said that?" His only answer was laughter from some in the crowd.

Sheriff Whittaker said in an irritated voice, "All right, if nobody knows this man, you can all break it up and clear out. We're not having a camp meeting here. Go on about your business."

As the crowd began to disperse with some reluctance, Glory said, "I'm going to leave my wagon here for now, Sheriff. You'll have Claude Lister come and get the body so he can take care of it?"

"Yeah, I guess," Whittaker said in a surly tone. "What are you going to do in the meantime, Mrs. MacCrae?"

"Mr. Jensen and I are going to get some lunch," Glory said. "Assuming that he's free to go."

Whittaker nodded, made a curt gesture, and said, "Yeah, yeah, that's fine. Remember what I said, though, Jensen."

"I intend to remember everything that's happened today, Sheriff," Luke said.

Let Whittaker make of that whatever he wanted to.

"Hold on a minute." Whittaker pointed at the corpse. "Nobody's told me how this hombre wound up dead."

Glory said, "I most certainly did tell you. This man was with a group that attacked my ranch headquarters last night. They shot up the bunkhouse and my house and tried to throw torches in the house to burn it down."

"Yeah, but who pulled the trigger on him?" Whittaker asked as his eyes narrowed.

Without hesitation, Glory answered, "I killed him."

"You're mighty quick to admit that."

"He was about to shoot Mr. Jensen, and I fired to save my guest's life. There's nothing underhanded about that, Sheriff."

"There'll have to be an inquest into both of these killings," Whittaker said. "You'll have to testify."

"Let me know when and I'll be here," Glory promised.

"All right, then," the sheriff said with a reluctant shrug. "I guess you're free to go, both of you."

As Luke and Glory turned away, Whittaker scooped Singletary's hat from the ground, dipped into a nearby water trough, and dashed the water into the deputy's face.

"Wake up, you blasted ox," Whittaker said. Singletary came up from the ground sputtering and cursing.

The two lawmen stood there talking in swift, angry voices, but Luke couldn't make out the words anymore as he and Glory crossed the street toward the Elite Café. He could feel a hate-filled gaze burning into his back, though, and he knew he had made a dangerous enemy in Whitey Singletary.

Since it wasn't long past midday, the café was still busy, but a couple of tables with blue-and-white-checked tablecloths were empty and Luke and Glory sat down at one. She loosened the chin strap of her hat and took it off, setting it on the table. Luke put his hat on one of the empty chairs at the table.

He was aware that they were the subject of a lot of interested stares from the other diners as a buxom young woman in a calico dress and a white apron came over to the table and said, "Good afternoon, Mrs. MacCrae. What can I get for you and your friend?"

"Two specials, Hazel, and coffee."

"Yes, ma'am. I'll bring the coffee."

When the waitress had gone, Glory said, "I hope it's all right I picked what to eat, Luke."

"You know the place better than I do," he told her. "As long as it's good."

"It will be. Hazel Anderson's mother is an excellent cook. Not as good as Teresa, mind you, but still good."

Hazel brought the coffee, then returned a few minutes later with plates that contained sizzling steaks, potatoes, greens, and a couple of rolls that steamed when they were broken open.

"You showed good judgment," Luke said after he had been eating for a few minutes.

"In this, perhaps, but not always, unfortunately."

Luke sipped his coffee and said, "Forgive me for being blunt, but opinions in this town seem to be divided when it comes to you. Some people seem to like you, but a lot of them don't appear to have much use for you."

"You're absolutely right," Glory said. "There are several reasons for that. Some of them knew Sam's first wife. She was much loved and admired around here, and they resent me for what they see as trying to take her place. After Sam died, it got even worse. They'd been willing to tolerate me for his sake, but now with him gone, I'm just the outsider who came in and took over his ranch. With some of the old-timers, just the fact that I'm an outsider is enough for them not to like me."

"Where you're from isn't exactly your fault."

"No, but they'll hold it against me anyway. Then there are the people who support Harry Elston. His ranch isn't as big and successful as the MC, but it's big enough that Elston wields a lot of influence around here. People try to curry favor with him, especially the ones who think that he'll win in the end and take over my ranch."

"Like Sheriff Whittaker," Luke commented.

"Precisely. By the way, I hope you have eyes in the back of your head. I wouldn't put it past Whitey Singletary to try to ambush you. Nobody's ever beaten him like that before. The wound to his pride is probably even more painful than his broken nose."

"It won't be the first time somebody's had a grudge against me."

Glory regarded him speculatively and said, "No, I imagine it won't be. You've been through some rough times, haven't you?"

"A few," Luke admitted. "They build character."

Glory laughed and said, "Indeed, they do."

A few minutes later, a short, pudgy man with a round, beaming face and slicked-down brown hair came into the café, looked around, and then started toward their table when he spotted them.

"Mrs. MacCrae," he said as he came up to the table.

"Hello, Claude," Glory said. "Luke, this is Claude Lister, Painted Post's undertaker. Claude, this is Luke Jensen."

Luke stood up and shook hands with the undertaker. He could have made some comment about how they were both in the business of death, but he didn't see any point in that.

"Mrs. MacCrae, the gentleman you brought in had

some money among his belongings," Lister said, "but not quite enough to cover my services. I was told you were in here, and I thought you might want to . . ."

"I'll cover the cost," Glory said. "Figure up a bill, and I'll stop by your place on the way out of town and pay it. And by the way, he wasn't what I would call a gentleman."

"By the time I see them, such distinctions usually don't mean much anymore. Can I assume you won't be attending the service . . . ?"

"Just put him in the ground," Glory said. "Where snakes belong."

CHAPTER 10

The lunch special included a bowl of peach cobbler, which was as good as the rest of the meal. When they were finished, Luke insisted on paying.

"But you're my guest," Glory argued.

"And you've fed me a couple of meals already. This one is on me."

Glory shrugged and agreed. Luke left the price of the meals and a generous tip for Hazel on the table. That cut into the dinero he had left, but he told himself that it didn't matter. Pretty soon he'd be collecting that five-thousand-dollar bounty on Glory, and he'd be flush for quite a while.

He just wished the thought of doing that didn't make something stir uncomfortably inside him.

As they stepped out onto the street again, he reminded himself that she had murdered her husband back in Baltimore, and there was a good chance she'd bushwhacked Sam MacCrae, too. He knew she was a good shot, so there was no reason to think she couldn't have plugged MacCrae in the back. Sure, she had saved *his* life by cutting down that night rider, but that didn't excuse her other crimes.

Did it?

That was a troubling question, but Luke didn't have time to ponder it. Sheriff Jared Whittaker was coming toward them, and as usual, the lawman didn't look happy or friendly.

"I've talked to Judge Marbright," Whittaker said without any sort of greeting as he came up to them. "The inquest will be at two o'clock tomorrow afternoon. You'll have to testify, and so will Jensen here. And Gabe Pendleton, too."

"All right," Glory said. "We'll be here, although I hate to have to make another trip into town so soon."

"Maybe you should have thought of that before you killed that man."

"If I'd stopped to think about anything, Mr. Jensen probably wouldn't be alive."

Whittaker grunted. It was obvious he thought that wouldn't be any great loss.

"How's your deputy?" Luke asked. Maybe it was a little petty, trying to get under Whittaker's skin that way, but he didn't really care.

"His nose is busted all to hell," Whittaker snapped. "Doc Fleming says he may never breathe right again."

"Maybe *he* should have thought of *that*."

Whittaker's shoulders bunched as he struggled to control his anger. Glory linked her arm with Luke's and said, "Come on. We still have to stop at the undertaking parlor."

Luke gave Whittaker a curt nod, said, "Sheriff," and then turned to go with Glory.

"Do you make a habit of going around poking hornet's nests?" she asked under her breath as they walked away from Whittaker.

"You're a fine one to talk after some of the things you said to that hombre."

She laughed.

"I suppose you're right. I just don't like the man. It's hard not to say things you know are going to irritate him. But he *is* the legally elected sheriff. There's only so far we can push him."

"You're sure he was elected legally? No irregularities in the voting?"

"None that I'm aware of."

"All right," Luke said. "I'll try to be on my best behavior from now on, but I can't make any promises."

"Neither can I," Glory said with a smile.

They went into Claude Lister's undertaking parlor, where Glory settled the bill for a pine box and planting the dead man.

"By all rights it should be Harry Elston paying for this," Glory said as she handed over the money.

"I wouldn't know anything about that, ma'am," Lister said. "A man in my business, he's sort of got to be neutral, you know? Sooner or later, I have responsibilities to both sides in any dispute."

"Of course," Glory said. "And since that man died on my ranch, I suppose I have some responsibility, too."

"What about his belongings?" Luke asked. "You said you found some money."

"Pocket change, not much more than that," Lister said.

"What about anything else? Letters, or anything else that might identify him?"

The undertaker shook his head.

"I'm afraid not. Tobacco, some loose ammunition, an elk's tooth lucky piece, a pocket watch, that's about it."

"So you don't have a name to put on the marker."

"No, he'll have to be buried as unknown, unless somebody comes in pretty quickly to let me know different. I'll be loading up the coffin and taking it out to the cemetery soon."

Glory said, "If you see Harry Elston, you might ask him. I doubt if he'll be in town today, though."

Again Lister looked a little uncomfortable. Glory shook her head and muttered an apology. She and Luke left the undertaking parlor.

"I should have held my tongue," she said. "I know that most of the people here in town are hoping that the trouble between Elston and me will be settled one way or the other before they're forced to take sides. They don't want a range war spilling over into Painted Post."

"Can't really blame them for feeling that way," Luke said.

"No, but it bothers me when people can see what's going on and yet they refuse to take a stand. When they're finally pushed into a corner, it may be too late."

Luke couldn't disagree with that sentiment.

Glory's wagon was still parked in front of the courthouse. The two horses in the team and the roan Luke had borrowed had had a chance to drink at the trough where Sheriff Whittaker had scooped up water to throw in his senseless deputy's face.

Luke untied the team while Glory climbed to the driver's seat. He swung up into the saddle, and they headed north along McDowell Street until it turned into the road that led up through Sabado Valley. Remembering how long it had taken them to reach the settlement that morning, Luke calculated it would be almost dark by the time they got back to the MC headquarters.

That estimate proved to be correct. They moved steadily, pausing now and then to rest the horses, and the sun had just dipped below the hills to the northwest when they came in sight of the ranch buildings. Luke knew that darkness fell quickly out here, but they were close enough now that they wouldn't have any trouble making it the rest of the way. The trail was easy enough to follow.

But as the gloom gathered, he heard hoofbeats up ahead, coming toward them. Ever since they had left Painted Post, he had been alert and watchful, studying the landscape around them for any sign of impending trouble. He didn't think it was likely they would run into an ambush this close to the ranch, but nothing was impossible.

He drew his Winchester from its sheath and held the rifle across the saddle in front of him. Glory had brought along her carbine; it was on the floorboard of the driver's box at her feet. Luke said quietly, "Better get that gun and put it on the seat beside you."

"What is it?" Glory asked.

"Horses coming."

But a moment later a familiar voice hailed them, and in a relieved voice Glory said, "That's Gabe. Someone must have spotted us, and he and some of the men came out to meet us."

Pendleton and three other riders loomed up out of the dusk. The foreman said, "Is that you, Mrs. MacCrae?"

"It is," Glory replied. "Me and Mr. Jensen."

Pendleton might not be all that happy he had come back from Painted Post with Glory, Luke thought. But he must have known that would happen, since Luke's horse was still here at the ranch.

Pendleton turned his horse to ride on the other side of the wagon from Luke. The other men fell in behind the vehicle. Pendleton asked, "What happened in town?"

"I turned the body over to the sheriff like I said I was going to. And then Claude Lister took charge of it. I expect that the man's been buried by now."

"I'll bet Whittaker was fit to be tied," Pendleton said.

"He wasn't happy, that's certain. But it was that deputy of his, Whitey Singletary, who caused the real trouble."

"Singletary," Pendleton repeated, sounding like the name tasted bad in his mouth. "What did that ugly, pale-faced polecat do?"

"He attacked Mr. Jensen and actually tried to cut his throat. There was quite a battle."

"Is that so?" Pendleton looked across the driver's seat at Luke. "You don't appear to be busted up too bad."

"I'll be sore in the morning, I expect," Luke said. "But Whitey's the one who's going to be wheezing through a crooked nose from now on."

One of the cowboys said, "You busted Singletary's nose? Good for you!"

"Yeah, it's long past time somebody handed that varmint his needin's," another man added. "He's been known to jump a cowboy who's had too much to drink and beat the stuffin' outta him, for no good reason."

The cowboy who had spoken up first said, "No offense, Jensen, but I'm a mite surprised you were able to whip him. Nobody else ever has, since he's been in Painted Post. He's half bear, half buffalo."

"It wasn't easy," Luke said.

The punchers started to heap more praise on him, but Pendleton interrupted them and said, "You fellas get on back to the ranch. Everything's under control. I'll see to it that the boss lady gets home safely."

"The boss lady can take care of herself," Glory said dryly.

"Yes, ma'am, I didn't mean otherwise."

The three cowboys rode on ahead and vanished into the gloom that was dispelled by a few yellow patches of lamplight from the buildings. A few minutes later, still accompanied by Luke and Pendleton, Glory drove the wagon up to the barn and stopped it. Ernie and Vince, the two young wranglers, were waiting and moved in quickly to take over the chore of putting up the wagon and unhitching the team.

Glory jumped down from the seat before Luke could move to help her. She looked up at her foreman and said, "You'll have to come back into town with us tomorrow, Gabe. Judge Marbright wants you to testify at the inquest into the killing, along with Luke and me."

"I don't like leaving the ranch," Pendleton said. "Who'll make sure all the work gets done?"

"We have a good crew. I think we can trust them to work without supervision for one day."

Pendleton gave a skeptical grunt and said, "Reckon I don't have any choice, if that's what the judge wants."

"It is." Glory turned to Luke. "You'll have dinner with me again this evening."

It wasn't a question. While Luke didn't much like being told what to do, even by a beautiful woman, he didn't argue. He was still trying to sort out how he was going to proceed here and what he was going to do about Glory.

It wasn't as easy a decision as he had thought it would be when he first arrived on the MacCrae ranch.

While Glory went into the house, Luke and Pendleton led their horses into the barn to unsaddle them and turn them into the corral. As they were doing that, Pendleton said, "It sounds to me like you're sort of a magnet for trouble, Jensen."

"How do you figure that?"

"Whitey Singletary jumping you that way. He's a bad man to have for an enemy."

"I've already been warned that he might try to bushwhack me."

"You think it's smart for you to hang around here? I mean, Mrs. MacCrae already has enough problems with Harry Elston. . . ."

Luke asked, "Are you saying that I'm just going to bring more trouble down on her head?"

Pendleton shrugged and said, "If you're crosswise with the law, it can't help matters."

"What about Elston trying to force her off the MC with all that rustling and raiding?"

"The boys and I can handle that," Pendleton snapped. "We don't need any help from a gunfighter."

Luke set his saddle on a sawhorse and said, "I don't recall that I claimed to be a gunfighter."

Pendleton snorted.

"What else can you be, packing two guns like that? You're sure no grub line rider."

"Never claimed to be that, either. As for Elston and his men . . . No offense, Pendleton, but I'm not sure how well you and the rest of the crew match up with Verne Finn and those other gun-wolves working for Elston."

"So it's back to you hiring your gun out to the boss." Pendleton made a disgusted sound and turned away. "Nothing but trouble is going to come of you coiling your twine here, Jensen. If you really want to help Mrs. MacCrae, you'll ride out when that inquest is over and put this part of the country behind you."

"We'll see," Luke said curtly. He knew, though, that he wasn't going to be leaving.

Not without Glory.

He left Pendleton quietly seething behind him and walked toward the house. This conversation had convinced him more than ever that the foreman thought of Glory as more than just the boss lady. He entertained dreams of someday marrying her and becoming the boss of the MC himself.

A wild thought suddenly occurred to Luke.

Was that dream so strong inside Gabe Pendleton that he would resort to murder to help it along? Were Pendleton's whereabouts unaccounted for at the time Sam MacCrae was bushwhacked?

He would have to talk to Glory about that, he decided, but he would need to be careful about how he phrased his questions. He couldn't just come out and ask her if she thought Gabe Pendleton might have murdered her husband.

For one thing, if she herself was guilty, more than likely she would be quick to cast suspicion on somebody else, even Pendleton.

Luke went into the house, wondering a little how he had talked himself into trying to solve Sam MacCrae's murder.

He unbuckled his gun belt and hung it on the peg near the door, then dropped his hat on the peg as well. Teresa came into the room and told him, "Señora MacCrae is freshening up. She asked that you wait for her in the dining room."

"*Gracias,*" Luke said. He went on, "Did you work for Sam MacCrae for a long time, Teresa?"

She looked a little surprised that he would ask her a question. As a servant, maybe she wasn't used to having a real conversation with a guest. But after a second's hesitation, she said, "*Sí*, I worked for Señor MacCrae and the first Señora MacCrae ever since they came to Sabado Valley, long before the town of Painted Post was there, long before the railroad came. In those days, this part of Texas belonged to the Apaches. My late husband, El Señor Dios rest his soul, was the *patrón*'s foreman. Together they fought the Apaches and the weather and the land to make this ranch what it is."

Luke had a feeling that might be the longest speech he ever heard from the old woman. He said, "You must not like it that the new Señora MacCrae is running the ranch now."

"It is hers by right," Teresa said. "That was Señor MacCrae's decision to make."

"Of course. If they were happy together—"

From one of the doors at the side of the room, Glory asked, "Luke, why are you questioning my house-keeper?"

He looked over at her, saw that she had changed into a dark blue gown that dipped low into the valley between her breasts. She was dressed for dinner, all right.

And maybe more.

CHAPTER 11

"I'm not questioning anybody," Luke said. "Just making conversation."

Glory's voice held a hint of coolness as she said, "If there's anything you want to know about me, or about my relationship with my husband, you can just ask me. I think there's a connection of sorts between us." She paused. "After all, I *did* save your life."

Luke inclined his head in acknowledgment of her point and said, "Of course. I meant no offense."

"None taken," Glory said as she came farther into the room. Her raven hair was loose tonight, instead of being put up as it had been the night before. It flowed around her face and onto her shoulders in a dark, lustrous tide. She went on: "Dinner will be ready soon. Until then, would you like a drink?"

"Sounds good," Luke said.

Teresa retreated to the kitchen. Glory went to the sideboard and poured drinks for herself and Luke. As she handed one of the glasses to him, she said, "I keep getting the feeling that there's more to you than is apparent, Luke Jensen."

"I could say the same about you, Mrs. MacCrae," Luke replied as he lifted his glass to her. She clinked hers against it, and they drank.

"What are your plans after the inquest tomorrow?" she asked.

"I haven't made up my mind yet. Your foreman wants me to leave."

"Gabe? Why would he want that?"

He couldn't tell if she was being disingenuous, or if she really wasn't aware of how Pendleton felt about her. He said, "I think he's a little jealous."

"Really? Of what?"

"Of the fact that I'm in here about to have dinner with you, and he's out there in the bunkhouse."

Glory looked surprised. She shook her head and said, "You can't be serious. Gabe doesn't have any interest in me. He's been courting a woman in Painted Post."

"Painted Post is half a day's ride away from here," Luke pointed out. "You're a lot closer."

"I'm also his employer."

"And until recently you were also his boss's wife. That doesn't always stop a fella from feeling things he knows he shouldn't."

"Well, I just can't believe that," Glory said. "I've never given him any reason to think—"

"A man doesn't always need a reason."

She turned to the sideboard and frowned as she poured another drink.

"I'm going to pretend we haven't had this discussion," she said. "I don't need anything else complicating my life right now."

"All right. I'm sorry I said anything."

Glory shook her head and said, "No, I asked. You just answered. But you didn't tell me what you plan to do."

"What would you have me do?"

She looked him squarely in the eye and said, "You could stay here and help me keep Harry Elston from running me off this ranch."

"Be your hired gun, in other words, the way Elston has Verne Finn around."

"It's not exactly the same. Finn's just a mercenary. You and I . . . Somehow it seems to me that we're kindred spirits. You live here on the frontier, but yet you're more than that."

Luke let a harsh note creep into his voice as he said, "Don't give me more credit than I've got coming. I'm not some pampered Eastern gentleman, and I never will be."

"If you were, I wouldn't want your help."

Luke had a little whiskey left in his glass. He tossed it back and contemplated everything they had just said. Despite his show of reluctance, Glory was really playing into his hands. If she hired him, it would give him the perfect excuse to stay here until he found the right opportunity to take her into custody . . . assuming he still wanted to.

Twenty-four hours earlier, he had been convinced she had murdered Sam MacCrae, along with Alfred Jennings back in Baltimore. Now he had begun to have nagging doubts about whether she was responsible for MacCrae's death.

And if she hadn't killed MacCrae, could he be absolutely certain that she had murdered Jennings? She had been charged with the crime, which meant the law in Baltimore believed her to be guilty, but lawmen sometimes made mistakes just like everybody else.

Luke tried to force his thoughts away from that possibility. It wasn't his job to determine guilt or innocence. That was up to a judge and jury. He would collect five grand just for turning her over to the law so she could stand trial. What happened after that was none of his business.

There was more to life than blood money, though. No matter how much he might deny it, he wanted to know the truth. One way to start might be to figure out who was really responsible for gunning down Sam MacCrae.

And all he could do was hope that Glory's beauty wasn't muddling his mind too much.

Teresa appeared and said, "Dinner is ready, señora."

"You still haven't given me an answer, Luke," Glory said as she looked at him.

"If you want me to stay for a while, I'll stay," he said. "That doesn't mean I'm working for you, though. We'll talk about that later, once we've seen how things go."

"So for now you remain my guest."

He shrugged and said, "If that's what you want to call it."

"That means after we've eaten, you can go out to the bunkhouse and gather your things. If you're a guest, you'll stay here in the house, in one of the guest rooms."

"Pendleton's liable not to like that," Luke warned.

"Gabe may be the foreman, but I still call the shots on this ranch."

Luke didn't figure there was any doubt about that.

Dinner was as good as it had been the previous night, but afterward Glory said that she was tired and had a headache, so she didn't suggest they have brandy to top off the meal.

"It's been a long day, and tomorrow will probably seem even longer," she said.

Thinking about the inquest, Luke said, "You may well be right."

"Teresa will show you to your room."

"If you're sure you want me to move in here."

"I'm not worried about my reputation, if that's what you mean," Glory said with a smile. "For one thing, most of the people in Painted Post who don't like me already consider me a hussy, and for another, having a she-wolf like Teresa in the house will insure that everything remains proper."

"The thought of anything else never crossed my mind," Luke lied.

He had thought about it, all right. Any man who laid eyes on Glory MacCrae would. But as much as he enjoyed the company of women, he wasn't a slave to the passions of the flesh and never had been.

Glory came over to him and rested her hand on his arm for a moment.

"Good night, Luke," she said.

"Good night."

She hesitated, and he knew that if he wanted to, he could lean down and kiss her. She probably wouldn't object.

But as she had said earlier, he didn't really need any extra complications in his life, either, so he just stood there giving her a faint smile until she turned away and vanished down one of the corridors.

As if she had been lurking, waiting for Glory to leave—which she probably had been—Teresa appeared from one of the other corridors and said, "This way, señor. Your room is down here."

In the opposite direction from Glory's room, Luke noted.

Teresa showed him to a room that was furnished with a comfortable-looking bed with a thick straw mattress, a woven rug on the floor, a small table with a basin and a pitcher of water, and a couple of chairs. Yellow curtains hung over the arched window. One wall had a portrait of the Virgin Mary on it.

"You will sleep well," Teresa said. "The Madonna will watch over you, and nothing will disturb you here."

Luke took that to mean he shouldn't disturb anyone else, either. He said, "*Gracias*, señora."

"The memory of Señor MacCrae will be honored!" she blurted out.

"I agree completely," he assured her. "I'll be back as soon as I fetch my things from the bunkhouse. You don't have to wait up for me, though. I can find my way back here."

"See that you do," she said.

He waited until her back was turned, then grinned as she swept out of the room. She might not like the new señora very much, but she was protective of Glory's honor anyway, because it reflected on the honor of the late Sam MacCrae.

Luke went out to the bunkhouse, pausing to put on his hat and buckle the gun belt around his waist again before he left the main house. When he entered the long, low building, he saw that the door to Gabe Pendleton's room was open. The foreman sat on a stool, cleaning his Colt. When he glanced up at Luke, he tried to make it casual but didn't quite succeed.

"You're back a mite earlier than I expected," Pendleton commented.

"Yes, but I'm not staying," Luke said. "Mrs. MacCrae has invited me to stay on for a while as a guest, and I took her up on it. She wants me to sleep in the main house."

"Is that all you took her up on?" Pendleton snapped.

"That was all that was offered," Luke said coolly. "Not that it's any of your business."

"Anything that happens on this ranch is my business."

"Right down to what the lady does in the privacy of her own home?"

Pendleton set the gun aside and stood up quickly. For

a second, Luke thought the foreman was going to take a swing at him. He hoped he wasn't going to have to fight Pendleton. His muscles already ached from the ruckus with Whitey Singletary in Painted Post.

"You like to push a man, don't you, Jensen?" Pendleton asked in a tight voice.

"Not particularly. But I have a habit of pushing back."

Pendleton glared at him for a second, then said, "I don't tell Mrs. MacCrae what to do with her personal life. That's her business. But I'll look out for her interests in every other way."

"Fair enough."

"I don't know what you're up to, Jensen, but there's something you're hiding. I'm sure of it. So I'm keeping an eye on you, and if you try anything funny, I'll be ready . . . and you'll be sorry."

"You've got me all wrong, Pendleton," Luke said, even though to a certain extent the foreman was right about him. He hadn't told the truth about why he'd come to Sabado Valley. He wouldn't reveal that until he was ready to make his move.

And that time wouldn't come until he had found out more about Glory MacCrae and the tangle of violence and tragedy that swirled around her.

He stalked over to his bunk, gathered up his meager possessions, and stowed them in his saddlebags. As he draped the saddlebags over his left shoulder, Ernie Frazier asked from a nearby bunk, "You're not pulling out, are you, Mr. Jensen?"

"Just moving into the house, Ernie," Luke said. "Mrs. MacCrae has decided that I'm a guest, not a member of the crew, so I need to stay in one of the guest rooms."

"Oh." Ernie didn't look very happy about this new development, either, and Luke recalled that the young wrangler seemed to have a crush on Glory. Once the word got around, this whole bunkhouse might be a hotbed of jealousy, he thought.

"'The face that launched a thousand ships'," he murmured, "'and burnt the topless towers of Ilium.'"

"Huh?" Ernie said with a frown.

Luke shook his head and waved away the question. He said, "Never mind. I'll see you, Ernie. I'm not leaving the ranch, just moving across to the house."

"All right, Mr. Jensen."

Luke wouldn't have been completely surprised if he'd found Glory waiting for him in his room when he got back to the house, but it was empty in the light of the single candle burning on the table. That was probably a good thing, he thought. He hung his saddlebags over the back of a chair, then moved the other chair close to the bed. He took off his gun belt and coiled it, placing it on the chair so that the butts of the Remingtons were handy if he needed them in a hurry during the night.

Once he'd taken off his boots, blown out the candle, and stretched out on the bed, it was a while before he went to sleep.

His brain was too full of questions, and answers were in short supply.

* * *

"How did you sleep last night?" Glory asked him at breakfast the next morning.

"Fine," Luke said, which was stretching the truth by a considerable amount. Not only had he had trouble dozing off, but once he did, his sore muscles had stiffened up, so that every time he shifted on the mattress, twinges of pain disturbed his slumber. He thought he was lucky Whitey Singletary hadn't battered him even more during their fracas.

Glory looked fresh and lovely in a denim riding skirt and white blouse with a brown rawhide vest over it. When Pendleton came in to ask her if she wanted the wagon team hitched up, she said, "No, just have Ernie or Vince saddle my horse instead. I'll ride to town with you and Luke."

Pendleton had his hat in his hands. He turned it over, fidgeting with it as he said, "It's a good long ride to Painted Post."

"I know, but we have plenty of time to get there before the inquest. We won't push ourselves or the horses."

"Whatever you say, ma'am," Pendleton responded with a nod. He left the house.

Glory looked at Luke over her coffee cup and said, "I still think you're wrong about him, you know."

Luke just shrugged. If Glory couldn't see how Pendleton felt, maybe she was being willfully blind.

When they came out of the house, Glory's big white horse was saddled and ready to go. Luke's dun was waiting, too. As he checked the saddle, Pendleton and three of the MC hands rode up.

"Are those other men coming along?" Glory asked

her foreman. "The three of us are the only ones who have to testify."

"Verne Finn and some of those other gunhawks would love to catch the three of us out alone between here and town," Pendleton said. "If anybody jumps us, I want to be able to put up a fight."

"Do you think Elston's men would try to ambush us?"

"Ma'am, after everything they've done, I wouldn't put anything past that bunch."

"I don't think I would, either," Glory said. She smiled at the three cowboys. "I hate to take you men away from your work, but honestly, I'll be glad for your company."

"It's our pleasure, ma'am," one of them replied.

The six riders left the ranch headquarters and followed the road southeastward through Sabado Valley. It was a pretty day, with some high, thin white clouds in the bright blue sky. Good weather was no guarantee there wouldn't be any trouble, though. Pendleton and the other men seemed to understand that. They spread out so they surrounded Glory, and their eyes never stopped moving as they scanned the countryside for any warning signs.

"From what Sam told me about the old days, it was like this before most of the Apaches moved across the border into Mexico," Glory said. "Any group that set out to go anywhere was well-armed and on the alert. You never knew what you might run into when you rode away from home."

"It'll always be that way," Pendleton said. "If it's not Apaches, it'll be outlaws, and if it's not outlaws, it'll be hired guns. There'll always be something out there that's dangerous."

"You don't think things will ever settle down and be peaceful?" Glory asked.

Pendleton spat and said, "Peace is just another word for your enemies trying to lull you to sleep. What do you think, Jensen?"

"'Man is born to trouble as the sparks fly upward,'" Luke quoted.

"Wouldn't have pegged you as a man to quote scripture."

"What's that?" Luke said as he nodded his head toward a long ridge on their left. A faint haze of dust hung in the air over there.

"Riders," Pendleton said. "Can't see 'em, but they're there."

"Maybe some bronco Apaches?"

Pendleton rubbed his jaw.

"Could be," he admitted. "Or it might be Elston's men. Either way, we could be riding right into trouble."

CHAPTER 12

Despite the obvious nervousness gripping Pendleton and the other ranch hands, the dust along the ridge never veered from its path. After a while, it even moved ahead of Luke and his companions, indicating that the other party was moving faster.

Pendleton noticed that, too, and muttered, "Wonder what they're in such an all-fired hurry about?"

"Maybe trying to get ahead of us so they can set up an ambush?" Luke suggested.

Pendleton started to curse, then caught himself with a glance at Glory.

"Sorry, ma'am," he said.

"Don't worry, Gabe," she told him. "With everything that's going on these days, I sometimes feel like letting out a few choice words myself."

By the time they came in sight of Painted Post, everybody's nerves were stretched taut, but nothing had happened. That was almost worse than if it had, Luke reflected. Like a day when the air was heavy and ominous with an impending storm, the continuing threat of trouble could make a man wish that all hell would go ahead and break loose, just to get it over with.

The sun was directly overhead, so it was still a couple of hours until the inquest. Glory reined to a halt in front of the Elite Café and said to the others, "We have plenty of time to get some lunch."

One of the cowboys said, "If it's all right with you, ma'am, they've got a free lunch down to the Buckhorn Saloon. We thought we might head that direction. . . ."

"And cut some of the trail dust at the same time?" Glory laughed. "What do you think, Gabe?"

"Don't get drunk," Pendleton told his men. "And stay out of trouble. If any Lazy EO hands happen to come in, steer clear of them. If you start a brawl, you'll land behind bars. You know Sheriff Whittaker will seize any excuse to throw you in the hoosegow."

"We'll behave ourselves, Gabe," another man promised with a grin.

"See that you do."

The three cowboys turned their horses and rode slowly along the street toward the saloon.

"You're not going with them, Gabe?" Glory asked.

"I'll stick with you and Jensen," Pendleton said. "I've spent enough of my life in smoky, boozy saloons."

"That's fine. We'll be glad for your company. Won't we, Luke?"

"Sure," Luke said. He actually didn't mind. Better to have Pendleton where he could keep an eye on him, rather than the foreman being off somewhere drinking and stewing and nursing a jealous grudge.

They went into the Elite and this time got the last empty table. The special today was beef stew, and it was very good, Luke thought. People in this settlement sure couldn't complain about the eats.

"How long have you worked for the MC, Pendleton?" Luke asked as they lingered over coffee.

"What business is it of yours?" Pendleton replied with a suspicious frown.

Glory said, "I think Luke is just trying to make friendly conversation, Gabe."

"That's right," Luke said. "I was talking to Teresa yesterday evening, and she told me that her late husband was Sam MacCrae's foreman when he started the ranch."

"That's right," Pendleton said with grudging civility. "I remember old Enrique Salazar. He's the one who hired me when I was nothing but a green kid. He was the ramrod, and Kaintuck was his segundo, back in the days before the old pelican got too stove up to make a riding hand. Reckon you could say I learned everything I know about being a cowboy from those two, although Salazar called us *vaqueros*."

With a wistful smile, Glory said, "From everything I've heard, they were quite a trio, Sam and Enrique Salazar and Kaintuck. They carved the MC out of wilderness and made it a real ranch. They had to fight the Apaches every step of the way, too."

"Sometimes I miss the old days," Pendleton said, "but I wouldn't go back to all that Indian fighting. It's bad enough having to deal with the varmints we have around these days."

Luke asked, "How did MacCrae get along with the other ranchers who moved into Sabado Valley?"

"There weren't any other ranchers at first. When they started showing up, they looked to Mr. MacCrae for leadership, since he'd been in these parts longer than anybody else. He was a well-respected man. Didn't have an enemy in the world."

"Until Harry Elston came along," Glory said. "Elston bought out one of the other ranchers, a friend of Sam's who was in poor health, and once he looked around he set his sights on the MC. He's one of those men who can't stand for anybody to have something better than he does. He'll take it away, no matter what he has to do to get it."

"So Elston's the only real enemy your husband had," Luke said.

"That's right. That's why there's never been any doubt in my mind that the man who killed him was somebody who works for Elston."

That made sense . . . on the surface. But sometimes a man's enemies were too close for him to see, Luke thought. Like a young, beautiful new wife, or a supposedly loyal foreman, or . . .

Was there any chance that they were in it together?

The thought made Luke look at them in a new light. He was convinced that Pendleton had feelings for Glory, but so far she had shown no signs of returning those feelings. She seemed to regard him as a valued employee, but that was all.

Maybe she was just better at hiding what she really felt than Pendleton was, Luke mused. He couldn't dismiss the possibility that they'd been sleeping together . . . and plotting together as well.

Or maybe he was seeing conspiracies where none existed. Regardless of what Glory had or hadn't done back in Baltimore, the situation here in Sabado Valley might be exactly what it appeared to be.

Glory slipped a gold turnip watch from a pocket in her riding skirt and opened it to check the time. It was a bigger, heavier watch than women usually carried, a man's watch, and Luke wondered if it had belonged to Sam MacCrae. As Glory snapped it closed, though, he caught a glimpse of some initials engraved inside the lid. He wasn't sure, but he thought they were *AJ.*

Alfred Jennings.

"We should be getting on down to the courthouse," Glory said as she put the watch away. She laid a five-dollar gold piece on the table and stood up. Luke and Pendleton were on their feet by the time she reached hers.

Word of the inquest had gotten around town and probably spread to the ranches in the area, too, and as a result Painted Post was more crowded than usual this afternoon. An inquest wasn't exactly the same as a trial, but it was interesting enough that Luke expected the courtroom to be full.

As they approached the courthouse, Luke saw several men leaning on a hitch rail where a buggy was tied. He recognized the men first, and then the buggy.

It belonged to Harry Elston, and the men leaning on the rail worked for him. Verne Finn gave Luke a sardonic grin.

Pendleton had seen the gunmen, too. He said, "Looks like Elston's in town for the inquest."

"That's no concern of mine," Glory said.

"Could that have been his bunch kicking up that dust we saw this morning?" Luke asked Pendleton.

"More than likely," the foreman replied. "There's a trail on the other side of that ridge that leads all the way through the valley and on up to Elston's ranch. Wonder why he decided to come in."

"I suspect we'll find out," Luke said.

Spectators had packed into the courtroom, and more stood outside. Luke, Glory, and Pendleton might have had trouble making their way through the mob if Whitey Singletary hadn't been stationed outside the doors of the courtroom. The burly deputy bellowed, "Get outta the way! Let those folks through!"

His voice was distorted by the heavy bandage over his broken nose. He glared at Luke with murderous hate in his eyes as Luke went past. He was tempted to make some comment, but setting Singletary off on a rampage wouldn't really accomplish anything.

Jared Whittaker was already inside the courtroom, standing to one side near the front of the room. He had his arms crossed over his chest and wore a scowl on his face that darkened when he looked at Luke. He didn't have any friends among the local lawmen, that was for sure, Luke reflected wryly.

Whittaker pushed away from the wall, walked over

to meet them, and pointed at some empty seats in the front row.

"Sit there," he said curtly. "The judge'll be here in a few minutes. And take your hats off. This is a civilized proceeding."

"I suspect that I've spent more time in actual civilization than you have, Sheriff," Glory said as she removed her hat. Luke and Pendleton took off their hats as well.

"Just because a town's got a lot of people in it doesn't make it civilized," Whittaker said.

"I'm surprised that we're actually in philosophical agreement on something, Sheriff," Luke told him.

Whittaker just glared at him and went back over to lean against the wall.

A few minutes later, a door on one side of the room opened, and Whittaker straightened and called, "All rise!"

Everybody in the courtroom got to their feet as Judge Hiram Marbright came in. He was a middle-aged, heavyset man with graying rusty hair and a face like a bulldog. Instead of judicial robes, he wore a brown tweed suit, boiled white shirt, and string tie. As he sat down behind his judge's bench, he picked up a gavel, rapped it sharply, and growled, "Court's in session. Sit down."

With a shuffle of feet, everyone in the room did so.

Marbright took a pair of spectacles from his coat pocket, unfolded them, put them on, and picked up a sheet of paper from the bench in front of him. He glanced at it briefly, then said, "This is the official inquest into the deaths of one Dave Randall and an unknown man hereafter referred to as John Doe."

Luke and Glory glanced at each other. Dave Randall was the dead rustler Harry Elston had claimed he'd fired. They hadn't known that Randall's death was going to be part of the inquest as well. That probably explained why Elston was here.

"This isn't a trial," Marbright went on. "We'll seat a jury, and then I'll hear testimony regarding these deaths. There won't be any lawyers or objections or folderol like that. We just want the facts, and then the jury will determine the disposition of the case."

The judge picked six men from among the spectators, evidently citizens of Painted Post with whom he was acquainted, and told them to take a seat in the jury box. Since there were only six of them, they all fit in the first of two rows of chairs inside the box.

"Our county coroner is Claude Lister," Marbright continued. "Are you satisfied with the jury, Claude?"

"Yes, Your Honor," Lister said.

"All right, then, you'll be the first one to testify. Come on up here."

Lister took a seat in the witness chair and Whittaker swore him in. Marbright asked the undertaker to tell the court how the two decedents had met their demise.

"They were shot, both of them."

"A single bullet wound to each, or multiple wounds?"

"Just a single wound apiece, Your Honor."

"Well, that was good shooting, anyway," Marbright said, which drew chuckles from some of the spectators.

"Do you have anything else to add? Anything unusual about the condition of the bodies?"

"No, sir. They were just dead, which is the way I nearly always get them."

Marbright frowned and said, "Nearly always?"

"Well, you remember, judge, when old Harvey Driscoll woke up just when I was about to embalm him."

"That was lucky for old Harvey," Marbright said. "Taught him not to pass out in an alley so drunk that nobody could tell if he was alive or dead!"

The spectators laughed again as the judge told Lister he could step down.

"I'll hear from Gabe Pendleton next."

Pendleton looked uneasy as he went up to be sworn in. When he was seated, Marbright asked him to state his name and occupation for the record.

"Gabe Pendleton. Foreman of the MC Ranch."

"Describe the incident that occurred the day before yesterday in which the deceased named Dave Randall lost his life."

"Well, Your Honor, some of the ranch hands and I were out checking the stock when we heard gunshots coming from the direction of a place we call Coyote Ridge. We went to see what the commotion was about, and when we got there, from the top of the ridge we spied some men around a branding fire. We knew they were rustlers, so we opened up on them."

"Just a moment. How did you know they were rustlers?"

"They weren't any of our crew," Pendleton said.

"Anybody else branding cattle on MC range is a rustler, plain and simple."

Marbright nodded and said, "All right. What happened then?"

"They jumped on their horses and took off. They were shooting back at us, and they were shooting at a rider out on the flat in front of the ridge, too. He had them sort of penned in, so we chased 'em along the top of the bluff. That fella Randall, he was one of them, and during the fight he got shot out of the saddle. From the looks of it he was dead when he hit the ground."

"Who fired the shot that killed him?"

Pendleton looked at Luke, but only for a fraction of a second. Then he said, "I couldn't tell you, Your Honor. There were so many bullets flying around, it could have been any of us."

Marbright frowned as if he didn't like that answer very much, but he didn't dwell on it. Instead, he asked, "Who was the other man you mentioned, the one who was also shooting at the alleged rustlers?"

Pendleton nodded toward the front row of the spectators' section and said, "That's him sitting next to Mrs. MacCrae. He says his name's Luke Jensen."

"What do you mean, he says that's his name?"

"Well, that's what he told us it was, but when you get right down to it, I don't know that for a fact. I don't have any reason to think he was lying about it, though."

"Is it possible Mr. Jensen fired the shot that killed Dave Randall?"

Pendleton hesitated, then said, "Sure, it's possible, I reckon. Like I told you, judge, I just couldn't say."

"All right. Step down, Mr. Pendleton, but don't leave the courtroom. I may want to ask you some more questions." Marbright swung his gaze to Glory. "Mrs. MacCrae, would you come up, please?"

After Glory was sworn in, the judge told her to describe the events of two nights previous at the ranch headquarters. Glory told him about the attack on the ranch and how she had shot "John Doe" to save Luke's life. The courtroom was absolutely still and quiet as she spoke. Some of the people in Painted Post might not like her, but everybody knew who she was and was interested in what she had to say.

"There's absolutely no doubt in your mind that if you hadn't killed that man, he would have killed your guest Mr. Jensen?" Marbright asked.

"Absolutely no doubt, Your Honor," Glory said. "Although I'd add that I wasn't necessarily trying to kill him. I would have been content just to wound him. In fact, I wish I had."

"So that you wouldn't have to live with the burden of having taken a man's life?"

"So that we could have gotten him to admit he was working for Harry Elston," Glory said.

The courtroom erupted in noise, but over the racket came the sound of Harry Elston's voice bellowing, "That's a damned lie!" Luke hadn't seen Elston among the spectators, but it was obvious the rancher had slipped into the courtroom after he and Glory and Pendleton had entered. Luke had known Elston was in town because he'd seen the man's buggy, along with Verne Finn and the other hired guns, so Elston's presence at the inquest came as no surprise.

Judge Marbright hammered so violently with his gavel that Luke thought the handle might break, and even so it took several minutes for the judge to restore a semblance of order in the room. When things finally quieted down enough for Marbright to be heard, he pointed the gavel and said, "Sit down, Mr. Elston, and count yourself lucky I don't have the sheriff throw you in jail for that outburst!" He turned back to Glory and went on: "Mrs. MacCrae, this isn't the time for such unsubstantiated accusations. We're just here to determine how those two men died."

"I think it's relevant, Your Honor," Glory said. "Those men died because they were following Harry Elston's orders to steal my cattle and burn down my home."

Quickly, Marbright pointed the gavel before Elston could leap to his feet and react. He said, "That's enough, Mrs. MacCrae. Step down."

"Thank you, Your Honor," Glory said coolly.

There was nothing cool about Marbright. Beads of sweat had popped out on his beefy face. Luke recalled Glory saying that the judge was an honest man, but even if that was true, Marbright found himself in an uncomfortable place, trapped between the two sides in a simmering range war. And all he could do was forge ahead.

"Mr. Jensen, you get up here," Marbright growled.

Luke stood up and went to the witness chair. Sheriff

Whittaker came over with the big black Bible and had Luke swear on it to tell the truth. Whittaker's instructions were curt. He didn't try to hide his dislike for the witness.

When Luke was seated, the judge said, "Your name is Luke Jensen?"

"That's right, Your Honor."

"What brings you to Sabado Valley?"

"I'm on my way to El Paso," Luke said. He had sworn to tell the truth, and he didn't consider that a lie. He probably would go to El Paso . . . sometime.

"How did you get mixed up in the fight with those so-called rustlers?"

"I was riding along minding my own business when somebody nearly parted my hair with a bullet," Luke said. "I could tell the shot came from the top of that ridge Mr. Pendleton was talking about. At the time I didn't know what was going on, but now it's pretty easy to see that the rustlers posted a lookout up there while they did their work with a hot running iron."

"You don't know that of your own personal knowledge, however."

"No, but it's the only explanation that makes sense, Your Honor."

Marbright waved a pudgy hand and said, "Continue."

"The rest of it happened like Mr. Pendleton said. I opened fire on the bunch when they took off, and so did he and the rest of the men from the MC Ranch."

"Do you know who killed Mr. Randall?"

"Not for certain, no."

Marbright leaned forward and asked, "What do you mean by that?"

"I thought I was the one who hit him," Luke said, "but like Mr. Pendleton told you, there was a lot of lead flying around."

That answer caused a stir in the courtroom, but it didn't escalate into a full-fledged commotion.

"If it was your bullet that struck and killed Mr. Randall, would you say that was self-defense, Mr. Jensen?" the judge asked.

"I would. I had already come under fire when I was minding my own business, and Randall and the rest of the bunch were still shooting at me."

Marbright nodded and said, "Let's move on to the incident at the headquarters of the MacCrae ranch that evening. No need to go through all of it again, but do you agree with Mrs. MacCrae's description of events?"

"I do, Your Honor."

"You're certain that the unknown John Doe was about to shoot you when Mrs. MacCrae shot him?"

"I was looking right down the barrel of his gun," Luke said. "I know it for a fact."

"All right. You can go back to your seat."

When Luke was sitting next to Glory again, Marbright addressed the members of the jury.

"What you men will do now is vote on whether or not the deaths of Dave Randall and John Doe were justified under the law, basing your decision solely on the evidence you've heard here today. You can retire to a separate room to deliberate if you want to, or if your minds are already made up you can—"

"Excuse me, Your Honor," Whittaker said. "I hate to interrupt, but I've got something to add to these proceedings."

Marbright frowned and said, "Eh? What's that, Sheriff? You want to give testimony? You weren't present when either of the deaths occurred, were you?"

"No, sir, I wasn't, but I have some information about one of the witnesses that might be of interest to the court."

Marbright looked skeptical and annoyed, but he said, "All right, it's irregular, but I suppose we can hear what you have to say. I warn you, though, if it's not relevant I'll instruct the jury to disregard it."

"That'll be up to you, Your Honor." Whittaker glanced over at Luke, who didn't like the self-satisfied smirk he saw on the lawman's face as Whittaker reached into his vest pocket and took out a folded yellow paper that Luke recognized as a telegraph flimsy. "This is a wire from Major John B. Jones of the Texas Rangers in San Antonio. I sent him a telegraph message this morning asking him for information about Luke Jensen. According to Major Jones, Jensen is a bounty hunter!"

CHAPTER 13

The spectators reacted to that, some of them loudly. In the minds of most people, bounty hunters ranked higher than rattlesnakes . . . but just barely.

Judge Marbright gaveled the room silent, then said, "Mr. Jensen's occupation has no bearing on these proceedings, Sheriff Whittaker. You're to be congratulated on your initiative in seeking information, but you've wasted your time and the court's time."

"Sorry, Your Honor," Whittaker murmured, but the sly smile on his face showed how insincere that sentiment was.

Luke was more concerned with the startled look that Glory was giving him.

Startled . . . and a little afraid and angry.

"The jury will disregard what Sheriff Whittaker just said," Marbright told the six men sitting in the box. "As I was saying, you can retire, or—" Marbright stopped as the juror sitting closest to him raised his hand. "Yes, what is it, Fred?"

"Your Honor, we already know how we're gonna vote," the man called Fred replied. "There's not a lot of point in us goin' into a room somewhere to do it."

The other members of the jury nodded their heads in agreement.

"Very well," Marbright said. "What verdict are you prepared to render?"

Harry Elston stood up and called, "Your Honor, am I allowed to speak here, before everything is official?"

Marbright frowned at him and said, "I didn't call you as a witness, Mr. Elston. What makes you think your comments would be relevant?"

"I knew one of the dead men," Elston said. "I don't deny that Dave Randall worked for me at one time. But I've had to sit here and listen to scurrilous accusations being thrown around about him and me, and I don't like it."

"I've already ruled that those accusations have no bearing on these proceedings."

"I know that, Your Honor, but everybody in this room heard them anyway. I'd like a chance to defend myself."

"I wasn't aware that you were on trial," Marbright said.

"My reputation may be."

Marbright considered for a few seconds, then waved a hand and said, "Go ahead."

Luke was actually glad that Elston had decided to butt in and bluster a little. It took folks' minds off Whittaker's revelation about him being a bounty hunter.

But in the long run, nobody would forget about it, least of all Glory MacCrae. Luke was pretty sure about that.

Elston said, "I want it known that Dave Randall wasn't working for me when he was killed. I fired him a week before that incident. If he fell in with some bad company and decided to steal some of Mrs. MacCrae's stock, that's nothing to do with me." Elston raised his right hand and poked angrily at the air with his index finger. "As for the idea that I sent men to the MacCrae ranch that night to attack the place, that's a blasted lie! I'm a businessman, Your Honor, and when I compete with somebody, I compete hard. But I don't resort to violence and lawbreaking to do it!"

Coldly, Marbright asked, "Are you done with your speechmaking, Mr. Elston?"

"I've said my piece."

"All right, sit down." Marbright turned back to the jury. "How do you rule on the deaths of these two men?"

Fred said, "We find that they were both lawful killin's, Your Honor."

Marbright nodded and picked up his gavel.

"So it will be recorded, and no charges will be filed." He rapped the gavel on the bench. "This court is adjourned."

A hubbub filled the room as the spectators got to their feet to make their way outside. Luke, Glory, and Pendleton stayed where they were for the time being. Luke wanted to say something to Glory, but the stony look she gave him convinced him to stay silent for the moment.

Pendleton wasn't that discreet. He glared at Luke and said, "A bounty hunter!"

"I never said I wasn't," Luke drawled.

"You never said one way or the other. You just let us think you were a drifter. What are you doing here, Jensen? Are you after some of that dirty blood money?"

"Look, I said I was passing through Sabado Valley, and that was true. It doesn't matter what my job is. I was riding along minding my own business when somebody took a shot at me. Everything that's happened since is because I took an interest in what's going on around here."

That wasn't completely a lie. He was intrigued by the mystery of who had ambushed and killed Sam MacCrae, and he definitely had an interest in Glory that had started out professional but had probably gone beyond that. He wanted to find out the truth.

"If it was up to me, I'd tell you to pack your gear and get out when we get back to the ranch," Pendleton said.

Luke looked at Glory and said, "But it's not up to you, is it?"

She didn't respond to him directly. Instead, she stood up and said, "I want to leave." She turned toward the doors at the back of the courtroom.

Luke and Pendleton started to follow her, keeping a little distance between them, but before they reached the doors, Sheriff Whittaker stepped in front of Luke and stopped him with a hand on his chest.

"You're not welcome in Painted Post anymore, Jensen," Whittaker said.

"That's funny. I never felt particularly welcome to start with." Luke glanced down at Whittaker's hand. "Take your hand off me, Sheriff. I haven't broken any laws."

"That's a matter of interpretation. I've still got a deputy with a broken nose."

"That's not my fault. He assaulted me first."

"We haven't put that to a test in a court of law."

Luke was getting impatient. Glory and Pendleton had moved on—but not before Pendleton had glanced back and seemed pleased that Whittaker had stopped Luke—and now they were out of the courtroom and he couldn't see them anymore.

"Sheriff, if you're trying to goad me into getting you out of my way by force so you'll have an excuse to arrest me, it's not going to work. I'll stand here all day if that's what you want."

With a disgusted grimace, Whittaker dropped his hand and stepped back, just as Luke had thought he might.

"All right, get out of here. Just don't forget what I said about not being welcome in Painted Post. Next time I see you in town, I'll throw you in jail for vagrancy."

Luke didn't respond to that. He just stepped around the sheriff and hurried out of the courtroom, hoping he could catch up to Glory and Pendleton.

On his way he passed Whitey Singletary, and once again the deputy glared at him.

"I ain't through with you, Jensen," Singletary said.

"I'll try to control my anticipation," Luke said off-handedly as he looked around for Glory and Pendleton.

The sound of a commotion attracted his attention, and when he looked in that direction, he saw people hurrying the other way. That wasn't a good sign. Luke increased his pace as the crowd continued to scatter, but he was going against the flow and that slowed him down. His frustration grew.

Suddenly, he broke out into the open, and as he did he spotted Glory and Pendleton. From the looks of it, they had been headed for the café, where their horses were still tied. Several men had confronted them, though, spreading out so that the two of them were halfway surrounded. One of the men called, "Dave Randall was a friend of ours, Pendleton, and you and your bunch murdered him!"

"He was no damn rustler!" another of the men yelled. "The MC crew is just a bunch of killers!"

Luke knew they were trying to spook Pendleton into grabbing his gun. As soon as he did that, the men would draw and open fire, and Glory would be cut down in the exchange of shots, too. He had no doubt that Elston had paid these men, although the rancher would deny it and they probably weren't members of his regular crew.

Moving forward quickly, Luke called, "If you're looking for the man who killed Dave Randall, I'm right here."

A gun cracked somewhere, and Luke felt the hot breath of a slug fan his cheek. Instantly, chaos filled the street as people who had been scurrying to get out of the line of fire now stampeded. Women screamed and men yelled curses. Luke saw the men who'd confronted Glory and Pendleton claw for their guns. Pendleton grabbed Glory by the shoulders and swung her to the ground.

Luke's hands flashed to the Remingtons. He was nowhere in his brother Smoke's class when it came to being a fast draw, but he possessed a natural grace and quickness that allowed him to get his guns out and fire faster than most men. The right-hand Remington bucked against his palm as he triggered it.

Blood flew in the air as the bullet shattered the left shoulder of the nearest gunman and twisted him halfway around. He didn't fall, though, and didn't drop his own gun. It came up as the man's face contorted in a snarl.

Before he could fire, Luke's left-hand gun roared. The slug punched into the man's chest and drove him back off his feet. Before he even hit the ground, Luke had already shifted his aim and fired both Remingtons at the second gunman. The two bullets ripped into the man's guts, doubled him over, and dropped him to the dirt in a bleeding, trembling heap.

Luke dashed forward, and as he did he felt something pluck at his shirt. Dirt erupted from the ground in front of him as a bullet plowed into it. There were still two gunmen trying to kill Glory and Pendleton. The foreman was on one knee, leaning over Glory to shield her with his own body as he returned fire. The Colt in his hand spouted flame, and one of the remaining gunmen staggered.

Luke dived to the ground as the fourth man fired at

him. The bullets hummed over his head. Lying on his belly, he fired both guns and saw the would-be killer jerk in a macabre dance as the slugs tore through his body. The man took several steps backwards and then collapsed.

Pendleton fired again. The only gunman remaining on his feet rocked back. The revolver in his hand erupted again, but his arm had sagged and the bullet just kicked up dust at his feet. Slowly, he toppled and landed on his side, curling around the pain that had to be filling his body, then lying still.

As the echoes of the shots died away, an eerie quiet settled over the street, which was empty now except for Luke, Glory, Pendleton, and the bodies of the fallen gunmen. Luke scrambled to his feet and ran to join Glory and Pendleton. He saw a bright splash of blood on the foreman's shirt and knew that Pendleton had been wounded, but the man was still alert and looking around for more trouble.

Luke stood over them and turned slowly, guns up, ready to fire if he spotted a threat. The battle seemed to be over, though.

"Mrs. MacCrae, are you hit?" Luke asked without looking down at her.

Glory pushed herself up on an elbow. Her breasts rose and fell rapidly under her shirt as she tried to catch her breath. She said, "No, I . . . I don't think so."

"How bad did they get you, Pendleton?"

Luke's question seemed to be the first time that

Glory realized her foreman was wounded. She cried, "Gabe!" and sat up to clutch his arm.

"I'm fine," Pendleton said, his voice tight. "Slug just grazed my side, that's all."

That might be true, but the wound was bad enough that Pendleton was losing a lot of blood, Luke saw when he glanced down. The crimson stain on the foreman's shirt was still spreading. Luke holstered his left-hand gun and reached down to grasp Pendleton's arm.

"Get his other arm," he told Glory. "We need to get him inside somewhere, before somebody else decides to take some more potshots at us."

"I don't need . . . any help, damn it!" Pendleton insisted, but the way his weight sagged against Luke's grip said otherwise. Luke could tell that Pendleton was on the verge of passing out.

Glory had hold of Pendleton's other arm. Together, they hauled him to his feet and steered him past the hitch rail toward the café. The door opened before they could reach it, and the pretty young waitress Hazel stood there holding it.

"Get inside," she urged them. "Hurry!"

They half-carried, half-dragged Pendleton through the door. Hazel told them to lay him on one of the tables. That was going to ruin the blue-and-white-checked tablecloth, Luke thought, but it seemed like the best solution.

He and Glory eased the wounded man down on the nearest table. Glory and Hazel took Pendleton's feet and lifted them onto a chair. Luke went back to the door and peered out. The four gunmen still lay where they had fallen. He was pretty sure all four of them were dead.

A quick scan of the street told him that no other bodies were sprawled in the dirt, and he was glad to see that. With so many bullets flying around, he had been worried that one or more of the bystanders might have been struck and wounded, maybe even killed.

Two men carrying shotguns emerged from the courthouse and ran along the street toward the café. Luke stiffened for a second, thinking they were about to be under attack again, but then he recognized Whittaker and Singletary.

Of course, the fact that those two were lawmen didn't mean he and his companions were safe, he thought. Both men bore grudges against him, and Whittaker might have decided it was time to throw in his lot all the way with Harry Elston.

Because of that possibility, Luke reloaded quickly, then eased into the doorway with a Remington in his right hand and called, "That's close enough, Sheriff!"

Whittaker stopped, crouching. The twin barrels of the shotgun he held were pointed toward the ground, but if they started to swing up, Luke was ready to put a bullet through the sheriff's arm and knock him out of the fight.

"Jensen!" Whittaker said. "Put that gun down, mister."

"Not until I'm sure the fight is over."

Singletary moved from gunman to gunman, covering them with his Greener and using a booted foot to roll them roughly onto their backs.

"These four hombres are dead, Sheriff," he reported.

"That satisfy you, Jensen?" Whittaker said.

Luke looked past the sheriff and saw Judge Marbright, Claude Lister, and several other men who looked like town leaders approaching. Confident that Whittaker and Singletary wouldn't try anything in front of so many witnesses, Luke pouched his iron and stepped out into the open.

"Are you planning to try to arrest me again, Sheriff?" he asked.

Whittaker scowled and said, "I'm not going to arrest anybody until I find out for sure what happened here. I was still in the courthouse when all the shooting started. It sounded like Santa Anna was invading again!"

Glory emerged from the café and said in a clear, angry voice, "I'll tell you what happened, Sheriff. Some of that dead rustler's friends tried to kill Gabe Pendleton and Mr. Jensen and me. They probably would have, too, if Gabe and Luke hadn't put up such a valiant fight." She paused, then added meaningfully, "And of course the local law was nowhere to be found when the attack took place!"

"I told you, I was inside the courthouse," Whittaker snapped. "Are any of you hurt?"

"Gabe is wounded. He needs the doctor."

One of the men with Marbright stepped forward. He had a black medical bag in his hand.

"I figured my services would be required," he said. "Where's the wounded man?"

Glory stepped aside and gestured toward the café's open door.

"He's inside," she said. "We put him on one of the tables."

"Good thinking," the doctor said as he hurried past her. She followed him into the café.

Judge Marbright had joined Whittaker and Singletary as they stood over the bodies. He put his hands on his thick hips and scowled down at the sprawled, bloody shapes.

"Who are these men?" he demanded. "Does anyone know them?"

Luke said, "They claimed to be friends of Dave Randall. I guess there's a good chance they were part of that bunch doing the brand-blotting the other day."

"Why come into town on the day of the inquest to settle the score?"

"Because they knew Mrs. MacCrae and Pendleton and I would be here?" Luke suggested. "Or maybe somebody paid them to."

Whittaker said, "Don't go spreading any more wild rumors. Things are bad enough without you blaming Harry Elston for this without any proof."

"How do you know there's no proof? Or are you just assuming that Elston's slick enough to make sure of it?"

Judge Marbright said, "That's enough, Mr. Jensen. I think we all know where you and Mrs. MacCrae stand on this matter. As Sheriff Whittaker points out, though, the law requires proof before it can act." He turned to Lister. "Claude, if you could fetch your wagon . . . ?"

"Of course, judge," the undertaker said. "I suppose these killings will call for another inquest."

"Yes, events are keeping us both busy," Marbright growled. He took a fat cigar from his vest pocket, clamped one end of it between his teeth, left it unlit, and heaved an exasperated sigh around it.

Glory came out of the café. Luke asked her, "How's Pendleton doing?"

"Dr. Fleming thinks he'll be all right. The wound is worse than what Gabe let on, though. The bullet did more than just graze him. It hit him in the side, broke a rib, and glanced off to go out his back. He's lost quite a bit of blood. The doctor says he'll be laid up for a couple of weeks, at least."

"That's too bad."

"Yes, for Gabe's sake, and it leaves me with a problem, too. I don't have a foreman. I'll have to promote one of the other men temporarily."

Luke wasn't going to volunteer to take on the job. He was no cowboy. And she wouldn't want him even if he did. Now that she knew he was a bounty hunter, she'd probably order him off the ranch as soon as she could. Regardless of what had really happened to Sam MacCrae, she still had that murder charge from back East hanging over her head. She was smart enough to suspect that was the reason Luke had come to Sabado Valley, even though he'd denied it.

The three MC hands who had come into town with them hurried up, hats in hands. One of them said, "We're mighty sorry we weren't here when the shootin' started, Miz MacCrae. We were still down the street at the Buckhorn and didn't know what was goin' on. We figured you was safe enough here in town."

"I should have been," Glory said. "Obviously, someone's getting desperate."

"Somebody said Gabe got shot . . . ?"

"He's in the café. The doctor is tending to him now."

"You reckon it's all right if we go in?"

Glory nodded and said, "I suppose. Just don't get in Dr. Fleming's way."

The three men hurried into the café. Glory turned to Whittaker and went on: "I suppose it's all right for us to return to the ranch when we're ready?"

"I'm not holding anybody," the sheriff replied. "You're free to go as far as I'm concerned. Judge?"

Marbright grunted and waved a hand to indicate that it was all right with him.

Glory looked at Luke and asked, "Are you coming back with us?"

"Do you want me to?" he asked bluntly. There was no point in pretending that things weren't different now.

"You and I need to have a talk," she said, equally straightforward.

Luke nodded and said, "Then I'll be going with you when you ride out."

He didn't know what Glory was going to say, but he certainly wanted to find out.

Something else had been nagging at his brain ever since the gunfire had erupted, and as he looked around the street he knew what it was. He remembered that first shot, the one that had come so close to his head as it started the ball. Something was wrong about it. It had come from behind him, not from any of the four hired killers in front of him.

He moved a hand to the side of his shirt, felt the little rip in it. Another bullet had done that, and he recalled how the slug had kicked up dust from the street in front of him. That shot had come from behind, as well, and the angle meant that it had been fired from a higher elevation. Luke's eyes narrowed as he considered the position where he'd been at that moment.

His gaze lifted to the roof of the courthouse. Somebody had been up there with a rifle, he thought, someone who had come too damned close to killing him, not once but twice. He could think of one very likely suspect, and as he did, he lowered his gaze to the ugly, scowling face of Deputy Whitey Singletary.

CHAPTER 14

Gabe Pendleton was hurt too badly to travel all the way out to the MacCrae ranch, even in the back of a wagon, Dr. Fleming decreed. He was going to stay in one of the bedrooms of the doctor's house until the bullet wound had healed and the broken rib had mended.

Pendleton had passed out from loss of blood, but when he regained consciousness in the doctor's house and found out what had happened, he objected strenuously.

It didn't do him any good. As he tried to sit up, Glory rested a hand on his shoulder and said, "You're going to do what Dr. Fleming tells you, Gabe, and that's final."

Muttering, Pendleton subsided and let his head sink back down on the pillow.

"What are you gonna do for a foreman while I'm laying here useless?" he asked with a bitter edge in his voice.

"I was thinking about giving the job to Rusty

Gimple," Glory said. "Temporarily, of course. You'll take over again as soon as you've recuperated sufficiently."

"Rusty's a good hand," Pendleton admitted grudgingly. "You'll need to keep a close eye on him and the rest of the boys to make sure they don't slack off, though."

"I will," Glory promised. "Don't worry, Gabe. The ranch will be fine. Temporarily."

Pendleton nodded, then looked over at Luke, who stood with his arms crossed on his chest and his shoulders against the wall. His black hat was tipped back so that some of his curly dark hair spilled out from under it.

"What are you still doing here, Jensen?" Pendleton asked. "I thought you probably would have lit a shuck by now, since nobody wants you around."

"It's still a free country, Gabe," Luke said. "Whether you believe it or not, I wanted to make sure you were all right."

"Well, now you know, so there's no reason you can't get on your horse and put this part of the country behind you. One of the boys can gather up whatever you left at the ranch and send it on to wherever you want it sent."

Glory said, "I don't want Mr. Jensen to leave just yet."

Pendleton frowned at her in disbelief.

"Begging your pardon, ma'am, but you don't want an hombre like this around. Bounty hunters are just about the lowest form of life there is. They always bring trouble with 'em, wherever they go."

"That may well be true," Glory said, "but I've asked him to stay anyway."

Her tone made it clear that she didn't want to continue having this argument.

Pendleton scowled but didn't say anything else. After a moment Glory went on, "I've told Dr. Fleming that you're to have whatever you need. You were wounded protecting me, so don't worry about the expense. The MC takes care of its own."

"Sure," Pendleton muttered.

"I'll be back in a few days to check on you and see how you're doing." Glory put a hand on his right shoulder and squeezed. "Just rest and get better, Gabe. That's your job now."

Pendleton jerked his head in a curt nod.

Glory glanced over at Luke. He straightened from his casual pose and eased out of the room in case Glory wanted to say something to Pendleton in private. She followed him out of the room right away, though, without any murmur of voices between her and Pendleton.

Dr. Fleming was in the front room. Glory spoke briefly to him, telling him again that she would take care of the expense of anything her foreman needed. Then she and Luke left the doctor's house, which was located on one of the side streets half a block from McDowell Street.

"Do you really want me to go back out to the ranch with you?" Luke asked as they walked.

"I'm not in the habit of saying things I don't mean," Glory replied.

"Yeah, I've noticed that about you."

"Some women like to talk around a problem and hope that the man she's talking to will figure out what she really means. To me that's always seemed like too uncertain a method. If there's something important enough to discuss, I'm going to come right out with it. Anything else is a waste of time and effort."

"All right," Luke said. "I'll take you at your word, then."

"That's the sensible thing to do."

They turned the corner and started along the boardwalk toward the Elite Café. Their horses were still tied at the hitch rail in front of the eatery. Before they got there, though, Luke saw Sheriff Jared Whittaker striding across the street toward them.

"More trouble coming, maybe," he said quietly.

"I see him," Glory said. She paused to let the lawman come to them, and Luke did likewise. As Whittaker stepped up onto the boardwalk in front of them, Glory asked, "Are you looking for us, Sheriff?"

"Yes, ma'am, I am," Whittaker replied. "Judge Marbright sent me to find you. He said for me to tell the two of you not to leave town. He's convening court again in half an hour. He's gonna go ahead and hold the inquest on these latest deaths."

"What?" Glory exclaimed. "It's only been a couple of hours since the shootings. Aren't inquests usually held a day or two later?"

"That's right, but the judge wants to get it out of the way today." Whittaker gave Luke a hard look. "And he says it better be the last inquest he has to worry about for a while."

"That's not up to me," Luke said.

"I don't know. Until you rode into the valley, Jensen, the last inquest we had around here was for Sam MacCrae's death. Beg your pardon, Mrs. MacCrae, for bringing that up."

Glory nodded but didn't say anything.

"But since you came along, six men are dead," Whittaker went on. "I don't call that a coincidence."

"I didn't start any of those ruckuses, and you know it, Sheriff. The jury at this new inquest is just going to render a verdict of self-defense again."

"That's as may be, but we still follow the law here in Painted Post, and the law says there has to be a proceeding. You two will have to be there."

"We'll be there," Glory said. "But tell Judge Marbright that it's a blasted inconvenience. By the time we're done here, it'll be too late to start back to the ranch today. We'll have to spend the night in town."

Whittaker shrugged as if to say that that wasn't his problem.

"Be at the courthouse in half an hour," he told them. "If you're not there, I'll come looking for you."

"We'll be there," Glory said again. She stepped around Whittaker and strode away, her attitude one of contemptuous dismissal. Luke followed her, trading cold stares with Whittaker as he passed the lawman.

"I hope there's a decent hotel here in town," he said to her as he caught up.

"There is," Glory said. "The Stafford House is comfortable enough, I suppose. I stayed there before, when I first came to Painted Post, and didn't have any complaints."

They went into the café. The table where they had put Pendleton earlier had a new tablecloth on it now, and all the blood that had leaked out of him had been cleaned up. Hazel and her mother kept the place spic and span.

The three MC punchers who had come into town with them that morning were sitting at one of the tables, eating apple pie and drinking coffee. They started to stand up when they saw Glory approaching, but she waved them back into their chairs.

"I hoped I would find you here," she told them. "When you've finished eating I want the three of you to head back out to the ranch."

"You're comin', too, ain't you, Miz MacCrae?" a lanky, redheaded cowboy asked.

"No, Mr. Jensen and I have to stay here in town. The judge has decided to hold another inquest today. We won't be riding back until tomorrow morning."

All three of the punchers protested. The redhead said, "Then we'll wait until tomorrow, too, so we can all go back together."

Glory shook her head.

"No, Rusty, I want all of the crew on hand and alert for trouble. With everything that's going on, Elston might decide that it's a good time to make another move against us. If he hit us with everything he has, he might have every head of our stock swimming the Rio Grande by morning. Where would the MC be then?"

"Out of luck, I reckon," Rusty admitted.

Glory smiled and said, "Besides, you're my new foreman while Gabe is laid up, so you need to be there to make sure things are done properly."

Rusty's eyes widened in surprise.

"Me, ma'am? You want me to take over as ramrod?"

"For the time being."

"You sure about that?"

"I am," Glory said. "Will you do it?"

"Well . . . Well, sure. It'd be an honor."

"I want men riding guard at all times," Glory said. "And you'll all need to be prepared for trouble."

"We'll be honin' for a scrap, ma'am," Rusty promised. A worried frown creased his forehead. "But you'll have to ride back out to the ranch by yourself tomorrow. That could be dangerous."

"Mr. Jensen will be with me."

Rusty turned a suspicious look on Luke and said, "We've been hearin' some things about you, mister."

"They're probably all true," Luke said, "but I'll keep Mrs. MacCrae safe. You have my word on that."

"You'd better mean it, elsewise you're liable to have a heap of mighty angry ol' boys lookin' for your hide," Rusty warned.

"We'll be fine," Glory said. "Come on, Luke. We'd better get over to the courthouse."

Word hadn't had time to spread much about this inquest, so it was sparsely attended compared to the earlier one. Harry Elston and his men seemed to have left town already. Luke wondered if Judge Marbright had instructed Whittaker to keep things as quiet as possible to diminish the chance of more fireworks.

As a result, the proceedings were just a formality. Another jury was sworn in, and Luke and Glory told their versions of what had happened. There had been plenty of witnesses to the gun battle, including some of the men on the jury, so their verdict that the killings had been justified was a foregone conclusion.

While he was testifying, Luke didn't say anything about how he suspected a rifleman hiding on top of the courthouse had been part of the fracas, too. He was going to keep that card close to his chest until he figured out exactly what had happened and hopefully had proof of it.

As they left the courthouse, Glory said, "If you can take care of our horses, I'll go on down to the Stafford House and get us rooms for the night. You can take the horses to Cramer's Livery."

"All right," Luke said.

"Tell Mr. Cramer to put the bill on my tab."

"You don't have to pay my way, you know. I don't work for the MC."

"That's right, you don't. But you've involved yourself in my troubles, and you helped save my life this afternoon. Those gunmen were after me as much as they were you and Gabe. Maybe more so. I think that gives me some responsibility." She paused. "You also lied to me . . . but we'll talk about that later."

With her usual brusqueness, she walked away, leaving Luke to deal with the horses.

He didn't have any trouble finding the livery stable. The proprietor, a short, bald man with a sweeping mustache, recognized Glory's horse right away and was impressed with Luke's dun as well.

"This fella may not be as much for looks as Miz MacCrae's horse," Cramer said, "but I'll bet he can run all day when he needs to, can't he?"

Luke felt an instinctive liking for the stableman. He nodded and said, "That's right. Take good care of him, will you?"

"You don't have to ask me twice."

From the stable Luke walked to the hotel, which he had taken note of earlier, and told the slick-haired clerk at the desk that Glory MacCrae had come in to get rooms for both of them.

"Yes, sir, Mr. Jensen," the clerk said as he snagged a key from the board on the wall behind him. "Room Seven. Top of the stairs to your right." A faint smirk tugged at his lips as he added, "Mrs. MacCrae is right next door in Room Eight. They adjoin."

"Is that so?"

"Yes, indeed."

Luke's voice hardened as he said, "That connecting door won't be getting any use, and I wouldn't want to hear any gossip about the matter, either." He leaned forward just enough to be menacing. "Is that clear?"

The clerk swallowed and moved back a step.

"Yes, sir," he said. "Very clear."

"See to it you remember," Luke said as he jerked his

head in a nod. He picked up the key the clerk had placed on the counter and turned toward the stairs.

As he went up, he wondered what was in Glory's mind. He knew she had been attracted to him, even though she hadn't acted on that impulse and probably wouldn't have. Ever since Whittaker's revelation during the first inquest, though, any feelings Glory had been developing for him had undoubtedly vanished. As a fugitive from the law, she wouldn't want anything to do with a bounty hunter.

And yet she'd insisted that he stay around so they could talk. Maybe the burden of guilt had gotten to be too much for her. Maybe she wanted to confess and get that weight off of her.

Luke couldn't make himself believe that. Not from a woman as bold and straightforward and convinced of the rightness of her own decisions as Glory MacCrae. Whatever had happened in Baltimore, he doubted that she felt much guilt about it.

The best way to find out what she wanted from him was to wait and see, he decided. The hotel had a dining room. Maybe they could eat dinner together there, or over at the Elite Café, if Glory preferred.

The door to Room Seven was unlocked. Luke went in and found it to be a perfectly comfortable-looking, if undistinguished, hotel room. The window overlooked McDowell Street and had a balcony outside it, too small for any purpose other than decoration. Luke hung his hat on one of the bedposts, poured some water from the pitcher into the basin on the table, and splashed it on his face. He was rubbing it in, feeling the weariness of the years and a life lived for the most part in hardship and danger, when he heard a soft knock on the door between his room and the adjoining one.

It seemed that his comment to the clerk about that door not getting any use wasn't going to turn out to be true, after all, he thought as he straightened. He dried his face, went to the door, and opened it.

Glory stood there, still wearing the clothes she had been in earlier, except for her hat. She hadn't expected to spend the night in town, so she probably hadn't brought along anything else. She said, "May I come in?"

Luke nodded and stepped back.

"Of course. I don't have anything to offer you to drink—"

"That's all right. I didn't come over here for a drink."

"I thought maybe we could have dinner in a little while—"

She interrupted him again by saying, "We'll have to see about that." Her right hand dipped into a pocket on her buckskin vest and came out with a two-barrel, over-and-under derringer much like the ones Luke carried. She pointed it at him, eared back the hammer, and went on: "That'll depend on what you have to say."

CHAPTER 15

If a man had pulled a gun on him like that, Luke would have taken it away from him before the hombre even got it pointed at him, let alone cocked. Glory had taken him a little by surprise, though.

He shouldn't have been shocked that she would threaten him like this. He knew from experience that she reacted quickly to danger and did what had to be done. Clearly, she felt that he was a danger to her . . . and considering the mission that had brought him to Sabado Valley, she was probably right about that.

Things had changed since his arrival here, though. At least for now, he was more interested in the truth than he was in the bounty on her head. He said, "Take it easy, Glory. You don't have to point a gun at me."

"No? Am I supposed to think that you don't give a damn about five thousand dollars? We haven't been acquainted for very long, Luke, but I already know you better than that."

"What do you want me to do, stick my hands in the air and beg for my life? That's not going to happen."

She looked at him intently and said, "I could shoot you, you know. I could put a bullet in your head, drag your body through that door into my room, and claim that you attacked me. Some people might not believe me, but they wouldn't be able to prove I wasn't telling the truth."

"You're not going to do that," Luke replied with a shake of his head. "You're too smart to kill the one person who's definitely on your side."

"On my side?" She laughed. "How in the world could I think that you're on my side? You know who I really am, don't you?"

"Yes, I do . . . Mrs. Jennings."

Luke knew he was taking a chance by saying that. Maybe she hadn't really been convinced that he was aware of her true identity and was trying to trick him into admitting it. But he was willing to run the risk because his instincts told him it was time for both of them to put their cards on the table.

Her reaction wasn't exactly what she expected. Angry lines tightened the muscles of her face as she said, "Don't call me that. I was legally married to Sam MacCrae. I was a widow when I married him."

"Only because you killed Alfred Jennings back in Baltimore."

"Is that what you believe?"

"It's what the wanted poster I read back in San Antonio told me. The one with that five-thousand-dollar bounty you just mentioned."

"And wanted posters never get anything wrong," she said contemptuously. "Lawmen never make mistakes."

"That thought *did* occur to me," Luke said.

"And greedy bastards never . . . never lie. . . ."

Unexpectedly, her face crumpled as she began to cry. That surprised Luke almost more than anything else she could have done. He had never seen anything from Glory except strength and determination. As her shoulders shook, she lowered the hammer on the derringer and tossed the little gun onto the bed.

"There!" she said in a voice choked with despair. "I'm unarmed. You can take me in now. You can take me back to Baltimore and watch them hang me, for all I care!"

Luke asked himself if she was acting, putting on a show for his benefit. He didn't think so, but it was hard to be sure of anything where this woman was concerned. She started to turn away. He put a hand on her shoulder and said, "Glory . . ."

She whirled back toward him. He tensed, ready to duck if she struck out at him, but instead she threw her arms around him and pressed her face against his chest as she sobbed.

He felt like telling her that it was too much, that she was overdoing it, but the way her body shook felt genuine. He supposed anybody could break sooner or later, no matter how strong they were. The strain of maintaining a tough façade could get to be too much.

Or maybe she was just skillfully playing on his emotions. It might take time to figure out what was really going on.

The best way to find out, he decided, was to play along with her.

He lifted his arms and put them around her. With one hand he stroked the fragrant, dark masses of her hair.

"It's all right," he murmured, the meaningless reassurance of any man trying to comfort a crying woman. "It's all right."

"N-No, it's not," Glory said. "He framed me, the son of a bitch!"

Now that sounded more like her, Luke thought. He said, "Who? Alfred Jennings?"

"No." Glory lifted her head and raised her tear-streaked face so she could look at him. "Alfred was a kind, wonderful man. I'm talking about his son, Hugh."

"I don't understand," Luke said.

She slipped out of his embrace, turned, and walked across the room before turning back toward him. She was pacing like a caged animal, he realized.

"Do you really want to hear the story?" she demanded. "Or are you just humoring me?"

"I really want to hear it," Luke told her. "I've got to know the truth before I decide what to do."

"You mean whether or not to turn me over to the law." Her voice was flat, hard.

"You *are* wanted on a murder charge. You came to Painted Post to hide out from it, didn't you?"

"I was hiding because I didn't want to hang or spend the rest of my life in prison for something I didn't do."

"Quite a few of the men I've taken in have tried to convince me at some point that they were innocent."

"But you didn't believe it, did you? That would have stood in the way of you collecting your blood money."

"If you really want me to help you," Luke said, "you might start by not insulting me."

"I didn't ask you to help me," Glory said. "I just asked if you wanted the truth."

Luke gestured to indicate that he was listening.

"All right." Glory raked her fingers through her hair, and even though that emotional gesture left it disheveled, she wasn't any less attractive for it. "I was Alfred Jennings's second wife, just as I was Sam MacCrae's. He was married for a long time to a woman named Prudence. Hugh's mother. She was a terrible woman, and she passed it on to her son."

"Is that what Jennings told you? Men sometimes aren't very objective when it comes to describing their wives. They're seldom really as good—or as bad—as their husbands make them out to be."

"No, Prudence Jennings really was awful. I saw it with my own eyes. I was . . . acquainted with them socially."

Something about the way she said that made Luke think there was more to the story, but he was willing to pass that over for now and get to her marriage to Jennings and his subsequent murder.

"Prudence made Alfred's life a living hell," Glory went on. "And Hugh was a real trial as well. He was always getting in some sort of trouble with women or gamblers or assorted lowlifes. Alfred had to come to his rescue with money many times. Prudence insisted that

Alfred take him into the business, and that just made things worse. Hugh wasn't just incompetent. He was a thief."

"But Jennings couldn't get rid of him because he was flesh and blood," Luke said.

"That's right. Then Prudence got sick and died after a short illness. Alfred couldn't fire Hugh then, of course, so soon after his mother died. So things went along the way they were."

"Until you moved in," Luke guessed.

Glory's chin jutted out defiantly. She said, "I didn't pursue Alfred or set a trap for him with my wiles, if that's what you're thinking. It was all his idea. But eventually, after a suitable time had passed, yes, we were married, and I planned to do my best to make sure the rest of his life was happy. I thought he deserved it."

"So what happened?" Luke asked.

Glory drew in a deep breath and blew it out. She said, "Alfred discovered just how much money Hugh had embezzled from the company. Without Prudence there to torment him anymore, he was ready to wash his hands of Hugh, ready to turn him over to the law. Hugh knew that . . . and he killed him."

Luke looked at her for a few seconds, then said, "Wait a minute. You're saying that Hugh Jennings killed his own father?"

"That's right."

"Then why did the police blame you?"

Glory began to pace again. She said, "I was upstairs. I knew that Alfred had summoned Hugh to the house to tell him that it was all over, and I suggested that I should be with him when they met. I didn't think Alfred needed to go through that alone. He said it wasn't a good idea, though. He knew that Hugh resented me, and he thought if I was there it would just agitate Hugh that much more."

She stopped, breathing hard again. If she was acting, Luke thought, she was one of the best at it he had ever seen, good enough that she ought to be on the stage.

"Too much time had passed," Glory went on. "I started to worry, so I went downstairs thinking that I ought to look in on them no matter what Alfred had said. But when I came into his study where he had been talking to Hugh, he . . . he was lying on the floor . . . with a letter opener stuck in his throat . . . and there was blood everywhere. . . ."

She put her hands over her face and began to cry again. Luke kept his distance this time and let her get through it on her own.

Finally, Glory was able to say, "I . . . I ran to him, of course, and I tried to see if there was anything I could do for him—"

"Which got his blood all over your hands."

She glared at him and snapped, "That's right. If you've already made up your mind you're not going to believe me, why are we wasting time with this?"

"I didn't say I've made up my mind. But I want to make sure I have all the facts straight in my mind."

"Yes, I got blood all over my hands, and my dress, too, while I was trying to see if he was still alive and if I could help him. That was when Hugh came in with some of his wastrel friends and acted shocked and yelled that I had killed his father. But I hadn't, of course. He had. Then he went out and found some of his crowd and came back with them so he could pretend to discover the body. I'm sure he planned to claim that I must have killed Alfred, but I'd unwittingly made it even easier for him. Now he had witnesses to swear that they'd found me kneeling beside Alfred's body with his blood all over me."

Luke nodded slowly and said, "I can see where that would look pretty bad, all right. What did you do?"

"Oh, I knew immediately what must have happened and what Hugh intended. He and one of his friends rushed at me. Hugh said they had to hold me while someone went for the police. I wasn't going to let that happen. I knew that Alfred had a loaded gun in his desk. I got to it first."

"You shot them?"

Glory shook her head.

"I didn't have to do that. Hugh and his friends weren't brave enough to charge a gun. I got out of there with nothing but the pistol . . . and Alfred's watch that I had slipped out of his pocket. I . . . I wanted something to remember him by."

"What about the hundred thousand dollars you're supposed to have stolen?"

"That was how much Hugh had stolen from his father's company. It was easy enough to cover up the theft by blaming it on me." Glory's voice was bitter as she added, "Everything worked out perfectly for him. It couldn't have been any better . . . except that I was still alive and knew what had really happened."

Silence hung in the hotel room for a long moment after Glory stopped speaking. Finally, Luke said, "It's a story worthy of a dime novel, but I suppose it could have really happened that way. I can see why the police charged you with murder."

Glory laughed, but there was no humor in the sound.

"It gets even worse than that, believe it or not. After everything I've told you, I might as well spill the whole thing. After I ran, it came out that Alfred had done some looking into my background."

Now they were getting to what he had suspected earlier, Luke thought.

"I said that I knew the Jennings family socially. They believed that I came from an old, wealthy Charleston family and that I was the widow of a British lord who'd been a blockade runner during the war for the excitement and adventure of it."

"Really?" Luke asked with a wry smile. "They actually believed that?"

"I was good at making them believe it. And it was true that my family was from Charleston. My mother ran the best tavern and whorehouse on the waterfront. As for my father . . . well, I don't really know about him. I suppose he could have been British, whoever he was. But I learned a lot at an early age about living by my wits."

"Did you have your sights set on Alfred Jennings from the start?"

"Actually, no." She gave that cold laugh again. "Believe it or not, Hugh was my target. But then I found out what a rotten louse he was, and even the likes of me didn't want to have anything to do with him. Prudence dying and Alfred taking an interest in me, that just happened."

"You didn't do anything to help the first Mrs. Jennings out of this vale of tears?"

She came at him fast, her hand flashing up in a slap aimed at his face. Luke was faster, catching her wrist before the blow could land. She stared into his eyes from a distance of mere inches and whispered, "You bastard."

"I just want the truth."

"And I'm giving it to you! Every word I've told you has been the truth!"

"Even the part where you admitted to being a lying swindler?"

She said, "Oh!" and jerked free from his grip. He let her go. She stepped back and went on: "Maybe if I'm going to hang anyway, I ought to kill you for being so damned obnoxious. They can only stretch my neck once."

"Go on with your story," he told her. "I'm still reserving judgment."

She snorted and said, "That's funny. Me, being judged by a bounty hunter. How much blood do *you* have on your hands, Luke Jensen?"

"I'm not the one wanted by the law."

"All right." She forced herself to calm down and continued. "I don't know why, but Alfred hired detectives to look into my life, and they found out the truth about me. Their reports were locked in his safe. I don't think he was ever going to use them."

"Unless you gave him a reason to."

"Maybe." She shrugged. "I said he was a good man. I never said he was a fool. I think if Hugh hadn't done what he did, though, eventually Alfred would have lost all his doubts about me, and he would have burned those reports and forgotten all about them. As it was, when Hugh opened the safe after Alfred's death, he found them and turned them over to the authorities."

"And you looked even guiltier than before," Luke said. "The reports gave you a motive for killing your husband. The police would think he was about to expose you for a swindler and throw you out."

"That's right. You can see why I had to run . . . and keep running."

"Until you got to Painted Post." Luke frowned. "Why here?"

"I was headed to California," she said. "I thought that's where the law would look for me. I figured that if I got off the train in some little town along the way and lived as quietly and discreetly as possible, I might be able to hide out and never be found."

"It didn't take me that long to track you down," Luke pointed out.

"That's because I didn't stick to my plan. I was going to get a job as a seamstress or a waitress or some other job like that. I was going to turn myself into a mousy little thing that no one would look twice at, let alone suspect of being a fugitive murderess."

Luke didn't say anything, but he thought that she never could have transformed herself into a mousy little thing that no one would notice. That just wouldn't have been possible.

Glory went on: "Instead of doing that, I wound up marrying the biggest rancher in this part of the state and landed in the middle of a range war. But when I met Sam, I couldn't resist him. I know what you're thinking, Luke. I found another rich man to marry and possibly swindle. But it wasn't like that. I swear it wasn't."

He didn't say whether or not he believed her. Instead, he said, "There's something I'm wondering about. You don't strike me as the sort of woman to just let this Hugh Jennings get away with murdering his own father, a man you claim to have loved. But by running away, you made sure he'd get away with it."

She shook her head and said, "No, I was just biding my time. I was going to save up my money and then try to find someone to get to the truth. When I married Sam, I admit that I thought his money would make it easier, once I'd finally told him everything. But I was waiting to do that until after things were settled with Elston, and then . . ."

"And then it was too late."

She sighed.

"Yes. Sam was dead. And I knew my first responsibility was to save the ranch he'd left behind. That's what he would have wanted. If that means war with Harry Elston, then so be it. My problems from before don't matter right now."

"So what is it you want from me?"

"Don't you see? I want you to believe me! I've been carrying this around—" Again she raked her fingers through her hair. "I want you to help me stop Elston from taking over the MC. If you do that, Luke . . . I'll do anything you want." She took another deep breath. "I'll even go back to Baltimore and face whatever's waiting for me there, once I know Sam's ranch will be safe."

"Safe for who? Does he have any children?"

Glory shook her head.

"So you're all he had left. The ranch is yours. You're a rich woman."

"I won't deny it."

"And you could use that money to fight the charges against you and expose Hugh Jennings."

"That's right."

"But only if you can protect the MC from Elston."

"You understand, Luke," she said. "You have the truth. The whole picture. The question now is . . . what are you going to do about it?"

CHAPTER 16

They ate supper in the hotel dining room. The table-cloth and the place settings were fancier than in the Elite Café, but the food—fried chicken, corn on the cob, and beans—wasn't as good. It was at least edible, though, and the coffee, thank goodness, wasn't bad, Luke thought.

He had told Glory that he would have to think about her question. She wasn't happy with that answer, but after spilling her guts to him the way she had, there wasn't much she could do except wait for him to make up his mind and hope that he believed her enough to throw in with her.

Not surprisingly considering everything that had happened, their dinner conversation was a bit strained. Luke was just as glad when the meal was over and they could go back upstairs to their rooms.

He told Glory good night while they were in the hallway outside Rooms Seven and Eight. She looked like she wanted to say something important, but then she just nodded slightly and told him, "Good night."

The door clicked shut behind her as she went in.

Luke went into his room, tossed his hat on the bed without lighting the lamp, and found one of the ladder-back chairs next to the small table. He picked it up and set it next to the door, which he left open about half an inch.

The corridor ended in a blank wall. No window, no side stairs. Glory's room was closer to that blank wall than his, so she couldn't leave without going right past his door. If she tried to light a shuck out of Painted Post in the middle of the night, he intended to know about it.

Fully dressed except for his hat, still wearing his guns, he leaned the chair back against the wall in the darkness. His eyelids drooped so his eyes were half-closed. He wasn't asleep, but after a few minutes he wasn't fully awake, either.

However, all it would take to make him instantly alert would be the scrape of a foot or the faint squeak of a floorboard on the other side of the door. Luke was confident that Glory couldn't get past his room without his knowing it.

Even though he hadn't told her about it, he had made up his mind how he was going to proceed. He wasn't prepared to believe her story completely, because he had heard too many people he knew good and well were guilty as hell proclaim their innocence, but he leaned toward believing that her stepson, Hugh Jennings, really had murdered his father.

He wasn't sure how she planned to go about proving

that, with or without his help, but for the time being that wasn't relevant.

First and foremost, he was going to help her protect the ranch from Harry Elston's rapacious grasp and get to the bottom of Sam MacCrae's murder.

None of that intruded on his thoughts as he leaned against the wall next to the door of his hotel room and waited for something to happen. Instead, he dozed lightly, with the experienced frontiersman's knack of snatching some rest whenever the opportunity presented itself.

When a tiny noise finally intruded on his hearing, it wasn't what he expected. Instead of coming from out in the corridor, the faint click he heard originated right there in the room with him.

In less than the blink of an eye, he was awake. Soundlessly, he eased the chair's front legs down onto the floor. The fingers of his right hand wrapped around the butt of the Remington holstered on his left hip. He slid the revolver from the cross-draw rig and looped his thumb over the hammer.

He didn't draw it back, though. That noise would have given away his position.

Breathing so shallowly that it couldn't be heard, he waited.

Several moments of silence went by. Then a floorboard gave a little as someone moved.

"Luke?" a voice whispered at last. "Luke, are you awake?"

Glory. That meant the noise that had roused him was the door between their rooms opening.

Luke still made no sound. She might have slipped into his room to shoot him or, more likely, slide a knife blade between his ribs. She wouldn't have him as an ally against Harry Elston if she did that, but on the other hand, she wouldn't have to worry anymore about him turning her over to the law, either.

"Luke, blast it, say something." Her voice was still a whisper. "I know you're bound to be awake by now. Why won't you—"

He heard a small thud and a muttered curse. More than likely she had banged her knee against the bed or the table in the dark, he thought.

"Luke! Blast it, are you even in here?"

He came out of the shadows, a moving patch of deeper blackness in the darkened room, and wrapped his left arm around her waist to jerk her back against him. As she gasped in surprise he laid the Remington's barrel against the side of her head, such a light touch she probably barely felt it. The gun's muzzle wasn't against her temple, but it was close enough to be a threat.

"What do you want?" he asked.

She trembled as he held her, but he got the sense that it was from anger, not fear. Her voice was certainly angry as she said, "What the hell do you think I'm doing? I came to see you."

"Why? To get me out of the way so I won't be a threat to you anymore?"

"Why do you think?"

He moved the arm that was around her. She wasn't wearing much, just whatever had been under her riding clothes earlier. When she twisted her head he felt the thick, tumbled mass of her hair brush his face and knew she wore it loose.

"Well, if you don't plan to kill me, then I'd say you're here to make sure I help you by bribing me with your fair white body," he drawled.

"You really are an unpleasant man," she said tightly.

"So I've been told many times. But am I wrong in my assumption?"

She hesitated before answering, but she finally said, whispering again, "No. No, you're not."

"You must think I'm pretty easily manipulated if you believe you can get me to do whatever you want just by falling into bed with me."

A short laugh came from her in the darkness.

"You're a man, aren't you?"

"Not any doubt about that."

"Why should you be any different from any other man I've ever met?"

"Because I am," Luke said. He holstered the gun, put that hand on her as well, turned her around toward him.

If he was wrong about her being armed, he might be feeling cold steel in his guts any second now, he told himself.

Instead, she seemed to melt against him, and with the unerring accuracy of instinct, her mouth found his.

It was a good kiss. Luke's hands and arms tightened on her in response. The bed was close beside them, and he knew that if he lowered her onto it, she wouldn't resist.

Maybe because she so fully expected it of him, he did

something else. He slid his hands from her waist up to her shoulders, broke the kiss, and moved her back a step.

"What's wrong?" she murmured. "I'll do whatever—"

"I know what you're prepared to do," Luke said. "And depending on how all this comes out, maybe someday I'll take you up on it, providing that you're still willing. But not now, Glory. Not when I'd never know if it was just because you thought you needed my help."

Her shoulders stiffened under his touch. She said, "Damn you, Luke Jensen. I finally make up my mind to come over here and you . . . you reject me!"

Luke chuckled.

"Hell of a note, isn't it?" he said.

Before she could respond, the hotel room window erupted in an explosion of shattered glass, flame, and noise.

Luke acted instantly. Since he still had hold of Glory's shoulders, he swung her to the side and gave her a shove that ought to have sent her sprawling on the floor next to the bed, although the room was too dark for him to see if that was where she wound up.

In a continuation of the same movement, he whirled around and drew both Remingtons. The opening where the window had been was a little lighter than the surrounding area because of the glow in the street from other buildings, and he saw something dark bulking against that faint illumination. Firing from the hip, he triggered the guns twice each and sent four slugs through the gaping hole. The shape jerked back and disappeared.

Luke knew better than to run to the window and look out. It could be a trick to lure him into making a better target of himself. Whoever had fired through the window had used a shotgun, but the would-be killer could have a confederate posted somewhere on the other side of the street with a rifle.

Instead, he backed toward the door, in a crouch with his guns ready to fire again. When he reached it, he pushed it shut with his foot and holstered the left-hand gun long enough to reach behind him and turn the key, just in case a second bushwhacker tried to bust in that way.

He was half-deaf from the scattergun's blast followed by the roar of the Remingtons, but he called, "Glory! Glory, are you hit?"

To his ears her voice sounded like it came from far away, but he heard the words clearly enough as she said, "I'm all right, Luke. What about you?"

"I'm fine," he said. "Are you on the floor?"

"Yes."

"Stay there."

They waited. Outside, people shouted questions, wanting to know what all the commotion was about. Luke heard footsteps hurry past in the corridor, no doubt other hotel guests wanting to get away from the scene of the trouble. Finally, after several minutes, somebody pounded a fist on the door.

"Open up!" Jared Whittaker called. "This is the sheriff! What's going on in there?"

Luke didn't fully trust Whittaker. It wouldn't surprise

him to find out that Whitey Singletary had fired that shotgun blast through the window, and Whittaker might be planning to finish what the deputy had started.

So he holstered his left-hand gun again, went to the door, and unlocked it, then stepped quickly to the side in case Whittaker tried to shoot through the panel. Instead, as Luke backed off with the other Remington leveled, the door swung open slowly and Whittaker asked from the hallway, "Who's in there, damn it? I told you, I'm the law."

Luke couldn't see Whittaker and knew the lawman was being cautious, too, hanging back out of sight.

"The only law I care about right now is in my fist, Sheriff," he said. "Come inside slow and easy, with empty hands where I can see them."

"Jensen! I should have known you'd be in the middle of this. Who have you killed now?"

"I'm not sure. Maybe nobody. Yet."

Light from a lamp at the end of the hall spilled through the open door. Whittaker stepped into the glow, and as Luke had told him, his hands were out in front of him, clearly visible. He wasn't holding a gun.

"I leaned my rifle against the wall out here, Jensen," Whittaker said as he came into the room. "Why don't you put away that revolver? Pointing a gun at a lawman is a crime in itself, you know."

Luke lowered the Remington but didn't holster it. He glanced at Glory, saw that she was climbing to her feet. She didn't seem embarrassed or upset about her skimpy attire, even though Whittaker's eyes flicked toward her, then lingered a little longer than was necessary.

As always, even under less than perfect conditions, Glory MacCrae was spectacularly beautiful.

She reached toward the bed, as if she were going to pull off the spread to wrap it around herself, then stopped as she saw the hole blasted in it. A little shudder went through her, and Luke knew what she had to be thinking.

If they had been in that bed, they would both be dead by now. Every now and then it paid to be chivalrous, he supposed.

"Well, I reckon I know some of what was going on here, anyway," Whittaker said dryly.

"Don't be obnoxious, Sheriff," Glory snapped. "And you might be wise not to jump to conclusions, either. My room is next-door. When I heard the shot, I ran in here to make sure Mr. Jensen was all right."

"Is that what happened, Jensen?"

"A gentleman never contradicts a lady," Luke drawled. "I'm fine, Mrs. MacCrae. You can go back to your room now."

"I'll decide when anybody can leave," Whittaker said sharply. "Somebody took a shot at you through the window, Jensen?"

"That's right. I fired back, and whoever it was disappeared. Maybe they're lying out there in the street where they fell right now."

Whittaker shook his head.

"This is the front of the hotel. If anybody was lying

in the street I would have seen them when I ran down here after I heard the shooting. How do I know you didn't get drunk or go loco and shoot out the window yourself?"

"For one thing, I don't have a shotgun," Luke replied in a tone of patient contempt. "You heard the shots, and you can see what happened to the bed where the buckshot hit it. You know a shotgun was involved. For another, look at all that glass on the floor. You've probably felt some of it crunching under your boots. It was blown in, not out, and that means it was broken from outside."

"All right, fine," Whittaker said. "Somebody tried to bushwhack you. Did you get a look at him?"

"Unfortunately, no. Just a glimpse of a shape. If I were you, though, right about now I'd be asking myself where that deputy of yours is."

Whittaker stiffened and said, "By God, I won't stand for you accusing Whitey of this, just because you've got a grudge against him—"

"I'd say the grudge runs the other way," Luke cut in. "I was the one who whipped him yesterday, after all."

"Well, I don't believe it, and I'd better not hear about you spreading rumors against him, either."

Glory said, "Just how long do you intend to make me stand here like this, Sheriff?"

Whittaker gave a little shake of his head, almost like he had forgotten she was there, although in her current state of undress that seemed impossible. He said, "Sorry, Mrs. MacCrae. You can go on back to your room."

"Thank you," she said coolly. "If you need me, you

know where to find me, but I can't tell you any more than I already have."

"Yes, ma'am." Whittaker waited until Glory had gone into the adjoining room, then turned back to Luke and said, "What was she doing on the floor when I came in here?"

"I told her to get down when you started hammering on the door," Luke answered without hesitation. "For all I knew, there was going to be more shooting, and I wanted her to get out of the line of fire as much as possible."

"I yelled out who I was."

Luke's shrug was eloquent.

With a frown, Whittaker went on, "You're still fully dressed, Jensen, right down to your guns, and it's obvious you hadn't turned in when the shooting started. What were you doing in a dark room like that?"

"It's not against the law for a man to sit in a dark hotel room, is it?" Luke asked. With a nod toward the chair where he'd been waiting earlier, he continued, "I like to sit and think. The dark helps."

"You've got an answer for everything, don't you?"

"Not everything," Luke said. "Some of the great philosophical questions still baffle me. Like the one about the bear in the woods."

Whittaker's jaw tightened in anger, but he said, "I'll take a look around town, ask some questions, see if I can find anybody who saw anything."

"You might want to start by taking a look out the window," Luke suggested. "The bushwhacker might have left something out there that would help you find him."

"Fine," Whittaker agreed grudgingly. He walked over to the window, glass crunching under his boots as he did so, like Luke had said, and peered out.

Luke struck a match, lit the lamp on the bedside table, and picked it up to carry it over to the window. He held it so that its light shone on the balcony.

A splash of fresh blood across the boards of the railing gleamed redly in the lamplight.

"I was pretty sure I winged him," Luke said. "That blood proves it."

"I reckon. The railing's not busted."

"It's low enough that he could have tipped over it and fallen without breaking it."

"How'd he get out here in the first place?"

Luke thought Whittaker sounded genuinely curious, which was a bit of a surprise. He said, "The easiest way would be to climb out on the balcony through the window of another room. I don't see a ladder anywhere, and it would take an ape to climb down from the roof. Although, I don't suppose that actually rules out Deputy Singletary. . . ."

Whittaker glared at him but didn't say anything.

There was nothing else on the balcony except the drops of blood. When Luke and Whittaker turned away from the window, a man with gray hair and a mustache who waited in the doorway asked, "Was anyone hurt, Sheriff?"

"It appears not, Mr. Stafford," Whittaker answered, the name indicating to Luke that this newcomer was probably the hotel's owner.

"Thank the Lord for that," Stafford said. "Mr. Jensen, you'll move to another room, of course. You can't stay here, not with that damage to the bed. Not to mention the, ah, smell of gunsmoke in the room."

"Like blood, it's a hard smell to get out," Luke said.

CHAPTER 17

Stafford led Luke down the hall to Room Three, which he said was empty for the night. When the hotel man opened the door, Luke immediately noticed that the window was open. Somebody had shoved the pane all the way up.

"Do you normally leave the windows open in vacant rooms?" he asked Stafford.

The gray-haired man looked perplexed as he shook his head and said, "No, not usually."

Whittaker was still standing in the hallway. Luke said, "Take a look, Sheriff." He pointed into the room. "Here's how that shotgunner got onto the balcony."

Whittaker came down to Room Three, looked through the door at the open window, and grunted.

"I suppose that's possible," he said.

Luke snapped a lucifer to life with his thumbnail and lit the lamp. He took it over to the window and held it over the sill. Something caught his eye right away. He motioned Whittaker closer and pointed it out.

"There's a little piece of cloth caught on a nail that didn't get hammered down quite all the way," Luke said. "Looks like it's from a pair of trousers. It must've torn when the bushwhacker swung his leg over the sill and stepped out."

Although Whittaker sounded like it pained him to admit it, he said, "You're probably right, Jensen. But that doesn't tell us any more about who the hombre was."

"It does if Singletary has on a torn pair of pants in the morning." Luke shrugged. "Of course, the fact that he'll have a bullet wound, too, is even better evidence."

Stafford said, "Are you talking about Deputy Singletary? You can't mean you think that he—"

"Anybody can run his mouth and say loco things," Whittaker interrupted harshly. "I warned you about that, Jensen."

"I'm just speculating," Luke said. "I think I have a right to, since it was me who nearly got blown apart by a shotgun."

"Speculate all you want, but keep it to yourself. I'm done here."

Whittaker left, stalking off with a ramrod-stiff back. Stafford said nervously, "I sure am sorry about all this, Mr. Jensen. If there's anything I can do to make things better . . ."

Luke shook his head.

"I don't blame you or your hotel, Mr. Stafford," he said. "Somebody's got a grudge against me, and chances are they would have come after me no matter where I was."

"Well, if there's anything you need . . ."

"Just some rest," Luke said.

That didn't come easy, though. For one thing, he was on edge from nearly being murdered, and for another, he wasn't sure what he had told Stafford was the truth. He had assumed that he was the bushwhacker's target, since the shotgun blast had been fired through the window of his room.

Maybe the gunner had been skulking out there on the balcony for a while, though. Maybe he had known that Glory was in Luke's room instead of her own. It had been dark in the room, but if the man's eyes had adjusted enough, he might have been able to make out both of them.

No, Luke decided, that wasn't what had happened. The would-be killer had known where the bed was located in the room and had targeted it, thinking that Luke would be asleep there. That meant he was familiar with the layout of the hotel's rooms. Probably somebody from Painted Post. Somebody with a grudge against Luke.

All the signs kept pointing to Whitey Singletary.

Maybe the morning would bring some new information to light. In the meantime, Luke closed the window, stuffed the pillows under the covers to make it look like he was sleeping there, then spread a blanket on the floor on the far side of the bed and stretched out there. The makeshift pallet wasn't very comfortable, but he had slept in worse places.

Besides, getting his hide filled with buckshot or .45 slugs would be even less comfortable.

* * *

The thought that he had misjudged the situation and that Glory might still be in danger nagged at him during the night, but when he knocked on her door in the morning she opened it almost immediately and didn't appear to be any the worse for wear.

"Did you get any sleep last night?" he asked her.

She shrugged and said, "A little. How about you?"

"Some."

"Actually, I laid awake most of the night with my derringer in my hand."

Luke chuckled and said, "We had the same idea. I had my hand wrapped around the butt of one of my Remingtons." He inclined his head toward the staircase. "You want to go down and get some breakfast?"

"Yes, please. I could use about a gallon of coffee, too. But let's go over to the Elite for it. Nobody in Painted Post makes better hotcakes than Mrs. Anderson."

That claim proved to be true. The hotcakes were fluffy and sweet, the bacon was crispy, and the hash browns were cooked perfectly. Hazel kept their coffee cups full of the hot, strong brew as well. By the time they finished the meal, Luke felt almost human again, and Glory seemed to be doing better, too.

She had settled the bill for their rooms before they left the hotel to walk up the street to the café, so all they had to do was head for Cramer's livery stable to pick up their horses.

Luke saddled his dun while Cramer got Glory's big white horse ready to ride. The liveryman said, "I heard about all the excitement up at the hotel last night."

"I'm not sure how exciting it was," Luke said. "It didn't make for a very relaxing night, either."

"No, I expect it didn't. A shotgun blast ain't exactly a lullaby."

"I'm sure you're up and about fairly early, Mr. Cramer. Have you seen Deputy Singletary today?"

Before Cramer could answer, Jared Whittaker strode into the livery barn through the open double doors and said, "I warned you about spreading rumors, Jensen."

"I just asked a question. I didn't spread anything." Luke finished tightening the cinches and stepped away from his horse. "But now that you're here, Sheriff, I'll just ask you, since you're the one in the best position to know. Is your deputy anywhere around town today?"

Whittaker glared at him, and for a moment Luke thought the lawman wasn't going to answer the question. But then Whittaker said, "As a matter of fact, I haven't seen him yet today. That doesn't mean anything, though. He hasn't been feeling very well since the other day, so I told him to take some time off if he needed to."

"Since I broke his nose, you mean."

"That's exactly what I mean," Whittaker snapped. "He's probably over at the boardinghouse where he has a room, getting some rest."

"Why don't we go see?" Luke suggested.

Again Whittaker looked like he wanted to argue, but Luke's suggestion was a reasonable one and he couldn't just disregard it. He jerked his head and said, "All right, come on. You'll see that you're wrong, though."

"One of us will," Luke said.

Glory was waiting in front of the livery stable. Luke

told her, "I'll be back in a few minutes. The sheriff and I are going to check on something."

"Does it have anything to do with what happened last night?" she asked.

"It does."

"Then I'm coming, too," she declared.

"That's not a good idea," Whittaker said.

"I think it is, and the last time I checked, this was still a free country."

"Might be better if it wasn't," Whittaker muttered, but he didn't try to stop Glory from walking along McDowell Street with him and Luke.

They turned onto one of the side streets, and the sheriff led them to a two-story frame house. A nice-looking, middle-aged woman with graying brown hair answered Whittaker's knock. He took off his hat and said, "Good morning, Mrs. Miles. I'm looking for Deputy Singletary. Does he happen to be here?"

The woman frowned and said, "I'm afraid I really don't know, Sheriff. I haven't seen him since supper last night. He didn't come down for breakfast this morning."

Whittaker shot a glance at Luke, then asked, "Did you go up and knock on his door to see if he was all right?"

"As a matter of fact, I did. He didn't answer, and I didn't hear anyone moving around."

Whittaker crammed his hat back on his head, then said, "If it's all right with you, I'm going to go up and take a look myself."

"Of course," Mrs. Miles said. "Do you think Deputy Singletary might be sick or hurt?"

"I hope not," Whittaker muttered. As the landlady moved aside, Whittaker stepped past her into the foyer. Luke followed, and so did Glory. Whittaker looked like he wanted to tell them to stay put, but he settled for saying, "You'd better stay down here with Mrs. Miles, Mrs. MacCrae."

Luke halfway expected Glory to argue, just on general principles if for no other reason, but she nodded and said, "All right."

"I'll need your key, Mrs. Miles," Whittaker said to the landlady. The woman reached inside a pocket on the apron she wore and took out a large brass key. Luke figured it would open every door in the house.

Whittaker went up the stairs with Luke right behind him. The sheriff obviously knew which room was his deputy's, because he went straight to one of the doors in the upstairs hall and hammered a fist on it.

"Whitey? Whitey, are you in there?"

When there was no response, Whittaker knocked again, but only silence came from the other side of the door.

"I don't think he's here," Luke said.

"All right, damn it," Whittaker snapped as he thrust the key into the lock and twisted it. "Let's find out."

He put his right hand on the butt of his Colt as he used his left to push the door open. Being ready for trouble like that was a habit every lawman got into if he wanted to survive for very long in a dangerous profession.

Luke didn't pack a badge and never would, but he had his hand on a gun, too, as he followed Whittaker into the room.

The sheriff stopped short and said, "Well, son of a bitch."

Luke moved slightly to one side and looked past Whittaker at the rumpled bed. Somebody had pulled the top sheet off and from the looks of it torn strips of cloth from it. What was left of the sheet lay in a bloody, wadded-up lump on the bed. Drops of blood were splattered across the other bedclothes.

Other than the furniture, the room was empty.

"I'll bet if we check the back stairs, we'll find more blood there," Luke said. "He made it back here, came in that way without waking anybody, and used that sheet to stop the bleeding, then tore pieces off of it to use as bandages."

"I've got eyes," Whittaker said in a grim voice. "I can see."

"After that, your guess is as good as mine where he went, but he knew he couldn't stay here in town, shot up like that. Not with me still alive to tell what happened at the hotel."

Whittaker shook his head and said, "You can't prove any of that."

"Singletary's not here to deny it, is he?" Given the sheriff's reaction to their discovery, which seemed genuinely surprised, Luke decided to play the other card in his hand. "That's not all of it, either. Yesterday, just as that shootout started in the street, somebody took a couple of shots at me from the roof of the courthouse. Do you happen to remember if Singletary was with you just then?"

"No, he—" Whittaker caught himself. "That doesn't mean anything. He was somewhere around there."

"Yeah," Luke said dryly, "up on the roof taking pot-shots at me. That's where he was, and you know it whether you want to admit it or not."

Whittaker turned to him and said, "Listen to me, Jensen. I didn't know anything about this. I don't mind admitting I don't like you. I didn't like you even before I found out you're a bounty hunter. And I don't have much use for Mrs. MacCrae, either. I think she's trying to make Harry Elston a scapegoat for her troubles. But I didn't have anything to do with trying to kill either of you!"

"You know, Sheriff, I almost believe you."

"It's the truth, damn it!" Whittaker paused and frowned, obviously thinking. "I wonder if there's some other explanation for all this. Whitey could've gotten hurt some other way. . . ."

"We both know that's not true," Luke said. "He was the one who fired a shotgun through that hotel room window last night. And now that I think about it, I've got a hunch I know where he went, too. Now that he's hurt, he's gone running to his real boss—Harry Elston."

"Maybe I need to take a ride out to the Lazy EO. That might be the best way to prove that you're wrong about all this, Jensen."

"Be my guest," Luke invited, "but don't expect that Elston will admit Singletary is there. He'll have him hidden out in some line shack or something. Elston will make sure you can't come up with any proof that he's involved. From everything I've seen since I've been here, he's very good at that."

"I want you to stay away from there," Whittaker snapped. "I won't have you harassing the citizens of this county."

"I'm going to see to it that Mrs. MacCrae gets back to her ranch safely," Luke said. "That's as far into the future as my plans extend."

"All right. Just remember what I said."

Whittaker turned and stalked out of the room.

Downstairs, the sheriff apologized to Mrs. Miles for the mess she was going to have to clean up in Single-tary's room.

"My goodness," the woman said as her eyes widened and she lifted a hand to her mouth. "Do you think the deputy is all right?"

"Well, he made it to his room and then back out," Whittaker said. "Does he still keep his horse in that shed of yours?"

"As far as I know."

"I'll have a look." Whittaker tugged on the brim of his hat. "Ma'am."

They left the worried landlady and went outside. Whittaker walked around the house to look in the shed. Glory, who had listened with great interest to what Whittaker told Mrs. Miles, said, "Do you think Single-tary headed for Elston's ranch after he failed to kill us?"

"That's what I told the sheriff," Luke replied with a nod. "I don't know where else he would go. Whittaker plans to ride out there and look for him."

"At least that's what he said he was going to do. Whittaker may be in Elston's pocket, too."

"I can't prove it one way or the other," Luke mused, "but I don't think he is. He wants to believe that Elston isn't behind all the trouble, but it strikes me as misguided support, rather than Whittaker being out and out crooked."

"Either way, he's no friend of mine."

"I think you're safe in saying that," Luke agreed.

Whittaker came back around the house. He said, "Whitey's horse isn't in the shed. Wherever he went, he's left town, I don't reckon there's any doubt about that."

"And that's what we're going to do," Luke said. "If you don't need us for anything else, Sheriff . . ."

Whittaker waved a hand and said, "Go ahead. I know where to find you."

Luke and Glory returned to the livery stable, where their saddled horses stood waiting. They said good-bye to Cramer and rode out of town on the Sabado Valley road.

They left the settlement behind and had ridden for a couple of miles when Glory asked, "Was what Sheriff Whittaker said true, Luke?"

"Which part? The man said a lot of things."

"About knowing where to find us. Are you still going to be at the MC if he comes looking for you, or are you going to leave once we get back there? You never did answer my question about your plans. Or about whether you . . ."

"Whether I believe your story about what happened with Alfred Jennings? I think I'm going to reserve judgment on that. There's one thing I know for sure, though: Harry Elston is a snake, and he's not to be trusted. Out here you never leave a dangerous snake alive. It might come back later to bite you."

"So you're going to help me save Sam's ranch?"

"It's your ranch now," Luke pointed out. "I don't want to see you lose it to a man like Elston."

A faint smile curved her lips. She said, "I'm glad to hear you say that, Luke. I really am. And when this is all over . . ."

"Then we'll figure out what to do about your other problem," he said. "Your five-thousand-dollar problem."

CHAPTER 18

They hadn't gotten an early start from Painted Post, so by midday they still hadn't gotten back to the MacCrae ranch headquarters, although Glory commented that they were already on her range again.

"We should have had Mrs. Anderson pack a lunch for us," she said as they rode. "That way we could have stopped and eaten."

"I could probably kill a jackrabbit and skin and cook it, if you're starving," Luke offered. "The meat's a little stringy and tough, but better than nothing."

She looked over at him and said, "You've really eaten jackrabbit?"

"And squirrel and prairie dog. True, none of them are what you'd expect to find in a fine restaurant in San Francisco, but when your belly is empty for long enough you'd be surprised what you might eat. The only thing I think I'd starve before I ate it again is armadillo." Luke shook his head. "That's just not good."

"I take it there have been times when your belly was empty?"

"Plenty of them."

"Bounty hunting isn't always a lucrative profession?"

"Not always. But it's always dangerous. That never changes."

They rode along in silence for a few minutes, then Glory said, "You're an unusual man. So cultured at times, so violent at others. But I suppose you're what life made you."

"I'd like to think I made my own life, instead of the other way around," Luke said.

"Yes, I suppose we'd all like to think that, but sometimes I wonder just how much control we're able to wrestle away from fate. Do we make our own choices, or do we just unwittingly follow the paths that some other force has laid out for us?"

"Free will or predestination, you mean?"

"Exactly!" Glory said.

It was one of the more bizarre moments of his life, Luke thought, riding across this rugged West Texas range with a stunningly beautiful fugitive who was wanted for murder, discussing theology and philosophy. His work had led him into some odd situations in the past, but this one was right up there.

Then everything got yanked back to normal by the crack of a gunshot and the whine of a bullet passing just over his head.

Luke reached over, slapped the rump of Glory's horse to send the animal leaping ahead, and heeled his dun into a gallop at the same time. He leaned forward in the saddle to make himself a smaller target as more shots blasted somewhere behind them. Glory cried out, but he was watching her and didn't see any sign that she was hit. He figured the cry was one of surprise and fear.

Ever since they had left Painted Post, Luke had been watching all around them, including their back trail. It bothered him that he'd let their enemies get behind him, but this country was covered with arroyos and little canyons, plenty of places for somebody to hide.

To tell the truth, he would have been a little surprised if they had made it all the way back to the MC *without* being jumped.

Part of him wished that Glory hadn't sent those three cowboys back to the ranch the day before. Her reasoning had been sound, though. Under the circumstances, it was entirely possible that Elston might launch a new offensive against the ranch. The new foreman needed the full crew on hand to protect the MC.

But that left Luke and Glory to make the return trip alone. Not sitting ducks, exactly, but tempting targets to be sure.

Luke twisted his neck to look over his shoulder. He saw three riders back there, pounding after them, smoke spurting from the muzzles of their guns as they fired wildly. They were too far back for handguns to do any good, a couple of hundred yards at least, but the excitement of the chase prompted them to burn some powder anyway.

The men on horseback hadn't fired those first shots. Those had come from a rifleman hidden on top of a small, rocky knoll Luke and Glory had passed a couple of minutes earlier. Luke knew that because when he looked back he saw the sun reflect from something up there, most likely a rifle barrel. When the bushwhacker had missed, then the other men had given chase.

Luke knew he was lucky the rifleman hadn't shot him out of the saddle. But was it really luck, he thought . . . or predestination?

A grim smile tugged at his lips under the mustache as he told himself not to worry about such things now. For the moment he had to concentrate on keeping himself and Glory alive.

"Up there to the left!" he shouted to her over the thundering hoofbeats. "That canyon!"

He had spotted the opening in the escarpmentlike bluff that formed the western edge of the valley, just below the rising hills. Boulders littered the mouth of the canyon. He and Glory could fort up in those rocks. They probably wouldn't have to hold off the attackers for long. Some of the MC cowboys were probably within earshot, and they would hurry to investigate the gunfire.

The big white horse was fast, but it lacked the stamina of Luke's dun and quickly began to falter at top speed. Glory urged the animal on, but Luke could tell it was already slowing. He pulled his Winchester from its sheath and called to Glory, "Keep going! Get behind those boulders and keep your head down!"

He hauled back on the reins and brought the dun around in a tight turn, then came to a stop. The Winchester flashed to his shoulder and he fired several rounds as fast as he could work the rifle's lever. He sprayed the lead toward the pursuers, who had cut down the gap between them and their quarry. Luke didn't expect to hit anything, but he came close enough to make the riders spread out and slow down a little.

That ought to give Glory enough time to reach the shelter of the boulders at the canyon mouth, Luke thought. Still holding the Winchester in his right hand, he yanked the dun's head around and jabbed his heels into its flanks. The chase was on again.

Glory was about fifty yards ahead of him now, and about fifty yards from the canyon as well. Another few moments was all she needed.

Without any warning, the white horse went down, its legs folding up beneath it. For a horrifying split second, Luke thought Glory was going to be crushed underneath the big horse. Then he saw her fly free from the saddle and crash to the ground several yards away from her fallen mount. She rolled over and the dust roiling in the air hid her from Luke's view.

"Glory!" he shouted. The dun never broke stride as he raced toward her.

Fear for her safety surged through him. Even though the horse hadn't landed on top of her, a tumble like that could easily break an arm or a leg . . . or a neck. He peered anxiously through the swirling dust, searching for a glimpse of her.

Then the dust parted and he saw her as she staggered to her feet and started stumbling around, obviously shaken but evidently not badly hurt. He veered the dun a little to approach at a better angle and shouted her name again.

This time she turned toward him and lifted her arms as the horse bore down on her. Luke slowed just enough that the impact wouldn't knock him out of the saddle as he leaned down to throw an arm around her and lift her off her feet. Glory flung her arms around his neck as he hauled her onto the dun in front of him.

"I've got you!" he told her.

But the incident had given the pursuers the opportunity to make up the ground they had lost a minute earlier when Luke opened fire on them. Now they were only a hundred yards behind, maybe less.

That wasn't close enough. Gallantly, the dun called on its remaining strength and dashed toward the boulder-littered canyon mouth. Luke galloped through a gap between two of the big slabs of rock.

He slowed the horse and swung Glory to the ground. She stumbled but stayed on her feet. Luke leaped from the saddle and landed running. He caught himself and turned to motion urgently at Glory.

"Get behind cover and stay there!" he told her. He cranked the Winchester's lever again as he ran toward the gap through which they had just ridden.

Pressing himself against the rock, he leaned out and drew a bead on one of the riders thundering toward them. The men realized their danger and tried to peel off to the sides, but they were too late. Luke tracked the man he had targeted and pressed the trigger.

The rifle cracked as it kicked against his shoulder. The man flung his arms in the air and slipped out of the saddle, but one foot was still caught in the stirrup. The horse dragged him across the rough ground.

If the bullet hadn't killed the pursuer, being dragged like that would finish the job. Luke worked the Winchester's lever and shifted his aim. He fired at one of the other two men, who had split up rather than staying bunched together. As far as Luke could tell, the shot missed. Both riders kept going without their horses breaking stride. They rode off at different angles, and he couldn't see them anymore from where he was.

As the echoes of the shots rolled across the prairie, Luke levered the rifle again and called, "Glory! Are you all right?"

Sounding a little breathless, she replied, "Yes, I . . . I think so." Then, as if it had just occurred to her, "Oh! My poor horse! Was he shot?"

"He's fine," Luke told her. From where he was, he could see that the big white horse had gotten up and wandered off to graze on some bunch grass. "He must've just lost his footing. He's moving around all right."

"Thank God. Where are Elston's men now?"

"Don't know. I can't see them from here. But I'm sure they're still out there. We'd find that out fast enough if we tried to leave this canyon."

"What are we going to do? We can't just stay here."

"We can for a while," Luke told her. "You said we were on your range, so some of your men might be within hearing of those shots. They'll come to see what it's all about."

Glory moved up closer beside him and said, "You're

right. We just have to wait. There were only a few of Elston's men."

"Yeah," Luke said slowly. "Seems like he would have sent more. . . ."

The skin on the back of his neck prickled, a warning sign that something was wrong. Why had Elston's men picked this particular place to jump them? he asked himself. There had been other spots along the trail from Painted Post that might have been better. And was it an accident that those first couple of shots from the rifleman hidden on the knoll had missed?

The hunch grew stronger in Luke that they had been trapped somehow, and what happened next confirmed that. A couple of horsemen raced into view, carrying blazing torches. It was like the attack on the ranch, Luke realized. Elston's men were trying to use fire to do their job for them.

He snapped the Winchester to his shoulder and fired, but it was too late. The men threw the torches toward the canyon mouth and hauled their horses around. One of them twisted in the saddle as Luke's bullet drilled his shoulder, but he had already done what he'd set out to do. The torches landed in clumps of dry grass and set them on fire.

"What are they doing?" Glory asked in a strained voice.

Luke didn't answer her question. He asked one of his own.

"Do you know if there's a way out at the other end of this canyon?"

"No, I . . . I don't. I'm sure I've been down here on this part of the ranch, but I don't remember. . . ."

Luke was willing to bet this was a box canyon. He looked around where they were and saw that the sides were too steep to climb. That went right along with what he suspected. Elston's men had herded him and Glory in here, like cattle going to the slaughtering pen.

The wind carried the first sharp tang of smoke to his nostrils. The flames were spreading quickly across the grassy flats in front of the canyon. They were about a hundred yards from the boulders where Luke and Glory had taken cover, and they advanced in that direction.

The wind wasn't blowing extremely hard, but it was strong enough to push the fire steadily toward them. The smoke began to thicken as the flames caught hold more and more. Gray and white masses of it billowed toward the canyon.

Glory coughed and said, "We'd better get out of here."

"They're waiting out there," Luke told her. "If we try to make a run for it, they'll throw enough lead to force us back in here. This is where they wanted us all along."

"But why?"

"Elston's being clever, or at least somebody is. It wouldn't surprise me if this was Verne Finn's idea. They want us dead, but they don't want it coming back on Elston. So they chase us in here and then start a fire to cut off our escape. We can't get out the other end of the canyon, so all we can do is sit here and wait."

"And burn to death?" Glory's voice held a note of panic. "I can't do that."

"We probably won't burn to death," Luke said. "The

smoke will get us before the flames do. But either way, when somebody finds us later there won't be any bullet holes in us. Nobody will be able to say that Elston had us killed. Some folks may suspect otherwise, but as far as anybody will be able to prove, our deaths will be accidental. It'll look like we took shelter from a prairie fire in the wrong place."

The smoke was starting to sting his nose and eyes now. Glory coughed again. Her eyes watered.

Luke pulled a bandanna from his pocket and handed it to her.

"Tie that over your nose and mouth," he told her. "It'll help a little. It'd be better if we had some water to soak it in, but we don't."

"Luke, what are we going to do?"

"We'll start by making sure there's no other way out of this canyon," he said. "Maybe they overlooked something."

Even as he spoke, he knew how high the odds were against that. Elston's hired killers would have checked it out themselves. This whole thing had been carefully planned to get rid of him and Glory in such a way that nothing could be proven against Harry Elston. Finn and the other gun-wolves would shoot them if they had to, but they really wanted the smoke and flames to take care of that chore for them.

Luke turned to the dun. He wasn't a cowboy by any stretch of the imagination, but he carried a rope on his saddle anyway. Sometimes he had to tie up prisoners, and he'd been known to tether them behind his horse and make them walk when he was bringing them in to the law. He untied the loop holding the coiled rope in place and then swung the rope hard against the dun's rump as he shouted at the horse. The dun bolted away, heading toward the canyon mouth.

The flames hadn't completely blocked the opening yet, so the dun had a chance of stampeding through there and reaching safety. It was a longshot, but not as long as the one facing Luke and Glory.

Glory tied the bandanna over the lower half of her face. Ignoring his own discomfort, Luke grabbed her hand and led her toward the back of the canyon.

There was enough grass in here for cattle to graze, enough to make a good-sized fire as it burned. It might not be enough for the flames to kill them, Luke thought, but the conflagration would generate enough heat and smoke to choke them to death.

The smoke was already thick enough to be a danger. The canyon's walls, which were about forty feet high, funneled it toward the two trapped people. As Luke and Glory broke into a run, they left the worst of the smoke behind them for the moment and gratefully dragged in lungfuls of cooler, clearer air.

The canyon was three hundred yards deep. The walls climbed higher the deeper they penetrated. Then they came to exactly what Luke had expected, a blank wall of stone. It wasn't completely smooth—the elements had pitted it here and there over the years, forming irregularities that might be useful as handholds and footholds— but it would take time to climb out of the canyon, time they didn't have, even if Glory was capable of it.

"Luke, we're trapped!" she wailed. She was on the

verge of losing her usual strength and composure, and Luke couldn't blame her for that. They had a terrible death staring them in the face.

Not only that, their deaths meant that Harry Elston would win. That just wasn't acceptable, Luke thought.

He peered up at the rock wall looming above them and realized there was one slim chance, but they had to act on it now. They didn't have any time to waste.

He had brought the rope with them on a hunch, and he was glad that he had. He started to shake out a loop.

"What are you doing?" Glory asked.

"If I can catch this rope on something up there, we might be able to climb out," he said.

"Luke, there's no time!"

"There's nowhere else to go," he said, and she couldn't argue with that grim truth.

He swung the rope, took aim with his eyes, and let fly.

CHAPTER 19

The first two tries didn't snag anything. The rope rose, hit, and then slithered back down in maddening fashion. Glory cried out in despair.

Luke didn't let it get to him. It was hard to stay cool-nerved when waves of heat washed over you and brought with them clouds of stinging, choking smoke, but right now he needed ice in his blood.

He coiled the rope, shook out a loop, and threw it again.

This time it caught on something. A rocky protuberance, a root, Luke didn't know. His eyes were watering and he couldn't see very well. But he knew the rope didn't fall back at his feet. He took a firm grip and leaned as much of his weight as he could on it, testing to see if it would hold.

When the rope didn't give, he told Glory, "Grab it and start climbing!"

"What's up there?" she asked between coughs.

"Don't know, but it's got to be better than down here!"

He held the rope while she took hold of it. She asked, "What are you going to do?"

"I'll be right behind you," he assured her.

Just because the rope had held his weight didn't mean it would support both of them. But again, there was no time for anything else. They had to risk it.

"I never climbed a rope before."

"Put your feet against the rock," he said. "That way not all your weight is on your hands. You're going to walk up the wall, understand?"

"Oh, Luke, this is crazy!"

"No, it's not. You can do it."

She gave him a wild-eyed look that said she couldn't, but she shifted her grip on the rope, lifted a foot, planted the sole of her boot against the rock wall, and pulled herself up. Once she started she had no choice but to raise the other foot and keep climbing.

She grunted with effort but managed to climb several feet. Luke didn't want to wait too long before he followed her. If the rope was going to give as soon as he put his weight on it, he wanted that to be when she wouldn't fall too far.

Although it didn't really matter, he thought. Killed by a fall, killed by the smoke, they were just as dead either way.

The rope held . . . at least for now.

"I'm with you," he called to Glory. "Just keep going, nice and easy. Don't stop. If you stop you won't be able to hold yourself in place."

"Luke, I'm scared!"

"Damn right! So am I. Just keep climbing."

He wasn't sure how high this rock wall was. They had to get completely out of the canyon. They couldn't just climb above the smoke because it was rising, too, getting thicker around them with every minute that passed.

But then he noticed something odd as he tried to keep his mind off the burning pain in his arm and shoulder and back muscles. Maybe it was wishful thinking, but it seemed to him that the smoke had started thinning instead of getting worse.

It was true, he realized after a moment. The canyon widened some at the top, and that gave the smoke more room to dissipate. That meant they were getting closer to safety.

"Keep going," he urged Glory. His voice was hoarse and painful now. "We're almost there."

"Luke!" That note of panic was back in her voice. "Luke, I'm at the end of the rope!"

"How far is it to the top? Can you see?"

"I . . . I don't know. Five or six feet?"

"Handholds. Can you find any handholds?"

"Let me—oh!"

Her startled, fearful cry made him think she had lost her grip and was about to come crashing down on top of him. He set himself, hoping against hope that he might be able to catch her.

She didn't hurtle down on him, though, and after a second he called, "Glory, are you all right?"

"I . . . I slipped." Her voice was more strained than

ever now. "My feet slipped. But I was able to . . . hang on to the rope. There's a little crack in the rock . . . I got my toe in it."

"Good! Find something like that to use as a hand-hold."

That five or six feet might prove to be insurmountable. Even though the smoke wasn't quite as bad, it still choked them and Luke felt dizzy from breathing so much of it. If he passed out, it was all over. That was probably true if Glory lost consciousness, too.

"I . . . I've got a hold," Glory panted. "Let me see if . . . I can pull myself up."

"One step at a time," Luke told her. "Steady, steady. Make sure you've got a good hold before you try going on."

He tilted his head back so he could watch her. His eyes streamed tears, so she was only a vague shape to him, a few feet above where he clung to the rope. She inched her way higher and higher. He moved up with careful steps until he was at the top of the rope, too.

"I'm almost there," Glory said. "Just a little bit . . . farther."

Luke heard her groan with effort as she pulled herself up again. Suddenly, he couldn't see her anymore, and he didn't know if the smoke was blinding him or if she had reached the rim.

A second later she called down excitedly, "Luke, I made it! There's a trail that runs on up into the hills. If you can make it, we can get out of here."

"I can make it," Luke told her. He stretched his arm above his head, found a rough spot where he could get a good enough grip to support himself, wedged a toe into a crack in the rock, and started climbing.

A couple of minutes later he rolled over the rim and lay on his back as his chest heaved and his muscles trembled. Glory stretched out on top of him, caught his face between her hands, and kissed him. Both of them tasted like smoke, but that didn't make the kiss any less urgent as his arms went around her and held on tightly.

The air was still thick with smoke around them. When Glory finally lifted her mouth from his, Luke rasped, "We need to get moving. Do you know these hills?"

"Some."

"As long as we're going away from the fire, that's all that really matters."

They climbed wearily to their feet and started up the trail. The terrain was rugged and they had to clamber over rocks and squeeze through gaps between boulders, but the important thing was that as they kept going higher, the smoke thinned more and more until the air around them was clear again. It tasted mighty sweet as Luke breathed deeply of it. He and Glory still coughed some, and it would likely take a few days for the damage to fade, but Luke knew they would be all right.

When they paused at a high point and looked back down, the smoke clogging the canyon looked deceptively like fog rising in a cool early morning. Luke hoped his horse had made it out of that hellish place. If the dun hadn't, that was one more score he would have to settle with Harry Elston, Verne Finn, and anybody else who was involved in this diabolical attempt on his and Glory's lives.

"How far is your ranch house from here?" he asked her.

"Five or six miles."

"We can walk it," Luke said with a nod. "We'll have sore feet when we get there, but they'll heal up."

She put her arms around his waist and leaned against him.

"You saved my life, Luke," she murmured. "I never would have gotten out of there without you. I'll do anything you want. I'll let you turn me in to the law so you can collect that bounty. I'll go back to Baltimore and face those charges."

"Let's don't worry about that now," he said gruffly.

"I told you the truth about what happened. We almost died back there. I don't want to leave this world with you thinking that I'm a murderer."

He cupped a hand under her chin and looked down into her eyes as he asked, "Why is it so important to you what I think?"

"Because you've risked your life for me and my ranch again and again. You're a good man, Luke Jensen. Your opinion matters to me."

"Well, for what it's worth . . . I believe you."

He actually did, he realized. Glory MacCrae might be a lot of things, but he didn't believe she was a killer.

"Come on," he said. "Let's get moving again."

As they started trudging through the hills, Glory said, "Lord, we smell awful. Will I ever get the smell of smoke out of my nose?"

"It'll take a while," Luke told her.

"What about my hair?"

He laughed.

"What?" she asked with a frown. "It's not funny. I really stink."

"There are worse things in the world than smelling bad."

"To you, maybe."

A short time later, another canyon opened in front of them. Glory paused when she saw it and exclaimed in delight. Luke thought it was a pretty place, too. A creek bubbled along the steep slope on one side of the canyon, cascaded over some rocks, and dropped down in a sparkling sheet of water into a small pool surrounded by junipers.

"It's beautiful," Glory said.

"It certainly is," Luke agreed.

"And more importantly, it's a chance to wash some of this awful smoke smell off of me."

Glory strode toward the pool, reaching for the buttons of her shirt as she did so.

Luke started to call out to her and tell her to stop, but then he reconsidered. They hadn't seen any sign of Elston's men since they escaped from the canyon that was now far below them. The killers probably thought their bodies were lying in there, choked to death by the smoke. It wouldn't hurt anything if they paused here for a short spell and cleaned up a little.

Besides, Glory already had her vest and shirt off and had sat down on a rock to remove her boots. With a smile, Luke went to help her.

* * *

Later, after they had scrubbed themselves and each other as clean as they could in the cold, crystal clear water of the pool, they washed their clothes and spread them out on rocks to dry in the afternoon sun. The warm rays dried Luke and Glory, too, as they stretched out on a grassy patch next to the pool.

With her eyes closed, Glory murmured, "After everything we've gone through, I think I could just lie here in the sun and sleep for a week."

"You'd be pretty blistered if you did that," Luke pointed out.

"I could move into the shade every now and then."

"Now you're talking."

They lay there in contented silence for a while longer. Luke felt drowsy, but a part of his brain remained alert all the time, along with his senses. Sooner or later Elston's gunmen would discover that they hadn't perished in the canyon after all, if they hadn't already, and when that happened the hired killers would come looking for them. Luke hadn't forgotten that he and Glory were afoot.

They didn't have his rifle or her carbine anymore, either. Glory's carbine was still in its saddle sheath on her horse, and Luke had left the Winchester below when he climbed out of the canyon.

But he had both Remingtons and a decent supply of ammunition in his pockets, plus his knife and the two derringers. Glory had a derringer, too, he reminded himself. They weren't exactly helpless.

She rolled onto her side and propped herself on an elbow. Luke saw her through his narrowly slitted eyes.

As she looked at him, she asked, "What are you going to do, Luke?"

"Hmmm? What am I going to do about what?"

"You know perfectly well what I mean. The reward that's posted for me. The murder charge."

He grinned and said, "Five thousand dollars is a lot of money."

She reached over and punched him on his bare shoulder.

"You said you believed me about what happened back in Baltimore!"

"Oh, I do, I do . . . but still, five thousand dollars is a lot of money."

Glory laughed, but then she grew more solemn as she said, "I'm serious, Luke. Should I let you turn me in? Should I go back and face whatever's going to happen?"

"Do you think you could prove your innocence at a trial?"

"With all the circumstantial evidence against me, and with the power and influence Hugh Jennings can wield now that his father is dead?" Glory shook her head. "I'd say the chances of that are pretty slim."

"That's what I was thinking, too. Taking your chances is one thing. Playing against a stacked deck—when the stakes are life and death—is something else entirely."

"I can't just keep hiding out for the rest of my life, though, looking over my shoulder all the time and never knowing when disaster is going to be right behind me."

"That's true," Luke said. "For one thing, to be blunt about it, you haven't done that good a job of hiding out.

I found you, and if I can, so can other bounty hunters. Maybe more importantly, those detectives your stepson hired can."

A little shudder went through her.

"I hate hearing Hugh referred to as my stepson," she said. "I can't bring myself to think of him that way. He was always leering at me and making comments when Alfred wasn't around. He wanted us to, well, you know. And all the time I was married to his father."

"He sounds like a real piece of work, all right. And we know he's dangerous, especially when he's crossed." Luke shook his head. "You seem to be in one of those situations where there just isn't a good answer."

"Maybe I should sell the ranch," she mused. "I could take the money and use it to start a new life somewhere. In Mexico, maybe."

"Elston might make you an offer," Luke suggested dryly.

"Elston! By God, I'll go back to Baltimore and put the noose around my own neck before I'll sell out to him. He made this personal when he attacked the MC. In fact, I've always thought he was responsible for Sam's death. Finn or one of those other gunmen bushwhacked him."

"I don't know," Luke said. "I'm thinking that maybe Whitey Singletary has been working for Elston all along without Sheriff Whittaker knowing about it. Singletary's a backshooter. I'm convinced of that."

Glory nodded and said, "I can see that. The man's a monster."

Luke would have agreed, but at that moment he

heard something that made him sit up straight and reach out a hand to the coiled gun belt and holstered Remingtons at his side.

"What is it?" Glory asked. She was smart enough to whisper the question.

"I heard what sounded like a horseshoe hitting rock somewhere not far from here," Luke replied, equally quietly. "I knew they might come to look for us, and I think they're here."

CHAPTER 20

He was acutely aware of his state of undress as he drew one of the revolvers and leaped to his feet. Up here in these hills, with ravines and rock spires and rugged bluffs all around, it was difficult to be sure where sounds were coming from, but Luke thought the warning noise he had heard had originated somewhere down the slope toward the canyon where he and Glory had almost died.

That would make sense, he thought. He told Glory, "Get dressed. We may have to move fast."

They should have been moving before now. He knew that, but he had allowed his own weariness, the idyllic surroundings, and Glory's loveliness to lull him into letting his guard down. It had been a stupid move, he told himself as he set the Remington on a rock in easy reach and started pulling on his clothes, which were still slightly damp.

When he was dressed, he buckled on the gun belt and jammed his hat on his head. He had been listening intently and hadn't heard anything else, but he knew he hadn't been mistaken about the earlier sound. Someone on horseback was definitely in the vicinity.

The rider might be one of Glory's ranch hands. This was MC range, after all. But they couldn't bet on that. The man might just as easily be one of Elston's hired gun-wolves.

Luke knew there were bighorn sheep in these hills. A game trail used by the animals twisted up the slope next to the waterfall. Luke pointed to it and whispered, "We'll go that way."

Glory looked at the trail with a dubious frown.

"Can we climb that?"

"We've climbed worse today," Luke said. "Come on."

With a sigh, Glory started up. Luke followed her. The going was easier than it looked like it would be, although they had to reach down and grasp handholds among the rocks so often that they might as well have been crawling.

They reached the top of the slope and saw that the trail followed the creek as it wound its way down from the upper elevations. The stream had to be spring-fed, Luke thought. These were just hills, not mountains, so there were no snowcapped peaks and no snowmelt to feed it.

The going was a little easier here. Every few minutes, Luke called a halt so he could listen again for sounds of pursuit, but other than that he kept them moving at a steady pace. He didn't hear anything, but he knew that didn't mean they were safe. The men who might be after them were experienced hunters . . . especially when it came to hunting other human beings.

During one of the pauses, Luke said, "It'll be dark in another few hours. If we can give them the slip until then, we ought to be safe. Can you find your way back to the ranch in the dark?"

"I don't know," Glory said. "Probably. Maybe. I've never had to navigate by the stars."

"I have," Luke told her. "We'll work together and figure it out."

She smiled at him and said, "I think I'm very lucky that you came hunting for me, Luke. Who would have thought that things would work out this way?"

"It's not what I had in mind when I rode into the valley," he admitted. "But life seldom works out the way we plan."

"I've been thinking. . . . What if the rider you heard was one of my men? Maybe instead of running away, we should be signaling for help."

He shook his head and said, "The same thought crossed my mind. But we can't risk it. There's an even better chance it's Elston's men looking for us."

"I suppose you're right," Glory said with a sigh. "I'm just getting tired. The past few days have been—"

As if to punctuate her unfinished sentence, a rifle cracked somewhere not far away, and the bullet struck the rock where she was sitting, missing her by mere inches before it ricocheted away with a sinister whine.

Glory let out a startled cry. Luke grabbed her and swung her behind a stone outcropping. It didn't provide much cover, but it was better than nothing.

"Stay there," he told her as he knelt behind a scrubby juniper. "Press your body back against the rock as much as you can."

"Luke . . ."

He heard the desperation in her voice as he twisted his head back and forth, searching for the source of the shot. He thought it had come from somewhere above them, which was a bad thing. That would mean some of the pursuers had gotten around them somehow and had been waiting for them. It was possible Elston's men knew these hills better than Glory did and certainly better than he did.

"We'll be all right," he told her. He made his tone as reassuring as possible.

"You don't know that," she said from a few feet away where she had her back pressed against the rock. "Luke, if we're about to die, I want to be certain that you believe me. About Alfred and Hugh, I mean. You weren't just saying that."

"I believe you. You're not a killer."

"That's right, I'm not. And if you come out of this alive and I don't make it—"

"No point in thinking about that," he broke in.

"Yes, there is," she insisted. "If I don't make it and you do, I want you to promise me that you'll let the authorities know who really killed my husband."

"They likely won't believe me," Luke said.

"I don't care. I just want the truth to be out there, whether anyone else believes it or not." Her voice softened as she added, "Right here and now, it's enough that you do."

Luke nodded. He said, "I give you my word. But it's not going to come to that—"

Another shot blasted, closer this time. A slug chewed splinters from the tree bark and sprayed them across his face. He felt the sting of one as it cut his cheek, but the brim of his hat protected his eyes.

He twisted to his left, saw two gunmen leaping from rock to rock as they charged down the slope at him. The Colts in their hands spouted flame. Luke had filled his hands with the Remingtons when he took cover. He lifted the left one and fired as another bullet whipped past his ear and struck the tree.

His shot caught one of the men in mid-air and slammed him backwards as blood flew from his chest. Luke fired again, this time at the second man. That bullet cut through the man's thigh and dropped him to the ground. He hit hard, striking his head against a rock as he landed, and didn't move again.

Those two attackers weren't alone. Luke threw himself down as another bullet sang over his head. This shot came from below. He rolled over, spotted at least three men among the rocks and trees along the creek bank. Lying on his belly, he lifted both Remingtons and began triggering them.

Firing up or down a slope was tricky, but the disadvantage applied equally. Luke missed with his first couple of shots, but then he tagged one of the gunwolves as the man tried to dart from one tree to another. The bullet shattered the man's shoulder and dropped him to the ground, howling in pain.

Luke's ears rang from the guns going off. A whiff of

powder smoke drifted to his nose. He shifted over so the juniper's trunk shielded more of his body as a bullet plowed into the ground a couple of feet to his right. The two remaining attackers had taken cover behind some rocks, and all he could do was wait for them to show themselves again.

"Luke, look out!" Glory cried.

His head jerked to the right. Another of Elston's men was creeping along the slope toward them from that direction. Now that he had been discovered, the man's beard-stubbled face contorted in a snarl and he opened fire with the revolver in his hand.

Luke felt the wind-rip of a slug past his ear as the Remington in his right hand roared and bucked against his palm. The gunman doubled over as the slug punched into his guts. He dropped his weapon and collapsed, and as he hit the ground he began to tumble down the slope. His fall came to an abrupt end as he landed in the creek with a splash. He lay facedown in the shallow, fast-moving stream, and the water around him began to take on a reddish tinge.

Rocks clattering down from above warned Luke that more trouble was on the way from that direction. He rolled over and saw a man about twenty feet up the slope from where he and Glory had stopped. The man had a Winchester in his hands. He jerked the rifle to his shoulder and opened up with it as soon as he realized he'd been spotted.

Luke had to roll swiftly to the side as the rifle rounds smacked into the ground where he had been lying. He fired both Remingtons and saw the rifleman rock back as the bullets hammered into his chest. He dropped the Winchester, pitched forward, and slid face-first down the slope about ten feet before coming to a stop.

The rifle landed a little closer than that to Luke. He holstered his guns and scrambled to his feet, then lunged for the Winchester. His movements exposed him to the fire of the men farther down the slope. Hot lead sizzled through the air around his head. He snatched the Winchester from the ground and worked the weapon's lever as he went down in a twisting fall.

In his eagerness to kill, one of the men downslope had stepped out from behind the boulder where he had taken cover earlier. Luke drilled him with the first shot from the repeater. Luke fired again and forced the other man to duck even lower behind the rock that shielded him.

"Hold it, mister! Drop the rifle or I'll kill the woman!"

Luke wasn't the sort of man to despair, but the harshly shouted command struck a pang in him. He turned and saw that one of Elston's hired killers had reached Glory. He stood in front of her now, pointing a gun at her as a triumphant leer stretched across his ugly face.

That leer vanished as two sharp cracks turned his face into a red ruin. He must not have realized that Glory was armed. She had gotten her derringer out while he focused his attention on Luke, and he probably never knew what hit him as she fired both barrels at him. The gun in his hand went off as his finger involuntarily jerked the trigger, but he had already fallen backwards and the bullet screamed harmlessly into the sky.

Luke couldn't see her very well from where he was,

but she peeked around the outcropping at him as she reloaded the derringer with cartridges from a pocket in her riding skirt. She looked pale and shaken, but she called to him, "I'm all right, Luke."

He waved a hand to let her know he heard her, then motioned for her to get back under cover as much as she could. Bodies littered the slope around them, but one of the gunmen remained alive and was still a threat. He might have more friends nearby, too.

"Hey, Jensen!" the man called. "You hear me?"

Luke scooted over behind the juniper again. The tree's trunk was scarred all over now from the bullets that had struck it.

"I hear you," Luke said, "but I doubt if I'm interested in anything you have to say!"

"Don't be so sure," the gunman replied from behind the boulder where he had taken cover. "You can still get out of this alive. All we really want is the woman."

"You think I believe you'll let me walk away after I've killed so many of you?"

The man made a disparaging sound and said, "Hell, we're all professionals here, ain't we? Anybody who sells his gun for a livin' knows he's gonna catch a bullet sooner or later. That's all part of it. The job is to bring the woman to Elston, and that's all I really care about."

"I thought Elston wanted us both dead."

"Orders have changed," the gunman said, and Luke could practically see the man shrugging. "Now he wants her alive. You, on the other hand, nobody gives a damn about one way or the other. Let me have Miz MacCrae, and you can ride away from here. Be stubborn about it and you'll die."

Luke frowned as he thought rapidly about what the man had just said. Now that he thought about it, it was true that all of the attackers' fire had been directed at him, not Glory, as if they were trying to keep her alive. And the man who had gotten the drop on her could have just blown her brains out then and there if her death was still the goal. Instead, that unlucky hombre had used her as a bargaining chip to try to get Luke to surrender.

Maybe there was some truth to what the gunman behind the boulder was saying.

"Better make up your mind, Jensen," the man called after a few moments of silence. "Our patience ain't gonna last forever."

"Seems to me like you just don't want to fight anymore," Luke goaded him. "You've seen how all your pards have wound up either dead or shot to pieces."

He heard the man spit.

"I told you, they ain't my pards. We just work together, that's all. Worked together, I should say. I won't deny, you are one big skookum he-wolf when it comes to killin'. But there's a dozen more men combin' these hills for you, and they're probably on their way here right now. They have to've heard all that shootin'."

That was right, too, Luke thought. The odds facing him and Glory weren't going to do anything except get worse as time passed. Maybe the moment had come to try some sort of subterfuge.

"What do you want me to do?" he asked.

"Throw all your guns out where I can see 'em! Then you step out with your hands in plain sight. Don't try for a hideout gun or anything like that. Like I told you, I don't have any real reason to keep you alive except to make things a mite simpler."

"Luke?" Glory whispered in a tone of disbelief. She had to be shocked that he was apparently considering betraying her.

Holding his hand where the man downslope couldn't see it, Luke motioned back and forth, hoping Glory would understand that he was telling her to disregard everything he had said and was about to say.

"All right," he called. "You've got a deal. Hold your fire now, while I throw these guns out."

He was going to match his speed with one of his derringers against the gunman. The man was going to be on the lookout for a trick, but Luke still thought he had a good chance. . . .

Glory's scream blasted that hope into smithereens. Luke heard something scrape in the rocks as he started to turn quickly toward her. A flashing shape above him told him that the gunman's "negotiation" had been nothing more than a distraction while some of the other killers crept down the slope behind him. A heavy weight crashed into Luke and drove him back against the juniper.

At close quarters like this, he couldn't bring the rifle into play. He tried to use the barrel as a club against the man who had tackled him, but the man ducked and blocked the blow with his shoulder.

At the same time, his fist dug painfully into Luke's

guts, striking in an uppercut that knocked the air from his lungs. Despite that, he might have had a chance if a second man hadn't tackled him around the knees and brought him down. The first man wrenched the Winchester from his hands and slapped the stock against the side of Luke's head. Rockets exploded redly behind his eyes.

He felt hands snatch his revolvers from their holsters. He might have reached for his knife or the derringers, but fists and booted feet thudded into him and filled him with pain. He heard Glory screaming and tried to summon up the strength to throw off his attackers so he could go to her aid, but there were too many of them. They were all over him, smashing and kicking until a tide of blackness rose up to wash him into oblivion.

Just before he passed out, he heard the rasping growl of Whitey Singletary say, "Don't kill the bastard yet." The crooked deputy chuckled. "We'll save that for later."

CHAPTER 21

Luke had never been caught in the middle of a buffalo stampede, but he figured that had to be about like what was going on inside his skull as he slowly regained consciousness.

He remembered being battered by Elston's men until he passed out. As far as he could tell, there were no gaps in his memory, despite the pain in his head.

But that was just the thing, he thought. If he couldn't remember something, he wouldn't know if any time was missing or not. Until he knew for sure, he just had to assume that was the case.

It probably didn't matter anyway. He was already a prisoner in the hands of his enemies. He was sure things could get worse—they always could—but they were pretty bad to start with.

Once he was awake again, he told himself that the first thing to do was take stock. He wanted to know if his arms and legs still worked.

Unfortunately, he couldn't tell because they seemed

to be bound so tightly he couldn't move. He took that to mean that he wasn't paralyzed, because if he had been, there wouldn't have been any point in tying him up.

The next step was figuring out where he was. Darkness surrounded him, but it wasn't complete. A faint luminescence filtered in from somewhere. He got the impression that walls loomed close around him. He managed to lift his legs slightly and then bring them down with a thud. The sound's echo seemed to confirm the impression that he was in a small area.

He was lying on hard-packed dirt. He could taste it in his mouth and feel it against his cheek.

At first, he felt as weak as if he'd been lying in bed sick for a month. But as he lay there in the darkness, the iron constitution that his rugged life had given him began to assert itself. Strength seeped slowly back into his muscles and bones. He was able to squirm sideways, and after only a couple of feet, he came up against a wall. His hands were tied behind his back, so he rolled over and felt the obstruction.

The wall was made of logs fitted closely together and then chinked. More than likely his captors had tossed him into a smokehouse, Luke thought. He sniffed the air, caught faint scents of both wood smoke and meat. The building wasn't being used for that purpose right now, but he was confident that it had been in the past.

Unfortunately, that bit of knowledge did absolutely nothing to help him in his current situation.

The effort involved in getting over here had worn him out, too. He lay there breathing hard and wondered if he ought to call out. He decided against it. No sense in letting his captors know that he was awake before he had to.

He might not have much choice in the matter, though, he realized a few minutes later as he heard a faint murmur that grew louder and turned into voices. Somebody was approaching the smokehouse.

A key rattled in a padlock, from the sound of it, and then hinges squealed and the heavy door scraped on the earth as it was pulled open. Lantern light spilled into the little log structure, and it was blinding to Luke's eyes after the time he had spent in the dark.

"Douse him," a harsh voice ordered. Luke didn't have a chance to tell the men he was already awake. One of them stepped into the smokehouse, bending to avoid hitting his head on the top of the low door, and threw a bucket of water in the prisoner's face.

Luke reacted instinctively, gasping and sputtering and shaking his head from side to side to get the water out of his eyes and nose. He heard a wheezing sound and realized after a second that it was somebody laughing.

"Drag him out of there," the same voice ordered, and this time Luke recognized it. It belonged to Whitey Singletary.

Hands took hold of Luke's feet. The back of his head bounced on the hard ground as a couple of the men with Singletary dragged him from the smokehouse. That set off new explosions of pain inside his skull. He did the best he could to ignore them.

"Howdy, Jensen," Singletary rasped. "Welcome back

to the world. Bet you figured you were dead, didn't you?"

Luke didn't bother answering the brutal deputy. His eyes were starting to adjust to the lantern light, so he looked around instead.

His surroundings were unfamiliar, but it didn't take much of an effort to figure out where he was. He saw barns, corrals, and in the distance a big, two-story ranch house with whitewashed walls and a porch that appeared to run around all four sides. Oil lamps hung on that porch at intervals and cast a lot of light, making it stand out in the night.

There was a small balcony outside one of the rooms on the second floor that looked like it had been added after the rest of the house was built. It didn't quite fit. Something about it seemed familiar to Luke, and after a moment he realized that it resembled a widow's walk of the sort that was found on seacoast houses in New England. No wonder it looked a little out of place here in West Texas.

He knew he was looking at the home of Harry Elston.

"Get him on his feet," Singletary ordered. "The boss is ready to see him."

The men who had dragged Luke out of the smokehouse took hold of his arms and hauled him upright. One of them hung on to him to keep him balanced while the other used a knife to cut the ropes holding his ankles together. Once his legs were loose, the man kicked them apart so that Luke was forced to stand on his feet. Until he felt the pain of blood flowing back into them, Luke hadn't realized how numb they had been. He tightened his jaw to keep from grimacing at the discomfort.

"He ought to be able to walk now, Whitey," one of the men said after a minute or so.

Singletary nodded and said, "If he falls down, we'll pick him up again. Let's go, Jensen."

The crooked deputy had stood slightly to one side with a shotgun in his hands while the other men dealt with Luke. He didn't appear to be injured, and Luke wondered for a second if he'd been wrong about Singletary being the one who had fired that shotgun blast through the window of his hotel room back in Painted Post.

But then as the group started toward the ranch house, Singletary grunted in apparent pain, and one of the hired killers with him asked, "Are you all right, Whitey?"

"Yeah, I'm fine," Singletary replied. "But I'll be even better once this son of a bitch pays for shootin' me last night. That bullet gouged a big hunk outta my side."

So he'd been right after all, Luke thought. Singletary had been the bushwhacker on the balcony. He must have bandages wrapped around his torso under his shirt.

He hoped they were taking him to wherever Glory was. He thought there was a good chance she was all right, since that gunman had said Elston's orders were for her to be taken alive, but Luke would feel better once he saw that with his own eyes.

Of course, they would still be in a mighty bad fix, but as long as they were alive they had hope.

Luke stumbled now and then, but whenever he did,

one of the men surrounding him grabbed his arm and steadied him. He wished he could make a grab for one of the guns they wore so carelessly. With his hands tied behind his back, though, that was hopeless. He'd just get himself killed sooner.

No, for now he had to just bide his time and wait for a better chance.

The walk to the house seemed longer than it really was, but finally they reached the three steps leading up to the porch. Luke stumbled again as he went up them, but this time it was on purpose. His legs felt stronger and steadier now, but there was no reason to let his captors know that. If they believed he was in worse shape than he really was, that might come in handy later.

As they started into the house, Singletary prodded Luke in the back with the twin barrels of the shotgun he carried and said, "You behave yourself in here, Jensen. Don't go sassin' your betters. The boss made it clear we can shoot you if we feel the need." Singletary chuckled again. "Or if the temptation is just too much to resist."

Luke didn't say anything. Trading insults with the deputy wouldn't accomplish a blasted thing. Singletary already wanted to kill him.

Not surprisingly, the big house's interior was opulently, even extravagantly furnished, with thick rugs on the floor, fancy wallpaper, paintings on the walls, crystal chandeliers, and expensive furniture. Luke's captors took him through a foyer with a gleaming hardwood floor, past a parlor, and down a corridor to a heavy oak door that one of the men rapped on and called, "We're here with Jensen, boss."

Harry Elston didn't call for them to come in. He jerked the door open himself and glared at Luke. He had taken off his coat, but otherwise he was dressed in a gray tweed suit and white shirt, with a string tie cinched tight around his thick neck.

"Bring him in here," Elston snapped as he stepped back from the door.

Singletary shoved Luke ahead. Luke stumbled on purpose again. That carried him into what appeared to be a combination office, study, and library. It was a big room with a lot of bookcases filled with leather-bound volumes. A large desk dominated one side of the room with windows behind it. Curtains closed off those windows at the moment. On the opposite wall was a fireplace with the mounted heads of wild game placed above it. Several paintings of sailing ships had been hung on the other walls. A pair of large, overstuffed armchairs sat near the fireplace.

Luke took all that in with a glance. He had hoped to see Glory in here, but there was no sign of her, only Elston. The rancher said, "Whitey, you stay. The rest of you men can go."

"Are you sure that's a good idea, boss?" Singletary asked with a frown.

"Jensen's arms are tied behind his back," Elston said coldly, "and a few hours ago he got a pretty severe beating. I think the two of us can handle him if he tries to give us any trouble."

Singletary jerked his head at the other gunnies and said, "You heard the man."

They filed out, leaving the three of them in the room.

Elston stalked over to the desk and took a cigar from a fancy wooden box with a gilt-edged lid. With his short, burly frame, he reminded Luke of a brown bear. He clipped the end off the cigar, put it in his mouth, and lit it with a lucifer. As gray smoke wreathed around his head, he looked at Luke and said, "You're a damned fool, you know that, Jensen?"

"So I've been told many times in the past," Luke said, "but I'm curious why you think so."

"If you had taken a look around Sabado Valley and gotten the lay of the land, you would have seen that you and I ought to be on the same side."

Luke shook his head and said, "I don't see how you figure that."

Elston puffed on the cigar for a moment, then said, "It's simple, really. Glory MacCrae stands in the way of what we both want. I want the MC, and you want a payoff. Blood money. You should have been working for me, helping me get rid of that bitch. It would have been a good arrangement."

"Except for the fact that I don't think I could have stood the smell," Luke said. He turned his head and looked meaningfully at Singletary, who glared and tightened his hands on the shotgun he still held.

Elston waved the cigar at Singletary to tell him to take it easy. He said to Luke, "Do you know what I did before I came to Texas and took up ranching?"

"I don't have any idea."

"I was a sea captain. Sailed the world over. Ran guns to ports in South America. Fought off Malay pirates to protect my cargoes in the South China Sea. Ruled over the hardest crews with a belaying pin and a strong right hand." Elston held up a clenched fist. "You don't think I'd let a *woman* stand in my way, do you?"

"I doubt if you ever met another woman quite like Glory MacCrae."

Elston shrugged and said, "You may be right about that. I'll give her credit, she's stubborn. Not to mention damned good-looking. But that doesn't matter, either. Anyone who defies me gets crushed, no matter what it takes."

"What gives you the right?" Luke asked as anger welled up inside him. "We have laws in this country, Elston, and it's not the law of the sea. You can't make anybody who crosses you walk the plank!"

Elston set his cigar in an ashtray on the desk and swung back toward Luke. His jaw jutted out belligerently as he said, "There's only one law, and that's the law of power! If you've got it, you're above all the other laws. They're for lesser people, fools like you who are willing to settle for crumbs when there's a banquet just waiting for you, if you're man enough to seize it!"

"You're out of your mind," Luke rasped. His throat still hurt from all the smoke he had breathed earlier.

Elston shook his head and said, "No, I'm the sanest man in the whole state of Texas. And I'm tired of arguing with you."

He turned to the wall and tugged on a tasseled cord that hung there. Luke supposed it rang a bell somewhere else in the house. He didn't know what the signal meant, but he knew he would find out if he waited.

He didn't have to wait long. Less than a minute later,

the heavy door opened again. Glory came into the room. Verne Finn was with her. The gunman's hand rested on her shoulder.

Glory's hands were tied, too, but they were in front rather than behind her and almost loose enough to free herself. When she saw Luke she cried out his name and ran toward him. Finn didn't try to stop her, and neither did Singletary.

She lifted her hands and caught hold of his shirt front. Pressing her head against his chest, she said in a voice choked with emotion, "I was afraid they had killed you."

"Not yet," Elston said. "But it can be arranged if you're determined to be stubborn, Mrs. MacCrae."

Glory's thick, dark hair was right under Luke's face. He bent forward and kissed the top of her head. Her hair still smelled faintly of smoke. It took a long time to get rid of that smell.

Time they might not have.

But for now he asked quietly, "Are you all right, Glory?"

"They . . . they haven't hurt me," she said.

"And we won't if you'll just cooperate," Elston said. "I've already showed you the sales agreement and deed to the MC I had drawn up. All you have to do is sign it, and this whole unpleasant affair can be over."

Luke didn't believe that for a second. Despite what Elston said about being above the law, he had broken too many of them just to let his prisoners go.

Glory signing that deed and giving her ranch to

Elston would be the same thing as signing their death warrant.

Luke saw that he didn't have to worry about her giving in to threats. She glared defiantly at Elston and shook her head.

"You'll never get your hands on Sam MacCrae's ranch, legally or illegally," she declared. "Even if I'm dead, my men will fight you. Gabe Pendleton will never let that happen."

Finn laughed and said, "I reckon you'll find that a bunch of cowboys are no match for me and my men, missy."

"Enough," Elston snapped. "I'm not used to begging. If we can't do this the easy way—" He stopped short and nodded to Finn. "Bring in our other guest."

With a lazy grin, Finn turned and left the room. *Other guest?* Luke looked at Glory, but she just gave a little shake of her head to indicate that she was as confused as he was.

Finn wasn't gone long. He came back into the room, and following him was a tall, handsome, well-dressed man with curly blond hair. He smiled at Glory, who stared at him with wide, horrified eyes.

"Hello, Gloria," the man drawled, then added mockingly, "Or should I call you Mother?"

Luke knew he was looking at Hugh Jennings.

CHAPTER 22

Glory cried, "No!" She slumped against Luke, evidently almost overcome with fear. He thought for a second that she was shamming, but then he felt her shaking and knew her terror was real.

How evil must Hugh Jennings be to provoke such a reaction in a woman as strong and defiant as Glory?

"It's so wonderful to see you again, my dear," Jennings went on smoothly, still smiling. "I was afraid we might never be reunited."

"How . . ." Glory gasped. "How did you—?"

"Find you? It really wasn't that difficult. I can afford to hire the best detectives in the country. I knew it was only a matter of time until they located you."

This was further proof that what Luke and Glory had discussed earlier was true. If she had stuck to her original plan and remained anonymous in some small settlement, instead of marrying the owner of the biggest ranch in this part of Texas and landing in the middle of a range war, she might have been a lot harder to find.

But it was too late to worry about that now. Hugh Jennings was here. Luke speculated that Jennings had arrived in Painted Post after his detectives informed him where Glory was, discovered that Elston had been trying to get rid of her, and come out here to forge an alliance with the rancher. That would explain why Elston's orders had changed abruptly from killing Glory to capturing her.

Glory seemed to be recovering some from the shock of seeing her murderous stepson. Her voice was stronger and touched with anger as she said, "What do you want, Hugh?"

"What I've always wanted, of course," Jennings said. "Justice for my father."

"If you want justice, you'll put a gun to your head and blow your brains out."

That prompted an arrogant laugh from Jennings.

"Not that old story again," he said. "The authorities know perfectly well that you killed my father. How can you expect them to believe otherwise when you were caught with his blood all over your hands?"

"He was only bleeding because you killed him."

"Then why did you point a gun at me and my friends and flee with all that money?"

"I never took any of Alfred's money! That was you. I wasn't going to be railroaded for something I hadn't done!"

Jennings smirked and said, "Those are bold claims from a woman with a history of being a scarlet adventuress and a criminal."

With a frown, Harry Elston said, "You two can snipe

at each other later. Right now I want this business of the MacCrae ranch settled. Mrs. MacCrae, if you sign your ranch over to me like I asked, I'll see to it that you don't have to worry about Jennings taking you back to face the law in Baltimore."

That blunt statement jolted Jennings right out of his smug, self-satisfied attitude. He looked surprised and said to Elston, "Wait just a minute! That wasn't the agreement we made. You said you'd turn Gloria over to me!"

Singletary shifted his shotgun so that barrels pointed more toward Jennings and growled, "The agreement is whatever the boss says it is, mister."

"That's right," Verne Finn added with an edge of steel in his voice.

Elston gave Jennings a hard look as he said, "I don't really care about your problems, Jennings. When you showed up this afternoon and explained who Mrs. MacCrae really is and what she's wanted for back in Baltimore, I figured I could use you to help me get what I want. All that matters to me is her ranch." Elston shrugged. "If I can persuade her to cooperate, that's the easiest way for me to get what I want. If she won't . . . well, then I guess you can take her back and let the law hang her. I'll buy the MC at auction when the taxes aren't paid. But it's more trouble and more expensive that way, so I hope I can convince her to be reasonable."

Glory asked, "Do you really think you can force me into selling the ranch to you, Elston, after you had Sam murdered? Sam MacCrae was worth a hundred of you!"

"I had nothing to do with your husband's death, Mrs. MacCrae."

"Maybe not personally, but you gave the order for him to be bushwhacked!"

Elston shook his head and said, "No, I didn't. That's the truth."

Oddly enough, Luke thought he believed the former sea captain. After everything else that had happened the past few days, Elston lying about Sam MacCrae's death didn't really serve any purpose now.

"You had your men rustle my cattle," Glory accused. "You sent them to try to burn down my house. And you've tried to kill Luke and me several times now."

"You can't prove any of that," Elston said blandly. "But if you're anxious to go into a court of law—with me knowing what I know about you now—I suppose we can do it that way."

Glory glared furiously at the rancher, but Luke knew Elston had her between the proverbial rock and hard place. He could hold the threat of Hugh Jennings and that murder charge over her head until she finally gave in and did whatever he wanted her to do.

After a long moment, Glory asked, "What happens if I sign that contract and deed?"

"Then I have what I want and the two of us have no further business. You'll be free to go."

"How much are you prepared to pay me?"

Elston puffed on his cigar, then said, "One thousand dollars."

Glory's eyes widened again. She said, "The MC is worth fifty times that!"

"One thousand dollars will buy you a train ticket to anywhere you want to go," Elston told her, "with enough left over for you to start a new life under a new name. If you stop and think about it, it's not a bad deal for you."

Jennings was red-faced with anger at what he had to consider a betrayal by Elston. He said, "You can't do that. This woman is wanted for murder!"

"Not in Texas," Elston said.

"I'll go to the law! I'll go to the Rangers!"

"That wouldn't be a smart thing to do."

Singletary pointed the shotgun even more toward Jennings and mocked, "Not a smart thing at all."

"You can't threaten me," Jennings blustered. "I know my rights."

"The only rights you have on this ranch are the ones I say you do," Elston pointed out. "Verne, why don't you take your guest back to his room? Make sure he's comfortable . . . and stays there."

"Sure, boss," Finn said with a faint smile. He put his left hand on Jennings's shoulder and his right on the butt of his gun. "Come along, mister."

"You tricked me," Jennings said to Elston. "You just wanted to use me as leverage to blackmail Gloria. You won't get away with this!"

Finn's hand tightened on Jennings's shoulder and swung him around. The gunman's eyes were as cold and hard as chunks of agate. Jennings must have read the looming danger in them. He swallowed hard and allowed Finn to steer him toward the doorway.

"This isn't over yet," Jennings said over his shoulder.

Elston didn't look worried about the veiled threat.

When Finn and Jennings were gone, Elston faced Glory again and said, "What about it, Mrs. MacCrae? You've heard my proposal. What do you say?"

"If I'll sign your damned document, you'll let me go?" Glory asked. "You swear?"

"Of course. It would be in my best interest for you not to be around here anymore."

"What about Luke?"

Elston shrugged and said, "Jensen doesn't mean anything to me. True, he's been damned annoying since he showed up—looking for you and hoping to collect that bounty, I suppose—and he's cost me a number of good men, but such expenses are necessary sometimes." A cunning look appeared on Elston's bulldog-like face. "Come to think of it, if you decide to go along with me, you might prefer not to have to worry about Jensen tracking you down again. That can be arranged."

"No!" Glory said quickly. "That's not what I meant. I don't want him to be harmed."

"Does that mean you agree to my proposal?"

"I . . . I . . ."

Luke hoped she wasn't foolish enough to go along with what Elston wanted. He didn't trust the rancher for a second. He still believed that he and Glory would be killed as soon as Elston got Glory's name on that paper. He stared at Glory and tried to communicate that to her without saying anything.

"I have to think about it," she said. "You're asking me to make a big decision here, one that affects the rest of my life. Give me tonight, anyway."

A look of annoyed impatience flashed across Elston's face. But he puffed angrily on the fat cigar for a second and then jerked his head in a brusque nod. He took the cigar out of his mouth and said, "You have until tomorrow morning to make up your mind. Cooperate with me or you'll go back to Baltimore to hang." He clamped his teeth on the stogie again and added, "And I'll collect the five grand reward on your head, too."

Finn came back into the book-lined room. He reported, "Jennings is locked in his room. He won't cause any trouble tonight."

"Good," Elston said. "Now you can take Mrs. MacCrae back to her room."

Singletary motioned toward Luke with the shotgun and asked, "What about Jensen?"

"Back in the smokehouse for now, I suppose."

"No," Glory said. "Luke stays in the house with me, or I'll tell you right now that there's no deal."

Elston grunted and said, "Really? You've gotten softhearted over a man who came here to take you in and collect blood money on you?"

"Luke knows I didn't kill Alfred Jennings."

"I don't care about that. And like I said, I don't care about Jensen, either. If you want him, you can have him."

Frowning, Singletary said, "I don't know if that's a good idea—"

Elston stepped toward the crooked deputy, bristling with anger.

"You don't give the orders around here, now do you?" he demanded.

"No, I reckon not," Singletary replied in a sullen voice. "I just don't trust Jensen."

"If he's locked in a room with Mrs. MacCrae, there won't be a damned thing he can do to cause us a problem. Just make sure that he *is* locked up, and that there's a guard outside their room at all times."

Verne Finn nodded and said, "We can do that, boss."

Singletary still had a surly look on his face, but he didn't say anything else except to order Luke to turn around. Then he planted the shotgun's twin barrels in Luke's back and forced him to follow Glory and Finn out of the room.

Luke couldn't try anything. At this range, the shotgun would blow him in half if Singletary squeezed the triggers. He knew that was exactly what the crooked deputy wanted, too.

Several more of Elston's gunmen waited in the ranch house's main room. They fell in with the others as the group went up to the second floor, then trailed behind while Finn and Singletary escorted Luke and Glory into a bedroom.

Finn went to the window and thrust the curtain back, then turned toward them and said, "There'll be two armed men outside the door all night. Not only that, but you can see that this window commands a view of the bunkhouse. A man with a rifle will be sitting outside watching the window, and he'll have orders to shoot you if you so much as poke your head out, Jensen. So don't start getting any notions about escaping. You can't do it."

"I'm just glad I'm not going back in that smoke-house," Luke said.

Finn chuckled.

"There you go," he said. "Look for the silver lining."

Finn left the room. As Singletary backed out, still holding the shotgun on them, he said, "If it was up to me, Jensen, you'd be dead already. And I'd have taken my own sweet time killin' you, too. Would've been mighty enjoyable."

"The only way you'd ever be able to kill me, Whitey, is if I was helpless," Luke said. "Or if you shot me in the back, the way you tried to after the inquest. The way you bushwhacked Sam MacCrae to curry favor with Elston."

Singletary grunted. The surprise in his piggish eyes told Luke that his guess was right. It was really the only explanation that made sense, considering Elston's insistence that he hadn't ordered MacCrae's murder. Singletary had come up with the idea on his own.

Apparently, Glory hadn't thought it all through and reached that conclusion yet. Her face flushed, and she stepped toward Singletary, saying in a coldly furious voice, "You—"

Singletary swung the shotgun toward her and snapped, "Stay back, lady. The boss wants you alive, but if I tell him you attacked me—"

"He'll probably kill you himself," Luke broke in. "At the very least he'll have Finn do it. You think you're a match for him, Whitey?"

"You just shut up! You run your mouth and get me all loco."

"I imagine that's not very hard to do."

A step sounded in the hallway. Finn said, "Singletary, are you coming or not?"

"Yeah, yeah," the deputy muttered. He glared at Luke and added, "I'll settle up with you. Just you wait."

He stepped out into the corridor and yanked the door shut behind him. The sound of it closing wasn't quite as final as that of a jail cell's door, but almost.

Glory turned to Luke and said, "Do you really think he did that? Bushwhacked Sam? Or were you just trying to get under his skin?"

"I'm as certain as I can be without having seen him do it," Luke told her.

"Did Sheriff Whittaker know?"

"My guess is that he didn't. Whittaker's quick to give Elston the benefit of the doubt, but I don't believe he's completely crooked. Singletary, on the other hand . . . He probably thought that if he killed your husband, that would put Elston in his debt. I think Whitey's got his eye on being sheriff, once Elston's running everything in the county."

"What a horrible man," Glory murmured.

"You won't get any argument from me." Luke turned so that his back was toward her. "Now, if you think maybe you can untie these ropes . . ."

"Of course." She worked the ropes off her hands and hurried to get to work on the knots. "I should have done this as soon as they left us alone. I was just so shaken by what you said about Deputy Singletary."

"At least now you know what happened to Sam, and why," Luke said, making his words as gentle as possible. "That's probably scant comfort, but better than nothing, maybe."

"Yes, it is." Glory muttered something under her breath, "These knots are stubborn."

"Take your time. We've got all night."

Glory kept working at the bonds, and eventually Luke felt them loosen slightly. Glory's efforts went faster then, and a few moments later the ropes fell away from his wrists. He groaned a little from the stiffness and soreness in his shoulder muscles as he brought his arms around in front of him again. His hands were so numb they were like lumps of wood. He couldn't even get them to work well enough that they could rub each other.

Glory took on that task as well, catching hold of his right hand with both of hers. She began massaging it. Pins and needles quickly turned into a rush of heat that felt like Luke had plunged his hand into a pot of boiling water. His lips drew back from his teeth as the blood flowed and feeling came into his hand, bringing with it pain.

"I'm sorry," Glory said.

"Don't be," he told her. "I'd rather it hurt now and be able to use it later."

Once enough feeling had returned that he was able to flex his fingers, she moved over to the other hand

and worked on it. Soon Luke was able to use both hands again.

He used them to draw Glory into his arms. She started trembling, and he held her until the shaking finally stopped.

She lifted her head from his chest and looked up at him, saying, "Elston's going to kill us, isn't he? No matter what he promised, no matter whether I do what he wants or not, he's still going to kill us?"

"That's what he's planning," Luke said, "but before this is all over, I think we're going to have something to say about that."

CHAPTER 23

Luke blew out the oil lamp that burned on the table and went over to the window. He edged the curtain back to look out. As Finn had told them, there was a good view of the bunkhouse from here. One of the hired killers sat just outside the building's door in a ladderback chair. He had a rifle across his knees, and he was watching the window. Luke didn't doubt that he was a crack shot with that Winchester, too.

"What do you see?" Glory asked from behind him.

"Finn wasn't lying. He's got a marksman keeping an eye on the window. Climbing out wouldn't be a problem, especially with that porch roof running all the way around the house. But that rifleman would drill me as soon as I threw a leg over the sill."

"Then we have to think of some other way to get out of here. The guards in the hall . . ."

"They probably have orders to shoot to kill, too." Luke sighed wearily and massaged his temples for a few seconds. His head still hurt from being knocked out earlier. He wasn't as young as he used to be, and the past couple of days had taken a toll.

He went on: "Elston is trying to set things up so that it would be impossible for the law to ever prove anything against him, even if the Rangers came in and investigated him. Your signature on that bill of sale takes care of that. If you just disappear, either by him giving you to Hugh Jennings or by . . ."

"Winding up in a shallow grave somewhere out on the prairie," Glory finished. "You can say it, Luke. I know how much danger we're in."

"If you just disappear, Gabe Pendleton will make a stink about it," Luke said. "Judge Marbright will insist that the sheriff look into it. Like I said, he might even call in the Rangers. Elston can ride it out as long as there's no proof that you're dead, but that's a complication he evidently doesn't want. So forcing you to sign is his best bet. But he can kill you and still get the ranch in the long run, so we can't underestimate what he'll do."

"Don't worry, I wouldn't put anything beyond that snake."

Luke was still looking out the window but not really paying much attention to what was going on out there. But then movement caught his eye. The rifleman outside the bunkhouse door had stood up. The man half-turned and appeared to call through the open door. A second later, two more of Elston's hired killers appeared. One of them ran toward the house.

"Something's going on," Luke said quietly.

Glory came up close behind him and asked, "What is it?"

"I don't know yet. Something seems to have spooked Elston's crew."

A moment later, a rider came into view, approaching the house. The guard must have heard the hoofbeats. As the man on horseback came closer, deeper into the light from the house, Luke recognized him.

Sheriff Jared Whittaker.

Maybe he'd been wrong about Whittaker, Luke thought. Maybe the sheriff was just as crooked as the deputy and had come to Elston's ranch to check in and find out if his boss had any new orders for him.

A door closed somewhere below. Harry Elston strode out into Luke's line of sight, accompanied by Verne Finn. Luke reached down to the sill and eased the windowpane up so he could hear what was being said below.

"Sheriff," Elston greeted Whittaker. "What brings you out here so late?"

"I'm looking for somebody," Whittaker replied.

"That deputy of yours? I haven't seen him."

Whittaker frowned. He said, "No, actually I'm looking for Mrs. MacCrae and that fella Jensen. They left Painted Post earlier today bound for the MacCrae ranch, but they never showed up."

Elston shook his head and said, "That's no concern of mine. I'm not the woman's keeper."

Whittaker thumbed his hat back. Elston hadn't

invited him to step down from his horse, and Whittaker didn't make any move to do so.

"Here's the thing," the sheriff said. "Some of Mrs. MacCrae's hands heard a lot of shooting this afternoon. They went to have a look and didn't find anything except a burned-out stretch of prairie. It was pretty obvious *something* had happened."

"Still none of my concern," Elston insisted.

"Then a while later Mrs. MacCrae's horse showed up at the ranch, and so did Jensen's dun. The dun had some burns, like it had galloped through flames, so it's likely the two of them were there."

Glory was close by Luke's shoulder, listening to the conversation, too. She clutched Luke's arm and whispered, "Thank God the horses got out all right."

Luke was relieved to hear that, too.

Whittaker went on: "Rusty Gimple is acting as Mrs. MacCrae's foreman while Gabe Pendleton is laid up. He rode to town and told me about Mrs. MacCrae and Jensen being missing, the shooting, the fire, and the horses showing up. He wanted me to look into it. He said he thought you might have something to do with everything."

"Why didn't you just tell him to go away?" Elston asked impatiently.

"Because I'm the law in these parts, Mr. Elston," Whittaker said. "And I'm getting a little tired of some people acting like that really doesn't matter."

"Good Lord," Glory breathed. "Is the sheriff finally trying to do his job?"

"It looks like it," Luke said.

Unfortunately, Whittaker's decision to be an honest lawman might have come too late.

"I have no idea about any of this," Elston said. "You've had a long ride out here in the dark for nothing, Sheriff. I haven't laid eyes on Mrs. MacCrae or Jensen since I left Painted Post."

"Are you sure about that?"

"I'm not in the habit of having my word disputed," Elston said angrily.

"Then you won't mind if I take a look around."

Elston hesitated for a second, then shrugged. He waved a hand and said, "Be my guest."

As Whittaker swung down from the saddle and the men started toward the house, Glory whispered, "We could call out to him, let him know we're here."

"If we do that, Finn will gun down Whittaker," Luke warned.

Whittaker stopped abruptly, which forced Elston and Finn to do likewise. The sheriff turned to them.

"Something you said struck me as wrong, Mr. Elston, and I just figured out what it is."

"No," Luke whispered. "Don't give it away, Whittaker."

The lawman didn't hear him, of course. Whittaker said, "When I rode in you thought I was looking for Whitey. If you've been gone from town since yesterday, how'd you know *he* was missing?"

The question seemed to take Elston by surprise. He didn't answer.

"Unless you'd seen him yourself," Whittaker went on. "Unless he's been here . . . or is here now. Unless he really works for you."

Elston sighed and shook his head.

"It's a shame you figured that out, Sheriff," he said. "Luckily, there'll be somebody else to step in and take over for you."

"What're you—"

"Whitey!" Elston called.

Singletary stepped out of the bunkhouse and rasped, "You always were a damn fool, Whittaker."

The sheriff spun toward Singletary and clawed at the gun on his hip. In a blur of swift motion, Verne Finn got behind him. The gun in Finn's hand came up and chopped down in a vicious blow that slammed into the back of Whittaker's head and drove the lawman to his knees. Finn kicked him between the shoulder blades and knocked him to the ground on his face.

Singletary came over and pointed the gun in his hand at the unconscious Whittaker.

"Let me kill him, boss," he growled to Elston.

"Not yet," Elston said. "We might be able to make some use of him. That bill of sale would carry even more weight if we force him to sign it as a witness. Put him in the smokehouse where we had Jensen earlier."

"We'll have to get rid of him sooner or later if I'm gonna be sheriff," Singletary argued.

"You'll never be sheriff if you don't do what I tell you," Elston responded sharply.

Singletary didn't look happy about it, but he bent

and took hold of Whittaker's collar. He started dragging the senseless man toward the smokehouse. Everybody in the yard between the main house and the bunkhouse had been watching the confrontation.

Including the rifleman assigned to keep an eye on the window of the room where Luke and Glory were being held.

That was why Luke was no longer there. He had taken advantage of the distraction a moment earlier and slipped out the window after telling Glory to stay put, and now he was stretched out on top of the roof. With his black clothes and dark hair, he was almost invisible in the shadows, free for the moment.

Free . . . but surrounded by a score of enemies who would like nothing better than to see him dead.

There was no point in thinking about that. Quickly, so that he could get out of sight before the rifleman spotted him, he wriggled backwards, deeper into the darkness, and then climbed up and over the roof's peak.

When he was safely out of sight, he paused to consider his next move. A memory of that little balcony shaped like a widow's walk came into his mind. With Elston's background as a sea captain, it was likely he was the one who'd had the balcony built onto the house. That meant it was probably outside the room where he slept. Luke thought the chances were good enough that it was worth checking out, anyway.

He made his way along the roofline, checking over the peak now and then, until he was even with the place where the balcony was. Even though the delay chafed at him, he knew it would be better to wait until the house had settled down and everyone had gone to sleep before he acted on the plan that was forming in his mind.

He hoped Glory wasn't going crazy with worry. There hadn't been any shouts or gunfire, so she probably figured that he was still all right and on the loose.

The lamps on the porch were still burning. That was actually a good thing for him, Luke thought. The light down below made the roof above the porch seem even darker. When an hour or so had passed and he hadn't heard any sounds from below for a while, he eased over the roof peak and started down toward the widow's walk.

He moved slowly, an inch or so at a time. The room where Glory was being held captive was at the other end of the house, so that helped his chances of reaching the balcony without being seen. The guard, who had resumed his chair by the bunkhouse, would have his attention focused on that other window. As long as his movements didn't catch the rifleman's eye, Luke knew he was safe from discovery.

Eventually, he reached the little cupola above the widow's walk. He leaned over the edge and studied what lay below it. The window that had been there originally had been replaced by a door. If it was locked, that might be trouble . . . but what would be the point of locking a door like that? Here in his own stronghold, Elston would be so confident of his safety that such a thing might never occur to him.

Luke twisted around, let his legs hang off the cupola's roof, then lowered himself and dangled from his hands for a second before he let go and dropped lightly to the balcony. His landing made enough noise that someone inside the room who was awake might have heard it, but there was a good chance it wouldn't disturb the slumber of anyone who was asleep.

As Luke leaned closer to the door, he knew the room's inhabitant *was* asleep. He heard loud snoring on the other side of the panel. He reached down to the doorknob, grasped it, twisted it.

It turned. With a faint click, the door came open.

The snoring continued as Luke stepped into the darkened room. He couldn't be sure the man sleeping here was Harry Elston, but he still thought that was a good bet. As silent as an Apache, Luke let the snores guide him toward the bed.

His leg bumped against the mattress, and the snoring abruptly stopped. Luke didn't wait any longer to make his move. He struck fast and hard, slamming a fist into the spot where he judged the sleeper's head to be.

That was only partially successful. His fist glanced off the man's head. Luke lunged on top of him and shot out his left hand. It found and closed around the man's throat, stifling a shout as it tried to escape.

The man wasn't going to give up easily. He bucked up from the bed in an attempt to throw off Luke's weight. A wildly thrown fist painfully scraped Luke's left ear. He tightened his grip on the man's throat and tried to choke him into submission.

That wasn't going to work. The man was strong and evidently had experience at brawling, another indication that he was Harry Elston. He jerked a leg up, hooked a calf across Luke's throat, and levered him to the side.

Luke hung on to Elston's neck, though, and dragged the rancher with him. Both men rolled off the bed and thudded to the floor beside it. Luke landed on the bottom. Anticipating Elston's next move, he twisted to the side so that the knee Elston tried to drive into his groin struck him on the thigh instead.

Even so, the impact was painful, and Luke's leg refused to work for a moment. He clung to Elston's throat with one hand, which wasn't easy because it was so thick and Elston's head was set low on his shoulders. With his other first, Luke hammered at his opponent's face.

Elston's hands were free, so he was able to strike at Luke with both of them. Sensing the blows more than seeing them, Luke jerked his head out of the way, but there were too many to keep dodging them. One of Elston's fists crashed into his jaw and made red rockets explode across his vision.

Luke knew that his life depended on winning this fight. Not just his life, either, but Glory's as well. He heaved himself up, rolled, and threw Elston to the side. Luke risked letting go for a second as he scrambled to get behind the rancher. His left arm looped around Elston's throat and he clamped down with it, grabbing that wrist with his right hand and adding even more strength to the grip.

Elston bucked and rolled, jabbed at Luke with his elbows, clawed at the forearm locked across his throat like an iron bar. But as the seconds ticked past, his struggles grew weaker. Luke kept the pressure on him anyway, just in case Elston was trying to trick him.

Finally, Elston stopped fighting. All his muscles went limp. Luke hung on, easing up just a bit so Elston could breathe but ready to apply the crushing pressure again if he needed to.

After several more minutes, Luke knew Elston was unconscious. He let go, pushed himself up on his knees.

Either nobody had heard the racket as they fell out of the bed or else hadn't thought anything about it. Working by feel, Luke reached out, found the sheet, and tore several strips off of it. He used them to bind Elston's hands and feet, then crammed a wad of fabric into Elston's mouth as a gag and tied it in place. Only when that was finished did he sit back and lean against the wall to catch his breath.

He and Glory were far from being out of trouble, Luke thought, but at least they had a bargaining chip of their own now in Elston. Assuming, of course, that's who the prisoner was, Luke realized suddenly. He figured he had better check to be certain.

He stood up, felt around, found a bedside table with a lamp and some matches on it. He made sure the door to the widow's walk was closed, then lit the lamp. Its yellow glow washed over the bound figure on the floor, revealing Harry Elston in a pair of long underwear.

Elston was starting to stir as consciousness returned to him. Luke rolled the rancher onto his back. In the light from the lamp, Elston saw and recognized him. Hate flared up and burned brightly in the man's eyes.

He made angry, muffled sounds through the gag in his mouth.

"You might as well take it easy, Elston," Luke told him. "We're going to be here the rest of the night . . . and it's a long time until morning."

CHAPTER 24

With Elston as his prisoner and Glory relatively safe for the moment—unless Finn or one of the other gunmen decided to check that other room and found Luke gone—he had time to look around the large, comfortably furnished bedroom. The bed where Elston slept was a four-poster with a thick mattress. Woven rugs covered most of the open floor space. A massive cedar wardrobe took up almost an entire wall.

Of much more interest to Luke was the gun cabinet on another wall.

A number of revolvers of various makes and models hung on pegs inside the cabinet. Luke even saw several single-shot flintlock pistols, old enough to have been carried by his brother's friend Preacher back in the mountain man days.

Racks of rifles and shotguns flanked the pistols. They tempted Luke, but he knew any gun work he had to do likely would be at close range. He found boxes of .45 ammunition in a drawer, so he loaded four Colts, even the chambers that rested under the hammers, and filled his pockets with more cartridges.

Feeling Elston's hate-filled eyes watching him, Luke hefted one of the Colts and quoted, "'I feel an army in my fist.' You know who said that, Elston? A German poet and playwright named Friedrich Schiller. And right now I know exactly what he meant."

Luke walked over to Elston and hunkered beside him. He let the muzzle of the gun in his right hand dangle in front of Elston's face.

"Come morning, you and I will be riding away from here," Luke went on. "Glory and Sheriff Whittaker are coming with us. And if your men want you to stay alive and keep paying them, they won't do a thing about it."

Again, Elston made furious noises through the gag.

"Actually, you'd be smart to go along with it," Luke told him. "You've made a lot of threats, and you and I know you're guilty as hell of ordering your men to try to kill Glory and me, but as you pointed out, what can the law prove against you? In fact, if you turned Whitey Singletary over to Whittaker and let the sheriff arrest him for murdering Sam MacCrae, you might be able to get away with everything else you've done. Of course, you'd have to back off and leave Mrs. MacCrae and her ranch alone from now on, but you've already got a good spread. You could learn to be satisfied with it."

Elston still scowled darkly at him, but Luke also saw something in the man's eyes that told him Elston was thinking seriously about everything he'd just said.

Luke still wouldn't trust him, no matter what deal they made, but as long as he had a gun to Elston's head, he thought he could get Glory and Whittaker out of here alive, which was a lot better than things had looked a few hours earlier.

Luke straightened, went over to a chair, and sat down. He still had three Colts tucked into his waistband and the gun in his right hand.

He didn't intend to let go of it until he and Glory and the sheriff were off of Harry Elston's range.

Elston was tied securely enough that Luke was comfortable with dozing off now and then, but he never went sound asleep and his senses remained keenly alert. When the sky began to turn gray in the east with the approach of dawn, he stood up from the chair and went over to the door that led out to the widow's walk. He opened it and looked out at the early morning, and as he did, he realized what day of the week it was.

"Sunday," he murmured, more to himself than Elston. "Sunday morning in Sabbath Valley. Appropriate for a day that'll be someone's salvation."

It remained to be seen, of course, exactly who would be saved . . . and who wouldn't be.

Just because it was Sunday, that didn't mean the work of the ranch would stop. Not all the members of Elston's crew were hired killers like Verne Finn. He had to have a number of actual cowhands working for him, too, and they would be up and about soon to take care of their morning chores.

A line of clouds hung over the eastern horizon. The

sun hadn't risen yet, but it was high enough now to turn those clouds red, as if they were billows of blood looming over the West Texas landscape.

Luke told himself not to think such grim thoughts as he turned back into the room where Harry Elston lay on the floor as his prisoner.

"All right, Elston," Luke said as he bent to take hold of the rancher. He grunted with the effort as he lifted Elston's solid, thickset form. "We're going out onto the widow's walk."

Luke had to untie Elston's ankles so he could shuffle out onto the little balcony. Elston didn't try anything, but Luke was ready if he had.

Once they were outside, Luke pulled the gag loose. Elston spat angrily to clear his mouth and throat, then loosed a stream of bitter curses before he finally paused and asked, "How did you know this was made to look like a widow's walk?"

"I've read about them," Luke replied. "Not that I've ever seen one, but you mentioned that you used to be a sea captain." A quizzical frown creased his forehead. "Do you have a wife, Elston?"

"I did," the man said through gritted teeth. "She died. And I wasn't there for her. The sea, the damned sea, kept me away from her. And that was when I decided to get as far away from it as I could."

Elston's words had the ring of tortured truth, and for a second Luke felt something. Not sympathy, no. A lot of people dealt with tragedy in their lives without turning into murderous, power-crazed madmen. But Elston's hatred was a window of sorts into a dark corner of the human condition, and Luke recognized that.

Down below, somebody shouted, "Hey! Hey, is that the boss?"

Luke put one of the Colts to Elston's head and told him, "All right, I want Glory and Sheriff Whittaker brought out here and horses saddled for all of us. And a fourth horse for you, since you're coming with us."

"I can't go anywhere like this!"

"It may be a bit humiliating, but you're decent enough in those long underwear."

The cowboy who had spotted them had turned and run back into the bunkhouse. Now more men emerged, Whitey Singletary among them. Luke didn't see Verne Finn. He wondered if the leader of the gun-wolf pack slept somewhere here in the house.

Luke prodded Elston with the Colt and said, "You know what to tell them."

Elston growled wordlessly, then raised his voice and called, "You men listen to me down there! Fetch out Mrs. MacCrae and the sheriff! Saddle four horses and bring them to the front of the house!"

One of the men ran into the main house. Luke heard the front door slam.

Singletary shouted, "Get out of the way, boss! We'll fill that bastard full o' lead!'

Luke eared back the Colt's hammer.

"My thumb is the only thing between you and eternity, Elston," he said. "If I die, so do you."

"Damn it, just do what I said!" Elston bellowed at

Singletary and the other men. "Bring out the prisoners, and get those horses ready!"

The men still hesitated. The front door banged again, and Verne Finn strode into view, wearing only a pair of jeans and carrying a revolver. He turned to look up at the widow's walk. In this bloody Sunday morning, the pale skin of his torso was red, making him look like Satan.

"I'm sorry, Mr. Elston," Finn said. "I don't know how Jensen got loose."

"It doesn't matter now," Elston snapped. "Just see to it that my orders are carried out."

"That's what you really want?"

"Yes, by God!"

Finn turned to the other men and jerked his head in a nod. They began to scurry around. Some of them headed into the barn to saddle the horses. Others headed for the smokehouse to get Sheriff Whittaker. Finn himself stalked back into the house, presumably to bring out Glory MacCrae.

"You won't be able to pull this off, you know," Elston said to Luke. "Something will go wrong. You'll wind up dead, and so will Mrs. MacCrae and the sheriff. Then we'll bury the three of you someplace you'll never be found. Whitey will take over as sheriff. I have enough influence among the county commissioners to make sure that happens. There might be a little stink . . . but it'll go away in time. It always does."

"Not this time, Elston. But like I told you, you haven't done anything that'll get you strung up, or even sent to prison for any amount of time. The best thing you can do is cooperate."

Elston just grunted and didn't say anything else. Luke could still feel the hatred radiating from him, though, like the shafts of crimson light that now shot up into the sky as the sun got ready to peek above the horizon.

The men returned from the smokehouse prodding a stumbling, hatless Sheriff Whittaker in front of them. Whittaker's hands were tied, but they were in front of him rather than behind his back as Luke's had been when he was in the smokehouse.

Other men led saddled horses from the barn. Then the front door of the main house opened and Verne Finn brought Glory out. He had hold of her arm, but her hands and feet were free.

"Luke!" she cried when she looked up and saw Luke and Elston on the widow's walk. "Luke, are you all right?"

"I will be once we get out of here," he told her. "Go turn the sheriff loose. Then the two of you get on a couple of those horses and get out of here."

"What about you?"

"Elston and I will be coming along directly," Luke said with a smile. "I want you and Whittaker clear first, though."

Even from where he was, he could see the familiar stubborn jut of Glory's chin as she said, "I'm not leaving without you."

"That's the only way this is going to work."

Glory hesitated, obviously wavering about what she should do next. Up on the widow's walk, Elston said, "That's pretty smart, Jensen. That's the one way you might be able to get the two of them out of here." With a sneer, he added, "I never thought a damned bounty hunter would be so blasted noble."

"People are usually capable of more than men like you give them credit for," Luke said.

"Yeah . . . that's why I can't let you get away with it."

Elston moved faster than Luke expected. He ducked his head and threw himself sideways, slamming against Luke and driving him into the railing around the widow's walk. The Colt went off as the impact jolted Luke's thumb off the hammer, but the bullet narrowly missed Elston's balding head.

With a sharp crack of boards breaking, the railing gave way as the weight of both men hit it. Luke and Elston toppled through it and crashed down on the porch roof. The fall wasn't very far, and the roof was sturdy enough that it didn't give. Both men rolled out of control to the edge and plummeted off.

Somehow Luke managed to hang on to the revolver as the ground came up and smashed into him. His brain and body were both stunned, but he forced them to work. He rolled over and lifted his head as guns began to roar. He had lost track of Elston, but he saw Jared Whittaker whirl and drive his clubbed fists into the jaw of the gunman next to him. As the man fell, Whittaker plucked his Colt from its holster and opened fire on Elston's gunnies clustered in the ranch yard.

From the corner of his other eye, Luke saw Glory struggling with Verne Finn. She hooked the fingers of her right hand into claws and dragged them across his face. Finn yelled in pain as she almost succeeded in gouging out his eyes. He backhanded her and knocked her away from him.

That gave Luke an opening, and as he came up on one knee he shouted, "Finn!"

Snarling, the gunman brought his revolver up and around and fired just as Luke triggered the Colt. Luke felt the heat of Finn's slug as it whipped past his cheek. Finn rocked back, though, as blood welled from the hole in his chest where Luke had drilled him. The pistol slipped from nerveless fingers as his knees unhinged and dropped him to the ground.

Luke surged to his feet. He lunged toward Glory, caught her arm, dragged her toward the house.

"Whittaker!" he shouted. "This way!"

The sheriff angled toward them at a run, the gun in his hand spouting flame as he did so. Elston's men had scattered, taking cover wherever they could, and they kept up a sizzling return fire. The air in the ranch yard buzzed with bullets like a swarm of angry hornets had been let loose in it.

Somehow Whittaker made it through that storm of lead and leaped onto the porch right behind Luke and Glory. Luke had emptied one gun and jerked out another. He used it to cover their retreat into the house. As he was the last of the trio to duck through the door, he slammed it behind him and thought fleetingly how lucky he was none of the guns tucked into his trousers had gone off when he fell from the widow's walk. That would have been a good way to get something important shot off. He hadn't broken any bones, either, as far as he could tell right now.

"Get them!" Elston roared somewhere outside. "I don't care how bad you have to shoot up the house! Just kill them all!"

Bullet after bullet slammed into the walls and the front door. Every pane of glass in every window exploded inward from the onslaught. Luke, Glory, and Whittaker kept their heads down.

"Glory, untie the sheriff," Luke told her over the gun thunder. When she had done so, Luke handed one of the Colts to Whittaker, along with a handful of shells, and gave Glory a couple of the guns as well. Each of them was now armed with a pair of revolvers. They made sure all the chambers were filled.

Some of the firing outside died away. In the relative quiet, Whittaker said, "They outnumber us by too much. If they rush us, we won't be able to hold them off for very long, even with this many guns."

"Maybe not," Luke said with a reckless grin, "but we can sure make them pay before we go down."

Glory said grimly, "If I can just get a shot at Whitey Singletary and settle the score for Sam, that'll be enough for me."

Whittaker raised himself high enough to risk a glance through one of the shot-out windows and said, "You may be about to get your chance, Mrs. MacCrae. Looks like they're getting ready to rush us!"

"I'd rather meet them on my feet," Luke said. He rose, kicked the door open, and went out with both guns blazing. Glory and Whittaker were right behind him, and their guns were roaring as well as they poured lead into the small army of gunmen charging the house.

That was when nearly two dozen men on horseback came boiling around the corner of the barn and smashed into the killers, taking them totally by surprise. Elston's men went down from the pounding lead of the newcomers' guns and under the slashing, steel-shod hooves of their horses. Luke saw the tall, lanky, redheaded figure of Rusty Gimple leading the charge. Old Kaintuck guided his horse with his knees as he fired right and left with a brace of old cap-and-ball pistols. Even the two young wranglers, Ernie and Vince, were with the group.

The MC cowboys couldn't have won stand-up gun-fights with Elston's hired killers, but in this melee they crashed through and over the gun-wolves and wiped out most of them in a matter of seconds.

Some of them escaped the lightninglike charge, though, and kept fighting. Whitey Singletary emerged from the roiling clouds of dust and gunsmoke that now obscured the ranch yard and lunged toward Luke, Glory, and Whittaker as the gun in his hand jetted flame.

They fired back, the three shots so close together that they sounded like one, and Singletary was jolted to a stop by the slugs that crashed into his chest. He stood there for a second, swaying, his pale face twisted in lines of pure hatred, before his eyes rolled up in their sockets and he pitched forward to lie there in the stillness of death.

That left Harry Elston. Holding a gun he had picked up, still dressed only in the long underwear, he walked out of the chaos and came toward Luke and the others. Elston stepped around Singletary's body. The gun in his hand was pointed at the ground.

"Elston, you're under arrest," Sheriff Whittaker called to him. "Drop that gun!"

Elston shook his head and said, "No."

"Don't be a damned fool, man," Luke told him. "Even after all this, you won't hang."

Elston smiled.

"You think I intend to spend one day behind bars?" he asked. "A man like me who spent his life on the open sea?"

Elston lifted the revolver, put the muzzle to his temple, and pulled the trigger.

That was the last shot of the battle of the Lazy EO.

CHAPTER 25

"I'm sorry, Sheriff," Rusty Gimple said. "After I told you about Miz MacCrae bein' missin', I didn't have faith that you'd really come out here and make sure Elston didn't have anything to do with it. So me and a few of the boys followed you."

Rusty and Whittaker were in the glass-littered parlor of Elston's house, along with Luke and Glory. Outside, the rest of the MC crew was gathering up the bodies of the dead gunmen and keeping an eye on the wounded survivors.

"I did ride out here, though," Whittaker said. "I don't like to admit it, but I took sides in what was going on around here . . . and it was the wrong side."

"You risked your life to try to help us," Glory told him. "And you fought beside us this morning. I think that's a start on making things right."

"I hope so," Whittaker said with a nod. "I should have figured out sooner just how crooked Whitey really was, though."

"That was a mistake, all right," Luke said. "But we all make them."

Rusty nodded and said, "Yeah, I sure did. When you rode up here and then didn't come back, Sheriff, I was more convinced than ever that you were workin' for Elston. So I sent one of the boys with me back to the MC to bring the whole crew. We were gonna bust in here this mornin' and find the boss lady, even if we got shot up doin' it."

"Instead, you got here just in time to save us," Glory told him with a smile. "I won't forget this, Rusty." She sighed. "But I don't know if it really matters. I won't be running the MC much longer."

Rusty frowned and asked, "Why in blazes not?"

Glory didn't answer, so Luke said quietly, "Hugh Jennings."

"That's right," Glory said. "He's locked in one of the rooms upstairs. Now that he knows where I am . . ."

"He could stay locked up for a while," Luke suggested. "Long enough for you to leave."

Without hesitation, Glory shook her head.

"I'm through running," she said. "I never did like the idea. It's time to go back and face . . . whatever's waiting for me." She stood up. "I'm going to go turn him loose. Luke, will you come with me?"

"Sure," Luke said. He wondered if he could get away with shooting Jennings. The man didn't deserve to live.

But Luke knew he couldn't do that. He was a bounty hunter—the lowest of the low, in the minds of a lot of people—but he wasn't a murderer.

Whittaker asked, "Who in blazes is this Jennings fella?"

"It's a long story, Sheriff," Glory said. "I'll tell you all about it later."

Whittaker looked like he wanted to argue and demand an explanation now, but he nodded and said, "All right. But I'll hold you to that."

He and Rusty went outside to see how the mopping up was going, while Luke and Glory climbed the stairs to the second floor.

"Do you know which room Hugh is in?" Glory asked as they started along the hallway.

"No, I—" Luke stopped short as he saw a door into one of the rooms hanging crookedly on its hinges. The doorjamb was splintered around the lock.

Somebody had kicked that door open.

That familiar cold prickle on the back of his neck warned him that someone was behind him. He stiffened and started to reach for the gun in his waistband when Hugh Jennings said, "Stop what you're doing, Jensen. Another move and I'll kill you."

"Hugh!" Glory started to jerk around, but Jennings stopped her with a harsh command.

"Turn around, both of you, but slowly," Jennings went on. "Jensen, lift your hands and keep them up."

Luke raised his arms and turned. Beside him, Glory turned around, too. Her face was taut with anger.

"You broke the door down during all the shooting, didn't you?" she said to Jennings. "Nobody heard you with that going on."

Jennings smirked over the revolver he pointed at them.

"That's right," he said. "I found this gun, too, and now I'm going to use it to kill both of you."

"I thought you wanted to take me back and put me on trial for a murder that *you* committed."

Jennings cocked his head to the side and grinned. He said, "That's the thing about trials. You can never guarantee how they're going to come out. And I don't need you going back to Baltimore and spreading a lot of wild stories about me. No, I think it'll be much better if you're dead . . . *Mother*. That way you'll be just another fugitive that justice caught up to, and the whole affair with be over and done with, forever."

"And you will have gotten away with murder," Luke said.

Jennings laughed.

"So what if I have? I've already gotten away with one, haven't I?"

"You mean Alfred," Glory said, her voice cold with hate.

"Of course. He should have known better than to threaten me. He was going to send me to jail over a measly hundred thousand dollars when losing it wouldn't have hurt him. What other choice did I have but to kill him?"

Luke said, "Reckon you could say that a little louder? I'm not sure Sheriff Whittaker heard it, standing down there at the bottom of the stairs like he is."

Jennings started to sneer again, the contempt evident on his face at what he must have thought was a trick, but then Whittaker said, "Oh, I heard every bit of it, clear as a bell."

Jennings's head jerked to the side. The gun in his hand followed, pulling out of line with Luke and Glory for a split second. Luke's left hand shot out and shoved Glory through the door Jennings had kicked open earlier, while his right flashed to the gun in his waistband. The Colt cleared and came up and roared just as Jennings jerked the trigger of his gun and sent a wild shot flying wide.

Luke's bullet struck Jennings in the chest and punched him backwards onto the stairs. His feet hit empty air and he fell, tumbling down out of control until his body came to a halt in a crumpled heap at the feet of Sheriff Jared Whittaker. Luke had seen Whittaker come in and approach the stairs. That was why he had goaded Jennings into confessing.

The lawman looked up at Luke and Glory, now standing at the top of the stairs as a wisp of smoke curled from the muzzle of the gun in Luke's hand, and said, "I reckon this has got something to do with that long story you were going to tell me, Mrs. MacCrae?"

"It has everything to do with it," Glory said.

Whittaker nodded.

"Don't worry," he said. "I heard plenty. You think the authorities back where you come from would take the word of a Texas sheriff about that confession this fella just spouted?"

"I think they'd take the word of an honest Texas sheriff," Glory said. "And I think that's what we're going to have in Painted Post from now on."

* * *

Several days later, Glory looked up at Luke as he sat on the back of the dun and said, "But you came all this way, did everything that you did, saved my ranch, saved my life . . . and you didn't get anything out of it! You should at least let me give you the five thousand dollars you would have earned as a bounty if you'd taken me in."

Luke smiled and shook his head.

"I got to eat my fill of Teresa's fine food," he said as he nodded and touched the brim of his hat in a salute to the little Mexican woman who stood in the doorway of the ranch house. "And I made some good friends."

He lifted a hand in a wave of farewell to Gabe Pendleton, Rusty Gimple, Kaintuck, Ernie Frazier, and Vince Halligan. The cowboys stood in front of the bunkhouse, Pendleton leaning on a cane since he was still weak from the gunshot wound he had suffered in town. He had insisted on coming back to the ranch, though, and was on the mend, anybody could see that.

Quietly, Luke added, "And I got some smiles and kisses from one of the most beautiful, determined women I've ever met in my life."

"You could have a lot more than that, and you know it."

"Maybe . . . but that's not the life I've made for myself."

"Isn't it a lonely life, though?" Glory asked as she reached up to him. "It's going to be a lonely life for me."

Luke clasped her hand and said, "I doubt that. I think

you'll have plenty of attention from Gabe and from Sheriff Whittaker. One of these days you'll probably have to decide between them. Just let the loser down easy, if you can. He'll be losing a lot."

"Luke . . ."

He smiled and shook his head.

With a sigh, she slipped her hand out of his. He turned the dun, heeled the horse into a trot, and waved again at the men in front of the bunkhouse as he rode away.

For a long time, whenever he rode away from a pretty woman who would have been glad for him to stay, he had told himself that one of these days he would settle down. One of these days he would have a family and a home and put the life of a bounty hunter behind him. No more cold nights sleeping on the hard ground, no more danger lurking in every shadow, no more waking up in the morning with the smell of gunsmoke clinging to him. Yes, one of these days . . .

But Luke Jensen knew that day would never come, so he put his eyes on the horizon and rode toward whatever was on the other side of it.

Turn the page for an exciting preview!

100 YEARS LATER, THE WAR FOR AMERICAN FREEDOM IS BEGINNING AGAIN

THE GREATEST WESTERN WRITER OF THE 21ST CENTURY

William Johnstone is acclaimed for his American frontier chronicles. A national bestseller, the legendary storyteller, along with J. A. Johnstone, has written a powerful new novel set in Texas—one century after the Revolutionary War. . . .

LIBERTY—OR DIE FOR IT

One hundred years ago, a thousand miles from Last Chance, Texas, American patriots picked up rifles and fought against British tyranny. That was Boston. This is Big Bend River country. There the enemy was King George III and his British troops. In Last Chance, it's Abraham Hacker, a rich and powerful cattle baron who will slaughter anyone who tries to lay claim to the fertile land and everything on it. For Last Chance, freedom is one intolerable act at a time, until wounded Texas Ranger Hank Cannan arrives in Last Chance. Seeing the oppressed citizens, Cannan is ready to start a second revolution. It's going to take a lot of guts. But one way or the other, Cannan is out to set Last Chance free—with bullets, blood, and a willingness to die—and kill—for the American right of freedom. . . .

DAY OF INDEPENDENCE

by *USA TODAY* BESTSELLING AUTHORS
WILLIAM W. JOHNSTONE
with J. A. Johnstone

On sale now, wherever Pinnacle Books are sold.

CHAPTER 1

Texas Ranger Hank Cannan was in one hell of a fix.

In fact, he told himself that very thing.

"Hank," he said, "you're in one hell of a fix."

He uttered that statement aloud, as is the way of men who often ride long and lonely trails.

About ten minutes earlier—Cannan couldn't pin down the exact time—a bullet had slammed into him just above his gun belt on his left side, and another had hit his right thigh.

In addition, after his horse threw him, he'd slammed his head into a wagon wheel and now, for at least part of the time, he was seeing double.

With so many miseries, Cannan reckoned that his future career prospects had taken a distinct downhill turn, especially since the bushwhacker somewhere out there in the hills was seeing single and was a pretty good marksman to boot.

The rifleman had earlier stated his intentions clearly

enough, but Cannan could not bring himself to agree to his terms.

Yelling across a hundred yards of open ground, the man had demanded Cannan's horse, saddle, guns, boots and spurs, his wallet, watch, and wedding ring, and whatever miscellaneous items of value he may have about his person.

"And if I don't?" Cannan called back.

"Then I'll kill you as dead as a rotten stump."

"You go to hell!" Cannan said.

"Ladies first," the bushwhacker yelled.

Then he laughed.

That exchange had happened a good five minutes ago, and since then . . . nothing.

Between Cannan and the hidden rifleman lay flat, sandy ground, thick with cactus and mesquite, but here and there desert shrubs like tarbrush and ocotillo prospered mightily.

The Texas sun scorched hot and drowsy insects that made their small music in the bunchgrass. There was no other sound, just a vast silence that had been scarred by rifle shots.

Cannan, long past his first flush of youth, gingerly explored the wound on his side with the flat of his hand. It came away bloody.

One glimpse at his gory thigh convinced him that he had to end this standoff real quick or bleed to death.

But the drawbacks to that plan were twofold: his rifle was in the saddle boot and the horse under that saddle could be anywhere by now, as was his pack mule.

The second, and much more pressing given his

present circumstances, was that the only weapon he had available to him was his old Colt .45.

Now there were many Rangers who were skilled with the revolver, fast and accurate on the draw and shoot.

Cannan wasn't one of them.

His colleagues rated his prowess with a Colt as fair to middling, but only on a good day, a nekkid-on-the-back-porch kind of good day.

Hank Cannan could never recall having one of those.

But most gun-savvy men allowed that he had at least the potential to be a widow-maker with a rifle—except now he had no rifle.

After his horse tossed him, he'd landed in a creosote bush and his forehead had crashed into an ancient wagon wheel half buried in sand. It had been the wheel's iron rim, still intact, that had done the damage and made Cannan see stars and, later, two of everything.

He'd hunkered down in the creosote bush and had propped up the wheel in front of him, where it provided at least an illusion of cover. But he knew he had to move soon before he grew any weaker.

His only hope was to outflank the bushwhacker and Injun close enough to get his work in with the Colt at spitting distance.

Cannan stared out at the brush flat, sweat running through the crusted, scarlet stain on his forehead.

He didn't like what he saw.

The ground was too open. Even crouched, he would present a big target. Two or three steps, and he'd be a dead duck.

Cannan sighed. Jane a widow after just six months of marriage, imagine that. It just didn't seem right somehow. He'd—

"Hey, you over there!" the bushwhacker yelled. "You dead yet?"

"Yeah, I'm dead," Cannan called out. "Damn you, I'm shot through and through. What do you think?"

"I'm a man gets bored real easy, and this here standoff is getting mighty tiresome. When do you reckon you'll pass away, if it's not asking an impertinent question?"

"By nightfall, I reckon. Depending on how I bleed, maybe a little sooner."

"Hell, that's way too long. I got places to go, things to do."

"Sorry for the inconvenience," Cannan said.

"Tell you what," the rifleman said.

Cannan said nothing.

"I'll take your hoss and leave you to die at your leisure. I can't say fairer than that. What do you reckon, huh? State your intentions."

"All I can say is that you're a good Christian," Cannan said. "Straight up an' true blue and a credit to your profession."

"Well me, I learned that Christian stuff from a real nice feller I shared a cabin with one winter over to Black Mesa way in the Arizona Territory. He'd been a preacher until he took up the bank-robbing vocation. We were both on the scout at the time, you understand."

"Yeah, I can see that," Cannan said. "Being on the scout an' all."

"Well, anyhoo, come spring I split his skull open

with a wood axe, on account of he had a gold watch chain I wanted. I'm wearing it right now, in fact."

"Well, wear it in good health," Cannan said.

There was moment's pause, then the bushwhacker said, "You're a right personable feller, a white man through and through, and it's been a pleasure doing business with you."

"You, too," Cannan said.

He wiped away sweat and blood from his forehead with the back of his gun hand, then gripped the blue Colt tighter.

He needed a break. He needed the drop. And right then neither of those things seemed likely.

But there was one option open to Hank Cannan, stark though it was.

He could die like a Texas Ranger.

Better one moment of hellfire glory, bucking Colt in hand, than to slowly bleed to death in the brush like a wounded rabbit.

But first . . .

Cannan reached into his shirt pocket and found the tally book and a stub of pencil that every Ranger carried.

He held the little notebook against his bent left knee and wrote laboriously in large print:

DEAR JANE, I THOUGHT OF YOU TO THE
LAST. I DIED GAME, AS A RANGER SHOULD.
     YOUR LOVING HUSBAND,
     Henry Cannan, Esq.

Cannan read the letter, read it again, and smiled, deciding it was crackerjack.

He tore the page out of the tally book, folded it carefully, and shoved it into his pocket where an undertaker was sure to find it.

Then he rose painfully to his feet, and, his bloody face set and determined, staggered toward the hidden gunman.

He planned to keep on shooting until the sheer weight of the bushwhacker's lead finally put him down.

They say fortune favors the brave, and if that is so, Cannan caught his first lucky break.

His ambusher, a big, bearded man wearing a black coat and pants, was in the act of mounting his horse and didn't see Cannan coming at him.

He'd also slid his rifle into his boot. A fatal mistake.

The Ranger tottered forward, then the bearded man turned his head and saw him.

He grabbed for the Winchester under his knee as Cannan two-handed his Colt to eye level and fired.

It was a "nekkid on the back porch" kind of day for Ranger Hank Cannan.

He scored a hit, then as the big man tried to bring the rifle to bear, scored another.

The bushwhacker's horse did not behave well.

A tall, rangy, American stud, it reared up and white, fearful arcs showed in its eyes. The horse attempted to shy away from Cannan's fire, and its rider cursed and battled to get his mount under control.

It was now or never for the Ranger.

A plunging, moving target is difficult to hit, and he missed with his third shot, scored again with his fourth.

Cannan had no time to shoot a fifth because the bearded man toppled out of the saddle and thudded onto the ground, puffs of dust rising around him.

Aware that he'd only one round left, Cannan, bent over from the pain in his side, advanced on the downed man. But the bushwhacker, whoever he was, was out of it.

Blood stained the front of the white shirt he wore under his coat, and the left side of his neck looked as though it had been splashed with red paint.

The man stared at Cannan with rapidly fading blue eyes that held no anger or accusation.

Cannan understood that, because he recognized his assailant as Black John Merritt, bank robber, sometime cow town lawman, and lately, hired gun.

Professional gunmen like Merritt held no grudges.

"I recollect you from your wanted dodger," Cannan said. "The likeness didn't do you justice."

"You've killed me," Merritt said.

"Seems like."

"My luck had to run out sometime, I guess."

"Happens to us all."

"I got lead into you."

"You surely did."

"I hope your luck doesn't run out."

Merritt licked his lips.

"Hell, got blood all over my damned mouth."

"You're lung shot," Cannan said. "Saw that right off."

"Figured I was."

Merritt had been leaning on one elbow. Now he lay flat and stared at the sky, scorched almost white by the merciless sun. He gritted his teeth against pain, but made no sound.

Then he said, gasping a little, "Who are you, mister?"

"Name's Hank Cannan. I'm a Texas Ranger."

Merritt smiled, his scarlet teeth glistening. "I should have suspicioned that. You boys don't know when you're beat."

"Goes with the job, I reckon."

Cannan lowered the hammer of his Colt and shoved it into the holster.

He felt light-headed, and the pain in his side was a living thing with fangs.

"Why did you decide to bushwhack me, Merritt?" he said.

"I was bored. It gave me something to do."

"You tried to kill me because you were bored?"

"Why not? I'm a man-killer by profession. Another killing more or less don't make much of a difference. I've already gunned more than my share."

"Merritt, I don't much like talking harsh words to a dying man, but you're a real son-of-a-bitch and low down."

"Truer words were never spoke, Ranger."

The gunman was barely hanging on, and gray death shadows gathered in his cheeks and temples. His gaze was still fixed on the sun-scorched sky, as though he wished to carry that sight with him into hell.

Merritt's words came slow, labored, like a man biting pieces off a tough steak. "Where you headed?" he said.

"I'm hunting a man. I go where he goes."

"What manner of man?"

"A man like you."

"Then he'll head for Last Chance."

"Where's that?"

"A town on the Big Bend, down by the Rio Grande."

"There are no towns in this part of Texas. Nothing for miles around but sand, cactus, and rock."

"Last Chance is there . . . due south . . . ten, twelve miles . . . hiring guns . . . gold . . ."

Cannan tensed as Merritt reached into his coat, but the man brought out only a gold double eagle.

"Ranger, take this," he said. "Make sure they bury me decent."

The coin slipped from Merritt's fingers and dropped into the sand.

"Promise me . . ." he whispered.

"I'll send you to your reward in a good Christian manner, Merritt," Cannan said.

But he was talking to a dead man.

CHAPTER 2

Black John Merritt was a big man, and heavy, and Hank Cannan had a hard time getting the gunman draped across his horse.

Cannon's own bay wandered back with the pack mule, but the Ranger was all used up and it was a while before he mustered strength enough to climb into the saddle.

After the gnawing pain in his side subsided a little, Cannan sat his horse and thought things through.

He'd lost Dave Randall's trail two days before in the deep ravine country up by Dagger Mountain. Figuring the outlaw might head for Mexico, Cannan had scouted as far south as the Chisos Mountains when Merritt decided to take a pot at him.

Now, at least one bullet in him, he was in need of urgent medical care. But around him stretched miles of hostile brush desert and raw, limestone mountain peaks that held themselves aloof and didn't give a damn.

As Cannan had told himself before, he was in a hell of a fix.

Unless . . .

Cannan stared at a sky slowly fading into turquoise blue at the end of the burned-out day, as if to seek the answer to the question he hadn't yet asked.

Could there really be a settlement due south of here on the big bend of the Rio Grande?

Cannan told himself that it was a ridiculous notion.

All this land would grow was a fair crop of rocks and cactus, and starving cattle would soon leave their bones on the desert sands, as would those who owned them.

If there really was a Last Chance, by now it was a ghost town inhabited by owls, pack rats, and the quick shadows of people long gone.

Cannan decided to take the gamble.

Last Chance was the only card he had left to play.

At best, he'd find a town. At the worst, a ruined roof to sleep under.

Or die under.

Hank Cannan would remember little of his ride south.

He'd later recall that the mule and the dead man's sorrel stud ponied well and didn't try to pull his arm out of its socket.

The yipping coyotes challenging the rising moon— he remembered that, and the far-off howls of a hunting wolf pack.

Cannan didn't remember trying to build a cigarette and cursing as both tobacco sack and papers fell from his weakening hands.

Nor would he recall staring at Black John's face in the moonlight, bone-white, the wide-open eyes glinting behind slate shadows.

And perhaps it's best that he'd never bring to mind Merritt's ghostly, hollow voice whispering to him that hell is not hot, but cold . . . colder than mortal man can imagine.

"You're a damned liar!" Cannan yelled. "You're burning in fire. I can feel your heat! You're making me burn with you."

Black John whispered that hell is a gray, soulless place, covered in ice, and it has a constant north wind that cuts and slashes like a knife edge, and leaves deep, scarlet scars all over a man's naked body.

Then Black John said, his voice like a death knell, "Feel them, Ranger . . . feel the winds of Hades . . ."

And Cannan did.

He was hot before, but now he shivered as an icy blast hit him, and it cut like a saber and stank of sulfur from the lowest pits of hell.

"Hell is a wind!" Black John screamed. "A wind that blows bitter from Satan's mouth!"

"Liar!" Cannan yelled. "Liar, liar, your pants are on fire . . . in hell!"

Then suddenly he felt burning hot again.

Then cold.

Then hot.

And when he rode into the moon-splashed town of Last Chance, windows stared at him with blank, emotionless eyes . . . and all at once the ground cartwheeled up to meet him . . .

And then Hank Cannan felt nothing . . . nothing at all.

CHAPTER 3

"Ah, the sleeping beauty awakes."

Hank Cannan thought he recognized the man's voice, but he lay still amid the soft comfort that surrounded him, unwilling to move.

"This may come as news to you, huh? But you're alive, Ranger Cannan. I saw your eyelids flutter."

Cannan opened his eyes and groaned.

"Baptiste Dupoix," he said. "Then I must be in hell."

"Close," the Creole gambler said. "You've been raving about Black John Merritt and a ghost town. But to set your mind at ease, you're in a burg called Last Chance, and you're a current resident of the Big Bend Hotel."

"What are you doing here, Dupoix?" Cannan said. "I thought I hung you years ago."

"No, you haven't yet had that pleasure," Dupoix said. "Though God knows you tried."

Cannan lifted his head off the blue-and-white-striped pillow and tried to rise to a sitting position.

"Here, let me fluff that for you," Dupoix said.

The gambler reached behind Cannan, pounded the pillow into shape, then propped it against the brass headboard.

He helped Cannan sit up and smiled, his teeth very white against his dark skin. "There now. Comfy?"

Two oil lamps, lit against the darkness outside, cast shadows in the room, especially in the corners where the spinning spiders lived.

"What the hell time is it?" Cannan said.

"Early. It's just gone six."

"Morning or night?"

"Dawn soon. When a sporting gent like me should already be in bed."

"But you postponed slumber to visit me, huh?" Cannan said. "Out of the goodness of your heart."

"Bad enemies are like good friends, Cannan. They're to be cherished."

"I've got a dozen questions," Cannan said, ignoring that last.

He lifted the sheets and saw that he was naked, but for the bandages around his waist and thigh.

"How I got here will be one of them," the Ranger said. "But first tell me what happened to the dead man I brought in."

"You mean Black John?"

"How many dead men did I have?"

"Only him, and he'll be sorely missed."

"I promised him I'd bury him decent."

"The nice folks of this fair town buried him, with all due pomp and ceremony, I assure you."

"When?"

"Why, two weeks ago."

Cannan was shocked.

"I've been lying in this bed for two weeks?"

"Uh-huh, that's what I said. The doctor told me you were at death's door." Dupoix grinned. "It was a mighty uncertain thing. Touch and go, you might say."

Cannan waved a hand around the hotel room. "Who did all this?"

"Not me, I assure you. My hypocrisy goes only so far. No, the town fathers put you up here. There are some really nice people in Last Chance."

Dupoix, a tall, elegant man who moved like a cougar, thumped a bottle of Old Crow and a couple of glasses onto the table beside Cannan's bed.

"I did do something for you, though," he said. "A couple young ladies of my acquaintance took care of you. You were out of it, but you did take nourishment now and again. Chicken gumbo mostly, made to a recipe handed down by my swamp witch grandmother back in Louisiana."

Dupoix poured whiskey into the glasses.

"It's a bit early, isn't it?" Cannan said.

"Early or late. It doesn't make any difference to a man confined to his bed. Oh, and remind me to tell you about my grandmother sometime. She's a very interesting woman."

"How did you know that I was the Ranger who brought in Black John?" Cannan said.

"From the description I got from the men who picked you up off the street. Big man, they said, maybe four inches over six feet with shoulders an axe handle wide and the face of a dyspeptic walrus. Who else fits that description?"

Cannan accepted a whiskey, then said, "Do you have the makings?"

"No, I've never succumbed to the Texas habit, but I can offer you a cigar."

"That will do just fine," Cannan said.

"I thought it might."

After Dupoix lit Cannan's cheroot, the Ranger said from behind a cloud of blue smoke, "Now tell me why you and I are breathing the same air in a town a hundred miles from anywhere."

"You first, Ranger Cannan, since you're feeling so poorly."

"I was tracking a feller—"

"Dave Randall. Yes, I know." Dupoix read the question on Cannan's face and said, "He's here in Last Chance." The gambler smiled. "And so is Mickey Pauleen."

That hit Cannan like a fist to the belly. "What's a killer like Pauleen doing here?" he said.

"Him, and Dave Randall. And Shotgun Hugh Gray. And a half-a-dozen other Texas draw fighters. But Mickey is the worst of them, or the best of them, depending on your point of view. The day after he arrived he shot the town marshal."

"And where do you come in, Dupoix?" Cannan said.

"I'm here for the same reason Mickey and them are here. For gun wages. Two hundred dollars a day until the job is done."

"What job? And who's paying you?"

Dupoix, elegant in a black frockcoat, boiled white shirt, and string tie, stepped to the window, then turned and said, "You've never forgiven me for that time in . . . what the hell was the name of the place?"

"Horse Neck," Cannan said.

"Yeah, Horse Neck. A benighted burg at the end of a railroad spur, as I recall."

"It was a hell-on-wheels tent town and I was sent there to keep the peace, Dupoix," Cannan said. "You ruined it for me and nearly got me kicked out of the Rangers."

"Cannan, those three gentlemen playing poker with a marked deck were asking for trouble. They took me for a rube."

"That's why you shot them, Dupoix, because your pride was hurt."

"They were notified."

"You left three dead men in the saloon, then lit a shuck on a stolen horse."

"The buckskin I left at the livery was a superior animal in every way to the one I . . . borrowed. Its owner got the best of that bargain."

Cannan held up his cigar, showing an inch of gray ash at the tip.

Dupoix picked up an ashtray from the table and laid it on the bed.

"You did take a pot at me, you know," he said. "My right ear felt the wind of your bullet. Now why did you do that?"

"I was aiming for the hoss," Cannan said. "My shooting was off that day."

"Ah, yes, as I recall you're no great shakes with a revolver."

"I wish I'd brought my rifle along. Then I would have hung you for sure."

"Suppose I tell you that those three Irish gents drew down on me first?"

"Wouldn't have made any difference, Dupoix. You took me for a rube and my pride was hurt."

The gambler smiled. "Touché, Ranger Cannan."

Dupoix refilled Cannan's glass then his own. He stepped to the window again and lit a cigar.

"You never answered my questions, Dupoix," Cannan said. "Why—"

"Am I here and who's paying my wages?" Dupoix said.

"Well?" Cannan said.

The gambler pulled back the lace curtain. "Look out there," he said. "A fair town with a schoolhouse and a church with a bell in its tower. It's got a city hall where the flag flies every single day of the year and the people dress in their best of a Sunday and go to worship."

Dupoix turned his head to Cannan and spoke over his shoulder.

"Last Chance was started by tin pans," he said. "They came here looking for gold, found none, and most of them left. But a few decided to stay and set down roots. In the early years they went through hell, but in the end they built something worthwhile."

"You still haven't answered my questions," Cannan said.

"Patience, Ranger, I'm answering them. Unless you're planning on going somewhere?"

"Funny, Dupoix. Go ahead."

"All right. Now, where was I?"

"You were talking about folks trying to build a town in a wilderness where there shouldn't be any town," Cannan said.

He suddenly felt irritable, from the whiskey or the pain of his still-healing wounds, he didn't know.

"The people of Last Chance worked together to irrigate the fertile bottomland with canals that carry water from the river. Despite droughts and floods and all the other things that plague farmers, they grew wheat, corn, oats, and now there's talk of planting cotton."

"They built their prosperity on farming?" Cannan said.

"Not entirely. They act as middlemen for Mexican trappers who supply them with fox, beaver, wolf, and bobcat fur. Last Chance also trades hogs, turkeys, and bees with Mexico for hard cash, and a few raise cattle on the floodplain farther along the river." Dupoix smiled. "You could say the hardy folks out there have turned this part of the desert into a Garden of Eden."

"Then why are you and the other gun hands here, Dupoix?" Cannan said.

"Because, Ranger Cannan, we're going to take it all away from them," Dupoix said.